A TRUE CRIME

CHARLOTTE BARNES

Copyright © 2024 Charlotte Barnes

The right of Charlotte Barnes to be identified as the Author of the Work has been asserted by her in accordance with the Copyright, Designs and Patents Act 1988.

First published in 2024 by Bloodhound Books.

Apart from any use permitted under UK copyright law, this publication may only be reproduced, stored, or transmitted, in any form, or by any means, with prior permission in writing of the publisher or, in the case of reprographic production, in accordance with the terms of licences issued by the Copyright Licensing Agency.
All characters in this publication are fictitious and any resemblance to real persons, living or dead, is purely coincidental.

www.bloodhoundbooks.com

Print ISBN: 978-1-916978-19-5

For Sally – the real Sally
Thank you for being a brilliant reader, proofreader, and friend

FROM THE WOODS

I would later learn from the police that it was hardly a mile. Though it felt like a marathon to find a house that didn't look like a threat. Of course, by then, everything did. I powered past trees and fallen trunks and frosted leaves in a winter greyscape. But it was the gnomes that would eventually help the detectives work out where we'd been held.

There were so many of them. A whole civilisation clustered in their red hats with their fishing rods and their toadstools, like characters stripped from a children's story – or a horror. I was panting minus three degrees temperatures into my lungs when I saw them. The world had fallen into a late winter slumber in the three days that we'd been away from it. Though the police doctor explained the lack of food, the lack of water would have made the temperatures harsher too. The late-night cramps and the shivers and shock wouldn't have helped either, they kept explaining. None of it mattered then, or since. I still ran and ran as fast as I could but paused to pant and stare, and try to find some sign that something existed beyond those woodlands. They must have seen some things, those gnomes. I've thought so many times since of the teenage fumbles and the drunken evenings they would have been able to bear witness to. Then there they were, quite suddenly, plummeted into the narrative of two girls who had been kidnapped; one who had escaped. I haven't been back to the woods since the police took me there that first time. But I've often wondered whether those huddles are still there, traumatised and dumbstruck where someone – I've wondered who – must have left them years before. Their broken tops and missing limbs the war wounds of officers who must have trampled through the space looking for evidence; clues that might have fallen into the cracks of the earth.

I've since thought of those gnomes as the signpost to society. It wasn't long after I started to run again that I found the edge of the trees, peeling away like the edges of damp paper to reveal a large field – another space I haven't been to since, as though a single side of that town is now exclusionary to me. The field was somehow less threatening, though, with fewer spaces for anyone to remain hidden. And so, like a creature set across a hot coal track, I tore across it until I found the cottage hidden on the other side. It was archetypal – another children's story motif that has been ruined by this tale – with its thatched roof and worn walls and the dribbles of steam that emerged from the open windows. That's how they heard me, before I arrived; a strangled animal calling into their kitchen. The Olssons – a Swedish couple, childless. They had moved to the United Kingdom six years before and had been living out a quiet existence in that time, until I arrived, and they emerged from their bottle-green front door one after the other. Their troubled faces were the first licks of real hope I saw after I'd escaped. And somehow, when I folded myself into Karin's arms like a paper doll in the palm of a spiteful toddler, I knew I'd done it: I knew that I'd survived.

ONE

Lena could always tell when something was wrong by how I fucked her.

She trod back into the bedroom with a steaming mug of something in each hand. When she sat on the bed, she did so gently. I thought there was an equal chance of that being to a) avoid spilling anything and b) avoid startling me. I was lying with one hand on my solar plexus, keeping time with my heartbeat – checking to see it was still there – and the other hand knotted into my hair. My eyes were near closed, and my face angled toward the ceiling, but somehow I was uncomfortably aware of each one of her movements. It was a strange superpower I'd brought out of the woods with me, this innate ability to sense an intruder – as though I was always, would always be, ready for one. I heard the knock of crockery as she set each drink down and felt the sink of the bed as she leaned in closer. She kissed from the brim of my forehead down to my chin and settled the crown of her head into the crook of my neck. I made no effort to hold her – but she wouldn't have expected me to, after.

Lena and I had been together for two years and I'd decided, somewhere six months into our messy courtship, that she was perhaps the most patient woman in the world. She'd grown up with a mother who suffered from a severe anxiety disorder – spurred by the absent father who worked more hours than he really needed to, simply to keep out of their house – and she assured me, as few as four dates in, there was nothing that would scare her away. I'd laughed and said, 'What about murder?'

She didn't know the story. But on date five I told her everything, like an ugly purge spilled across the table for two in the backroom of Benedicto's. Neither of us had looked back after that, but she'd realised by date six that I was a woman who would always have a hard time looking forwards. The book might help with that, one counsellor had told me; though of course, it might make everything that bit worse, another had said.

Lena tucked an arm across my midriff and made a soft noise. She did this, sometimes, when she sensed that I'd drifted away – as though making herself my kite string. She'd taught me the word *whiffle* – aimless talk; a breathy noise – and we swapped them like codes in these quiets, an implicit acknowledgement of the moment. When I didn't answer she split through the silence with speech. 'People are going to love the book, Sal.'

A noise fell out of me then – one I didn't have a single word for. But I suppose it was a cynical sort of laugh. 'I wasn't thinking about the book.'

'You big liar.'

I shifted so I could look down at her. 'How are you so certain that I was thinking about it?'

'Easy,' she craned up to kiss my cheek in a soft peck,

'you've been thinking about the book solidly for eight and a half months.'

'Sometimes I think about other things...' I moved further onto my side, then, at such an angle that I could ease her back against the bulk of the mattress. My teeth were against her jawline when she pushed back.

'Sal, don't.'

It never felt like rejection when she did this but still I said, 'I'm sorry.'

'Don't be.' She struggled upright and reached behind her to where the drinks were on her bedside. 'But you're anxious, I know. Have your tea, we'll have breakfast, then we'll get you ready.'

I took the drink from her and made a ripple across its surface with a breath that came out minus three degrees shaky. The smell of the tea filtered through me on my in-breath. 'Is this herbal?'

Lena huffed. 'Yes. The last thing you need today is caffeine.'

Duke moved around the booth like a butterfly subjected to shock therapy. He was always more nervous for these things than I was. But then, being kidnapped and held hostage for three days straight as a teenager was likely to have adverse effects on your panic response to things as an adult. Still, I could have lived without the intermittent bursts of, 'Sally, are you okay?' and 'Sally, do you need anything?' When he was the one out of the two of us who looked like they might need to gargle Rescue Remedy and lie down in a darkened room.

'Sally,' a stranger's voice caught me, and I was glad of

the distraction from Duke and his flurries. The man behind me was tall and dark and handsome, and if I'd been inclined towards that sort of thing then I'm sure I would have folded over to impress him. But I found myself in a strange landscape these days; where people were more likely to treat me like the person who needed to be impressed. Since the early announcements for the book – the next big thing, as Duke told anyone who would listen to his marketing schemes for me – people had started to treat me like a precious ornament to be passed around and admired at length. I was a snow globe of sorts, rendering those in close contact desperate to shake me to see what might come tumbling out. The snow replaced by winter leaves; the typically happy scene at its core replaced by two teenage girls; one of them dead, the other one, me.

'Zade, right?' I held out a hand.

'Right. Honestly, Sally– Do you mind if I call you Sally? It's a genuine honour to meet you. We're so glad to have you on the show with us today. It'll be great. Great, great, great.'

I withdrew my hand and resisted the urge to wipe a palm down the front of my jeans. He was skin-sweaty nervous; there was a sheen of it on his forehead too. I had to hope he was better at leaving dead air during a radio show than he seemed to be during real-life conversation.

'Duke said you ran the questions by him already?' I asked, for something to say. But as if being summoned–

'Sally, sweets, these are the ones I emailed over last week?' Duke appeared and placed an arm around me; his palm cupped my shoulder and I felt the heat of his nerves. *Why are* you *all nervous?* I thought, not for the first time during radio interviews. But then there were times, too, during my more sympathetic moments, when I thought their nerves might be justified. I was, after all, a valuable commodity. *And one that's likely to break.*

I tight-smiled. 'Of course, I remember.' I turned back to Zade then. 'I'm really looking forward to talking about the book. Thanks for having us.' I'd come to think of Duke and I as a unit by then. He'd bought into the concept of the book from its early days; he'd seen the early drafts; he'd fenced the late-night phone calls where all I could do was sob over the scene I'd written that day – and that same scene had then padded through the walls of my home, pulled back the duvet and clambered into bed alongside me, or sometimes between me and Lena. The memories were breathing things.

'Shall we get you all kitted up?' Zade nodded to the recording suite behind us where his colleagues were already positioning microphones. 'They'll throw a fit if we're late starting. Knocks the whole day out.' He trod around me to lead the way, then held the door open. Though I noticed that he didn't permit Duke entry.

'He can't come in with us?' I asked over my shoulder.

Zade looked as though I'd scrunched up quantum physics and thrown it at him in a wet paper ball. 'Of course,' he rushed out, then, 'of course, if you need... Of course.' He backtracked and welcomed in Duke, who cocked an eyebrow at me before taking his natural place in the room: on a chair out of the way in a corner, but close enough.

People danced around with their headsets and their speakers and their, 'Now, talk into this here...' as though I wasn't on my fifth round of radio interviews for the month. The book was two weeks away from being published and yet it had already been nominated for Best

Debut at the Named in Nonfiction Awards. Duke had been hauling my ass around to studios up and across the city since that announcement.

'Right, Sally.' Zade tucked himself into a seat opposite me. 'We'll start with a quick introduction about the book. I'll whizz through that, then read your bio from...' He turned over a proof copy and glanced at the back cover, where a hasty biographical note had been written. Out of the entire book's worth of content, that had perhaps been the most challenging thing to cobble together – second only to the Acknowledgements page. I didn't have much to say about myself when the proofs had gone to print. But I'd sure as shit had a lot of people to thank.

'All of that sounds great.'

'And you'll be reading from the book?' Zade asked, then looked at Duke. I followed the stare to Duke's corner where he nodded, then glanced across to me. 'You'll be reading from the book,' Zade said again.

'Apparently so.' I reached into my bag on the floor and pulled out my own thumbed copy. There were three extracts now so often read that I thought I'd be able to recite them with my eyes closed and a clamour of panic at my throat. But I knew that someone would be taking pictures, somewhere, of the studio, and an author holding their book would make for a better Instagram post than one staring into the abyss half reciting, half remembering the worst thing that had ever happened to them. So I opted for the paperback.

In the corner of the room an unnamed man held up three fingers. 'Everybody ready?' Though he didn't wait for an answer before folding his fourth finger, third, index, nod. Go.

'Good afternoon, everyone, you're listening to Zade

Kennedy on *Talk Truth To Me* and today we're joined by an exceptionally special guest. Genuinely honoured to have her in the studio. Sally Pober is the hot, hot, hot debut name on everybody's lips these days and today she's joining us to talk about her upcoming true crime novel–'

I hated them calling it that: a novel. As though it were a story being told. As though anybody could make up such a fucking hideous thing.

TWO

I threw open the living-room window and Duke took it as a sign. He pulled a packet of Marlboro Gold from his back pocket and worked free a single smoke. With the butt rested between his lips, he reached back into the same pocket to ferret free a lighter and then he sparked up for me. He handed it over with a disapproving look and I rolled my eyes.

'If she asks, you didn't get that from me.'

I pulled a greedy inhale and then spoke through the plume. 'Who else would I have gotten it from?'

He shrugged, his head already buried between the pages of an intimidatingly large planner. 'You could have some stashed somewhere.'

'Please,' I paused to inhale again, 'like Lena doesn't know every inch of this place.' During the worst of my panic attacks, she had had to check every square space of the apartment. There was no drawer, closed door or cupboard left unaccounted for. *Apart from those in the office.* Lena's thorough inspections had since made Duke my only source of secret cigarettes. But at least I always knew there wasn't a killer in my home. I fidgeted on the window ledge and stared down into the street, busy with cars and bodies. 'How are the ticket sales then?'

'I haven't checked today.'

'Liar.'

'I genuinely haven't had the chance, Sal. Do you want me...' He petered out and stayed silent until I turned to look at him. 'Where are you?'

'Here.'

'Liar.' Duke cocked an eyebrow at me and crossed the space. There was room for him on the window ledge, too, and he lifted himself onto the cold wood of it. 'The interview was too much?'

'It was fine.' Zade was nothing. He was a tailored personality designed to pull in listeners. *But isn't that exactly what you are now, Pober?* I heard the mocking tone of my own thoughts and somehow felt deserving of the derision. 'Smoke with me,' I said, 'it's sad to smoke alone.'

'Ha,' he was already reaching for the packet, 'you just want an excuse for if she comes home early.'

As if summoned then, there came the click, click, click of the front door locks being dismantled down the hallway.

'Talk of the devil.'

Lena looked up and smiled, then frowned, tutted. She was such a disapproving parent sometimes – which I sort of enjoyed. 'You're not meant to be doing that.'

I made a show of bringing the smoke to my lips and taking such a deep inhale that it singed my throat. I was such a difficult teenager sometimes – which I think she sort of hated. 'I think you'll find the deal was that I'm allowed one a day, as a treat, when I'm a good pet for Duke.'

'If you were a pet you'd be in behavioural classes by now,' he answered through his own smoky exhale.

'How did the interview go?'

'It was fine,' I parroted, and flashed Lena a smile.

She joined us by the window and came close enough to kiss the side of my head. 'The pair of you smell disgusting. Do you want coffee?'

'Please,' Duke answered before I could, and he must have clocked my expression. 'Sally, doll, don't think me rude but you look like you need it, and we've got an afternoon of planning ahead.' He gestured with the thick book. 'I need to run through dates with you to make sure your shit mess of a diary matches with mine.'

'Why do I keep you?' I dubbed the whittled cigarette out on the outside wall of the building and dropped it into the water-logged ashtray that lived on the outer ledge. Lena had her back to us, so I leaned forward and plucked Duke's cigarette from his mouth while he was midway through taking a drag. I pressed my index finger to my puckered lips and winked.

'I'm sure there are one or two reasons, if you think hard enough.'

'So where are you off to first?' Lena shouted in from the kitchen, with an accompaniment of whirrs and shushes as she booted up the coffee maker. She'd banned me from instant. Nothing but the strongest, she'd said. *Strong coffee but no cigarettes*, I thought as I put my contraband to my mouth.

'Birmingham then Manchester the day after,' Duke was flicking through pages, 'Leeds, Glasgow, Edinburgh–'

'I've never been to Edinburgh,' I interrupted him.

'Well, a new book is the perfect excuse for it, isn't it?' He flicked another page. 'Then we're migrating back down this neck of the woods, past home and all the way through to London. That's the longest stay, I think. We're waiting for one or two venues to confirm.'

Lena appeared with a coffee mug in each hand. When she saw me still perched on the window ledge, still smoking, she flashed a sceptical look. 'That can't be the same one.'

'I'm a slow burn.' I smiled as I crossed the space and took a mug from her. 'Have you been to Edinburgh?'

'Once.'

'Want to go again?' I asked, my tone playful, though it was undercut with something more serious. Lena couldn't get the time off work to come on a book tour with me, which, logically, I knew was reasonable. Illogically, it had been the source of as many as three late-night arguments already. I didn't leave for another week, which meant there was definitely time for a fourth.

'What's security like at each of these venues?' She looked around me to speak to Duke.

It felt like I'd been cut free of the conversation so I wandered back to my perch and let the pair of them enjoy their coordinated panic. It wasn't the first time that Lena had raised this subject with him, with me, with him again – now. They chattered for so long that I'd nearly emptied my mug – and the cigarette was long gone – by the time I felt drawn back in.

'Where did you go?' Lena came to stand next to me and pushed my hair back to get a clear look at my face. I never knew where I went exactly when people asked that question; somewhere cold, somewhere with gnomes. 'You know it's just because we care about you, babe.'

I smiled. 'Everything will be fine,' I assured her. This was the only time that I was the more careless one out of the two of us. I might have worried about intruders in my home – the man who might hide behind the curtain, leaving only his feet protruding from the bottom hem for me to spot on the way to the bathroom – but Lena was more concerned about the people beyond my home. The Man, as everyone referred to him now. That shadow figure who lingered like a fairy tale spectre; cursed and relegated to the banished lands where he might plan his return, any day now. *Any day...* I thought as I promised again, 'Really, everything will be fine.' I closed the window and crossed to the open-plan living room where Duke had taken over the coffee table. 'Talk logistics to me.'

'I'll make more coffee,' Lena suggested, but her preparatory actions became background noise. Duke talked and talked over the click and stir of her and I listened and listened until bees swarmed my ears, and soon Duke was background noise too. It didn't matter where we were going, or when. I was as much a tailored personality as Zade now, I knew. I would be a good victim in this; I would go where these grown-ups told me.

It was 1.36am when Lena came out to find me. I was perched on the same window ledge with Birdy curled up beside me. Lena had dropped her and collected her from the groomers earlier that day, while Duke had been making a desperate attempt at organising my diary – the diary that he bought me; the diary that I seldom used, much to his dismay. Now, it was full of notes in his handwriting, and Post-it notes from Lena that said things like: *When you see this, remember you're loved.* Though she didn't only hide them in my diary. I'd found one in the alcohol cupboard half an hour ago when I went to pour out a generous gin. That gin was with me in the window, too, and I was alternating between sips of that and long pulls on a vape. It didn't have the same ring to it as smoking, but at least I could do it without a reprimand.

I saw Lena in the outer edge of my vision but I kept my eyes straight ahead, one hand working at the soft, tight curls on Birdy's back.

'You can take her on the tour with you if you want,' Lena said eventually.

'I'm considering it.' I sipped at the gin and held back a wince. I didn't want to show the weakness of needing a mixer. 'Duke said that he'd be fine with it, he can arrange it with the hotels or whatever. There'll be someone he can ask to walk her and stuff and... I don't know. Is it unfair?'

'She'll be living her best life.' Lena lowered herself to the floor and sat cross-legged at an angle where she could see me. She nodded at the dog. 'I know my place.'

'She's my therapy,' I answered.

'I know that too.' A long pause elbowed between us then, while I sipped and smoked and sipped and– 'Do you want to talk about why you're up in the middle of the night?'

I shrugged. 'It was a busy day, wasn't it? Hard to shut off when it's all,' I made a swirling motion around my head, 'fluttering around you like a rogue horde of something.'

Lena laughed softly. 'You're such a writer sometimes, Sal.' I frowned. 'Most people would just say their brain was busy.'

'Okay,' I inhaled hard on Raspberry Ripple, 'my brain is busy.'

'Duke told me they've got security scheduled at every event, and the hotels are aware of the situation too,' she said then, answering a question that I hadn't asked – and wouldn't have asked. 'Do you still have the meeting with–'

'Day after tomorrow.'

'Do you want me to come with you?'

I shook my head and concentrated on kneading the fur that bunched and gathered around Birdy's ears, no matter the grooming. 'I'm fine on my own.'

'Don't I know it,' she said, *almost* under her breath, but nowhere near quiet enough for me to miss it. 'Do you want quiet, babe?'

Somewhere between the top of my gin measure and its bottom I'd lost sense of what I needed – and what I'd hoped would be at the bottom of the glass. It usually helped with sleep on the nights when there was a horde, an army, a throng – *a busy brain,* I tried to correct myself, but busyness felt too domestic a term for something that felt like an invasion. I wasn't tired. But there was another interview waiting on the other side of sunrise for me, this time with a podcast, and Duke had me booked into a studio in the afternoon to record another extract from the book. 'Something from the meatier parts,' he'd said at the time and then looked horrified with himself for having phrased it that way. I hadn't said anything. Years ago, I might have corrected someone. Now, people anticipated my outrage – even though I was long past it – which often meant they beat me to the punch of reprimanding them. *Besides which,* I thought, *isn't the guilt we put on ourselves worse than anything anyone can gift us?*

I needed to remember that line. My notebook was on the coffee table somewhere, under A3 sheets and promotional materials galore. If I went to write it down, Lena would call me a writer again. I almost didn't like the job title; its hidden meaning: I am a person who makes things up.

Lena struggled up onto her knees and kissed Birdy on the head, before standing fully. She kissed the crown of my head then, too, and paused to inhale, how a mother might with an infant. 'I know what will shut your brain off, if you're still struggling to sleep after another gin.'

'That's a generous offer,' I answered with a forced smile. She didn't want me when I was like this, though, and I couldn't blame her. But we kept up the façade of sex being a fix-all. 'I'll come to bed soon, I promise.'

She was already treading across the laminate, back towards our room. Her feet made a gentle sucking sound as the warmth of her soles conflicted with the cold apartment. It had never been good at holding the heat, which was one of the things I liked about the place. Even though on nights like this, the cold reminded me too much of being somewhere else.

THREE

Already, and in such a short space of time, too, I'd come to expect people to give a shit when I walked into a room. Radio hosts and podcasters and agents and– They'll do that to you. But when I said my name to the woman sitting behind the front reception desk at the police station, she looked back blankly and only handed me the sign-in sheet. Wordlessly, too. She couldn't even extend the usual human pleasantries that we've come to expect from reception staff, as though it's part of their remit. When I handed the sheet back she glanced down at it before setting it beside her. Then she extended a, 'I'll let them know you're here,' and turned back to whatever was beaming out from her computer screen.

I didn't take a seat; I lingered. There were posters and pictures and odds pinned to the walls, which gave me something to busy myself with. I read as many of them as I could in the short time I had for it. It wasn't until I was partway through reading an infographic about the dangers of drugs that I caught a real whiff of what the woman had said: *Them?*

From somewhere behind me a door swung open and I snapped around to catch sight of Harry. Harry, who looked older every time I saw him now, and I hated what time was doing to him. Granted, my early memories of him were tainted with tears and tiredness and tender conversations where he was asking for more and more, always more, about the man who had kidnapped me – us. So there was a chance my childhood memories of him were somewhat blinkered. Maybe he'd always been this old. But I was sure that leaving the force had done something to him – and I wasn't convinced it was a good thing, from the pillowcase puffiness beneath his eyes, and the way the grey of his hair far outweighed the dark brown of it now.

'How you doing, Sal?' He crossed the space and pulled me into a hug that I wasn't braced for. I remained rigid for it. It was a thing that happened when people touched me unexpectedly. My counsellor was working on it.

'I didn't realise you were going to be here for this,' I said when he unleashed me. 'Not that I'm complaining,' I rushed to add then, realising that the cut of my tone might have implied it was a problem. If anything, it was the opposite. DS Worsley and I had never exactly warmed to each other. She thought I was a problem. Though she was probably right about that, albeit, perhaps, in the wrong ways. 'She didn't want to see me on her own then?'

He smiled; a fatherly smile, with a frown fighting its way out. 'Don't take it personally, Sal. She just wanted someone with more experience on the case to listen in, that's all. Ready?' He gestured towards the door and I took a step towards it. Harry held the door open for me and it came back like muscle memory: walking through the door, treading to the office, walking through another door, no, I'm okay for a drink, thank you, of course, I'll sit here, is that okay– 'Sally?'

I turned and caught a worried look on him. 'Sorry.'

'Don't be. There's a lot happening.' Harry sat opposite me on the government-approved sofa when we were settled in the room. I wondered where their budget was for these things. They'd never had comfortable furniture, always in their uniform blue with boxy stature. I imagined it all as the build-it-yourself kind that came complete with internet instructions that didn't make sense. Again, it gave me something to overthink while we waited for Worsley.

'The book seems to be doing well,' Harry offered, with a deliberate questioning intonation hanging at the end of the comment. 'You must be pleased?' He shook his head. 'Maybe pleased is the wrong word.'

I forced out a smile. He was trying, in a fatherly way again, too, with that optimistic expression that sang out how desperate he was for an easy conversation to just walk in and take a seat in the room with us. The tension wasn't his fault though. It was the setting, the occasion; it was all wrong. Harry and I should be having this conversation over coffee, or tea – *herbal tea*, I remembered, he hated caffeine at this time of day – without Worsley offering her handbook comments on the matter. But every scene needs something to move it forwards, and Worsley would do that at least.

'Did you read it?' I asked eventually, when the silence started to feel too heavy. He nodded, slowly, his smile still fixed in place. 'And?'

Harry sucked in so much air that I thought the room might empty of it and it made my lungs flutter panic. 'I think you're an exceptionally brave young woman, Sally Pober, and I think a lot of other people are going to agree with me on that.' He leaned across the narrow space between us and gave my right knee a soft squeeze, like testing the texture of a bread roll, it was tender and deliberate, then he dropped back. 'You did good, kid.'

I closed my eyes and stole back some air from him for my own greedy breath. My lungs were shaking then, and in my head I could remember, 'You did good, kid,' at the end of those final interviews. He would always tell me, 'You did–'

'I'm sorry for keeping you both.'

My eyes snapped open when Worsley entered the room. She was loaded up with folders, flailing sheets of paper and an empty water bottle; the hard plastic kind that you should refill throughout the day. Writing the book had given me a flavour for details; you could tell a lot about that woman from what she brought into the interview suite with her. She was bland but dedicated; everything the police force wanted in a superior officer.

'That's okay,' Harry answered, 'Sally and I were just talking about the book.'

'Oh,' Worsley looked at me then, 'you've done a job and a half with it, Sally, really. Very brave, the bits I've seen.'

The compliment wormed into me and did uncomfortable things to my stomach. I hadn't sent her a copy. I glanced at Harry and cocked an accusing eyebrow.

'I shared some extracts with DS Worsley.'

'I'm glad you both enjoyed it,' I answered. I wouldn't give him a proof of any future books, I decided then.

'Now, I know you're really busy at the moment,' Worsley struggled to offload her belongings onto a side table in an orderly fashion, 'but I thought it was worth having a quick chat through things like security, changes in the case and so on.' She took a seat next to Harry, and I couldn't help but notice how close their knees were to touching.

'There have been changes in the case?' I latched on then, but I looked to Harry, not her, and he was quick to ease my rise.

'It's more that there *haven't* been changes in the case,' he clarified. 'DS Worsley wants to talk through the possibility that your book might *cause* changes in the case. Isn't that right, Mich– DS Worsley?' He autocorrected out of her first name but I noted the intimacy of it. I imagined them Harry-ing and Mich– *Michelle? Is that it?* over drinks with my manuscript between them. I was self-centred enough to buy into the snapshot of them both there, and I didn't like that about myself. I could thank – *blame* – Duke for it though.

'There is a concern that telling the story, encouraging people to revisit the case, might bring out some things.' Worsley spoke to me softly, like I was still a teenager; like my toes were still numb from the cold and my stomach was still howling from the restriction of three days without nutrients. Sometimes I let that happen, even now, just for the familiarity of it. My counsellor was working on that too.

'Now, it's two-fold. There's the possibility that reading the book, hearing your talks on the book, will help people remember things they might have forgotten, or neglected to mention the first time around. Then, there's the possibility that–'

'It'll draw him out,' I auto-filled the sentence. And for a full five seconds, no one said a word.

'Yes,' Harry eventually stepped up with an answer. 'That's obviously a concern.'

'Okay... okay.' I let another pause spread. 'What do you need?'

Worsley fidgeted forwards, closing the space between us all slightly, and I resisted the urge to lean back. 'Your agent, Duke, is it?' She waited for a nod from me. 'He's already given us the completed outline of the tour, as it stands. He assures us that he's got security measures in place, too, but, as I understand, you don't want any sort of round-the-clock assistance?'

I huffed a laugh. 'A bodyguard?'

'We don't need to use that word,' Harry answered, pre-empting my derision.

'But yes,' Worsley added.

'No, you're right, I don't want one person following me around everywhere I go. Given that we're talking about precautions for someone who may or may not try to kidnap me a second time, the prospect of already having one person tail me is more than enough, without paying for a second person to do it.'

'Sally...' Harry's tone was a cautioning one then.

'What?'

'We're genuinely just concerned for your safety,' Worsley crept back in with her soft tone and I wondered whether she had children. I chanced a look at her left hand: no wedding ring; no ghost of one. 'There are some services we can recommend, if you change your mind, and for the sake of my conscience I'd like to email those details over to you, if that's okay?'

I looked at Harry, who frowned so hard his forehead looked like scored concrete.

'Of course. If you have Duke's email address, it's best

to copy him in. He won't be leaving my side in the coming weeks, so I'm told, so he's a good point of contact to have.' Worsley looked relieved at that. 'Is there anything else?'

'I mean,' she fidgeted again, 'it might also be worth considering that these kinds of books can bring out all sorts of...'

'Everyday crazies.'

Worsley smiled. 'Thank you, Harry, but that's not the phrase I was looking for.'

'If writing a book has taught me anything, it's that sometimes there really is only one way of saying things.' I tried to lift my tone, tuck my palms flat beneath the tension of the room and raise it like a magician mid-act. When both of them smiled – Worsley *nearly* laughed, though it may have only been a sharp exhale – I knew that I'd pulled it off. 'There are going to be the die-hard fans who appear, swallow the case whole, then tell *me* what I got wrong about it. Those crazies, right?'

Harry snapped his fingers. 'Got it in one.'

'It's okay,' I assured them, 'if things get really crazy then at least I'll get a sequel.'

'I'm not sure that's funny,' Harry answered.

'It isn't.' Worsley turned around to start reorganising the mess she'd brought in with her. She kept her tone light as she continued – even though it didn't quite match the contents: 'I'd like to avoid a starring role in a true crime book, which means that I'm actively looking to keep you out of another one too. So I hope you didn't have plans for a follow-up.'

'Nothing in the pipeline just yet.' I threw my hands up in mock defeat and thought: *Like I had plans for any of this...*

FOUR

There were two sets of parents to contend with: mine, and hers. I started with my own, to get the easiest out of the way. Lena had offered to come with me but I told her I'd take Birdy instead – as though those two women in my life were interchangeable somehow, and I suppose in many ways they were.

The drive from city to country was always a head-clearing one. There were times when, especially on bad days, I would haul myself into the car, feel the gears churn and whir and anger on the drive, out of polluted air and into a landscape that still boasted an organic green in its fields, rather than a tailor-made one. I would coast along to my parents' home with the dog in tow and the windows down and I would park up on their drive, wait for my lungs to fill, only then to drive home again. *Escapism is a funny thing, isn't it?* I thought as I tucked Birdy into her car seat, before treading round to my own side of the vehicle. It would take just under two hours to get there, and on the drive I oscillated between the radio and Spotify. When I flicked back to Radio 4 and heard my own name – 'Today we're talking true crime on the show with the debut novel from Sally Pober, and aren't we excited?' – I opted for my Release Radar instead. I was becoming sincerely concerned with my name usage; that so many strangers might say it, and it would eventually lose meaning, in the same way that words sometimes do when you write them out too often: like 'woods' or 'gnomes' or 'victim'.

I was thirty minutes away from my parents' drive when their landline cut through my speaker system with an incoming call. It would be Mum, I knew.

'Hiya,' I shouted upwards. Her hearing wasn't what it once was.

'Hello, love, are you on your way?'

I huffed. 'More than on my way. I texted Dad when I left.'

'Oh, Vince, where's your bloody...' She spoke away from the handset and I imagined Dad with his head buried between the folds of a tabloid. 'She's on her way, she texted you.' I didn't hear his reply. 'He's been in the garden, love. Whereabouts are you? Far?'

'Another half an hour or so.'

'I'll wait twenty minutes and get the kettle on. Your dad bought pastries.'

My stomach turned over with an animal growl and Birdy's head shot up. I glanced down and caught her, head tilted to the side in a question, and then reached over to her with a pat of reassurance. I hadn't been eating much again, and she was the only person who knew. Though, I wagered, she wouldn't mind me feeding her scraps of puff pastry underneath Mum's kitchen table.

'That's great, really kind. We'll see you soon then.'

'Love you, Sal.'

'Love you too.'

She always made sure it was the last thing she said. On the morning I'd gone missing. *No, on the morning* we *went missing*. And even that wasn't right. On the morning we were taken, Mum and I had argued. She'd said I wasn't concentrating enough on school, on the prospect of universities, on life beyond being a teenager – as though any teenager in modern history had ever had the forethought to imagine life beyond those perfect years. She'd told me that I needed to get my act together and start taking life more seriously. Then a man had herded me into the woods with my best friend and told us to get into the dirt and mud of an underground hideaway that he'd cleared out with the intention of finding teenagers just like us and–

I slammed on my brakes at a junction. I was only five minutes away now and I thought of calling again, though I knew Mum would already be busying herself with trying to find teacups and saucers that matched. So instead I trundled through the beginnings of their village at a steady twenty-eight miles an hour; one hand on the wheel, the other kneading at Birdy's right ear which had an unfathomably large knot in, considering she'd been groomed within the last week too.

'How do you manage this?' I asked her, and she rolled her eyes – like I'd probably done to my own mother when I was the same age equivalent.

When we pulled up on the drive Birdy's back straightened, bent and straightened again in a cat-like stretch. Then she climbed over me to get to the open car door. She was out and on the porch before I'd even locked the car. Mum swung the front door open for us on my approach. She wandered out with arms stretched crucifix wide and wrapped me in a tight hug.

'I'm so glad you could come home for a bit, love, especially before you go.' She gave my cheek a hard kiss as she pulled away. 'Excited?'

'For the book tour or the pastries?' I joked.

She reached forward and made a tight vice around my upper arm. 'I don't know about excited for the pastry, but it looks as though you need it. Get in,' she nudged me ahead of her, 'your dad's in the kitchen.'

I took the cue and walked in, and soon found Dad – Birdy on lap, eating crumbs out of his palm. His eyes widened when he saw that I'd seen, and I smiled. There were still four full pastries on the plate in front of them both.

'She's allowed crumbs, you're all right.' I kissed the top of his head and then walked around to take a seat opposite him. Birdy didn't follow; she'd pledged allegiance to the pastry-keeper, and Dad had been desperate for a pet since I'd moved out so I wouldn't rob him of it.

'I see you've lost your dog,' Mum said when she joined us. I noticed the proof copy of my book tucked underneath her arm. I'd written it with them out of the room; which is to say, I didn't give anyone a chance to read anything until it was too late to amend the parts that might lacerate them. It felt like deceit but I'd been told it was good practice.

'I see you've brought the book.' I forced a smile. I had no idea what was coming, but I was getting used to that feeling. The critics had started to pour in, pile on, share their thoughts about the book too. And I'd known it was only a matter of time before people who knew me – *really* knew me – started to look for themselves between the pages and the spine cracks of the story.

Mum set it down on the table. 'Don't worry yourself, love, I'll sort the tea.' She lightly tapped Dad on the top of his head as she walked behind him and headed to the sideboard where cups were laid out.

'I can't move.' He gestured underneath the table. When I looked under I saw that Birdy – who had only seconds ago made her exit from Dad's lap – had instead made a home for herself across his feet. 'It would be dreadful to interrupt her.'

'Dreadful,' Mum parroted. 'Sugar?'

'Still no,' I answered. I hadn't taken sugar in my tea since I was seventeen, and yet... I looked up in time to catch Dad eyeing the book. 'Thoughts?'

He sucked in a greedy amount of air and I felt panic blossom in the core of my chest. *Here it comes.*

'I think the way you use language is very clever, Sal. That figurative stuff you do throughout, with the metaphors and whatnot, very clever stuff.' He flashed me a tight smile then, and I waited him out. 'And the way you describe the old house, that's really touching, accurate too.' They'd moved – we'd moved – after the kidnapping. None of us could stand to be quite so close to the area where it had all unfolded – or the pitying looks from neighbours that I was getting whenever I left the house, went to school, tried to live. 'And the, ah– And–'

'And you haven't read it.'

'And he hasn't read it,' Mum confirmed, as she set a tea tray down on the table. There was a brilliant bright-magenta pot in the centre of the tray with three cups piled on top of each other alongside it, three saucers beneath them, a squat milk jug – and a sugar bowl that no one would use, but Mum was a sucker for a full set of something matching. 'I have though.' She leaned forward and kissed the back of my head as she crossed behind me, then she took her own seat. 'And I think it's bloody exceptional.'

A blossom flowered, drooped and shed its leaves, and breathing became noticeably easier. 'Would you tell me if it was shit?'

'Ha,' Dad scoffed, 'of course she bloody would.'

Mum threw him a judgemental look. 'Pour the bloody tea, make yourself useful.' She reached over and felt for my hand then. 'I think it's brilliant and I think you're a brave girl– Woman, you're a brave young woman, for having written it.' She squeezed too tight, three times close together, until I smiled back at her, as though she'd pressed a magic combination to get the expression out of me.

I huffed out a laugh. 'Where the hell did you get *figurative language* from?' I asked Dad as he poured out our measures of tea. 'Have you been googling literary terms in your free time?'

'Now, Sal,' he pushed a cup and saucer towards me, 'I haven't been– Have a pastry,' he nudged the plate of those towards me too, 'I haven't been looking at literary terms, but I have been looking at reviews.'

I picked at the corner of a pecan plait. 'Can I ask why you haven't read it?'

He swapped a look with Mum and from the corner of my eye I saw her shrug. 'Honestly, Sally, it's– Selfishly now, it's too much for me. I can't– I don't think I can hack revisiting that time. And it's fine that you can,' he rushed to add, 'it's your story, sweetheart, and I think people should know, and people should– They should be aware, that these things happen. But,' he tapped his chest, 'it broke my heart, that time away from you, that not knowing. And I'm not altogether sure the knowing, the reading all about it, I don't know that that would make that break much easier, even now.'

'He still thinks you're brave for having written it, don't you, Vince?'

'Oh, fucking hell, Sal, the bravest wench that I know.' I smiled. He hadn't called me a wench since I was girl, and I wondered which part of his protective fatherly instincts had dredged the word up. 'Have a pastry, Lucy,' he told Mum before he forced a reciprocal smile for me, 'I can't have mine until you lot have yours. That's the rule, isn't it?'

'Please,' Mum leaned forward to take a plate, 'you're only standing on ceremony because we've got company.'

Their comfortable chatter became background noise; a hum of home comfort that receded underneath a wave of something other, that I couldn't give a name to. *Am I relieved?* I didn't come back around until I heard my name mentioned again. It fell out of Mum's mouth along with flecks of pastry, projected so far that I saw one or two land on my leg and I held back the urge to brush them away.

'Sorry?'

'Sal, will you stay for your dinner? We were going to have fish and chips,' Dad asked, but from Mum's expression I had a feeling that wasn't the only key part of the conversation I'd missed. 'I'll finish my brew and then have a drive out to the shop,' Dad said, as though I'd answered.

'I'm sorry?' I said again to Mum.

'I asked whether you'd spoken to Peter. About the book.'

'Oh.' A strangled animal sound fell out of my stomach. Dad said something about how hungry I must be. Mum shushed him. Birdy nudged me. Mum grabbed my hand. Dad stood up. Mum said– Mum said–

'Love?' She shook my arm softly.

'No, sorry,' I snapped back into the room, 'no, I haven't spoken to Peter. I will, before I leave for the tour. I will.' I must have repeated it three times, making a mantra of it; I was promising myself as much as I was promising Mum.

FROM THE WOODS

Karin held me how my mother must have done once. When I'd gone running into her room in the early hours of a morning, screaming of monsters stashed beneath the springs of my mattress. Now the monsters – monster, singular – was a different breed, and that bit more real. I'm sure I must have tried to explain it all to them – the kind Olssons, who welcomed me into their home and fed me full of tea and soft questions – but as for what I said, I can't remember. That information was swapped in smoke mouthfuls between them and the police, I'm sure, like teenagers passing tokes of something sinister between themselves. I do remember crying, though, and rocking, and that Karin shushed me with a great deal of tenderness. Meanwhile, Per's voice was an echo somewhere in the back of the house while he panicked down the phone to the operator, telling them that a young girl had arrived on their doorstep in a state of great distress and– All of the other details he felt pertinent at the time. Though I was soon to learn that pertinent was a relative term. That what I thought was important – *I survived, I survived* – would be lesser or only of equal importance to other details – *What can you tell us? What do you remember?*

Karin and Per were blissfully out of touch with the world. Everything about their existence spoke to the archetypal off-the-grid lifestyle that so many of us whimsically longed for, without making any substantial steps to obtain it. But, because they had indeed done that impossible thing, it meant they had no idea who I was when I arrived. A retelling of the stork with a swaddled baby, a crow or blackbird, bird of prey, had deposited a fully formed teenage girl on their doorstep. And they had no idea that entire search teams had been looking for me and Emma for days by then. Though of course, I didn't learn that until much later either. And in those hurried harried moments that follow a great shock, they weren't to know that Emma was still out there somewhere, stashed in the woods.

'Sip this, slowly, girl, slowly,' Karin said, holding the steaming mug for me. My hands were locked cold. That, or I was holding on to this sudden freedom so tightly – still thinking, somewhere, in the hollow of my starved stomach that it mightn't be real. 'Another sip, girl, slowly, still.'

I hadn't managed to tell them my name, they told the police. Once I had panted breath back into my lungs and once they had swaddled me in blankets, I had only managed to tell them one thing, one piece of information that everyone would agree *was* pertinent: 'Man,' I told them. 'Man' and 'Woods'.

FIVE

Aster didn't believe in colour. But she did believe in music. In the time we had been seeing each other, she had often handed me what I assumed was her work phone equipped with a ream of Spotify playlists for me to select from. I thumbed through the options that afternoon and tried to make a strategic decision for something that wouldn't give my mood away. I didn't feel like sharing anything. The sessions were advised, though, and they were something that Duke, Lena, my parents insisted on – especially when it became clear that the book was going to be The Book that so many people were waiting on. There were times when I envisioned them all in a group chat together, titled: Sally's Impending Breakdown, which was something I thought they were all braced for at any moment. Though who could blame them?

I chose a solo piano rendition of Einaudi's 'Experience' and pressed the repeat icon before handing the phone back to Aster. She eyed the track, smiled and placed it next to the Bluetooth speaker that the instrumentals were already pouring out from. She said nothing then, only leaned back in her chair with her hands folded neatly in her lap like a parent, or a priest awaiting a confession. It would have been much easier to have these sessions with a decorated screen between us – and if I knew that she wouldn't someday divulge everything that was said, too, of course. I wasn't sure that the therapist's oath was quite as binding as a clergyman's; where the pronounced morality lay around and within each figure.

Aster glanced at the clock. The second hand was making me flinch, intermittently; not every second but perhaps every five. It seemed louder than the music, though logically I thought that was unlikely. Perhaps the second hand of the clock wasn't making a noise at all, and it was only an internal metronome, monitoring the tick-tick-tick of the seconds. At least it wasn't accompanied by the scratch-scratch-scratch of Aster's pen. There was a small recording device sitting on the table in between us, at my request. I found it distracting, to have her writing her notes during our sessions proper. There had been so many interviews: police; journalists; police again; journalists; pol–

'Sally, are you in the room?' she asked at last.

I smiled. 'Metaphysically?'

'I see you're literally here, though I have to admit...'

First thing this morning I had called Aster and let dead air populate the line for a full ten seconds before hanging up. I knew that she would know it was me, whether through witchcraft or a caller ID system. She was right, too, in the assumption that I had been calling to cancel; to avoid stepping into the room. The white of it was enough to induce a migraine. Everything glass and polished to the point of compulsion and it had, more than once, made me wonder whether Aster didn't have her own neurotic behaviours tucked into the side of that mustard armchair – one of a few splashes of colour in the bright hollow she had designed here. The armchair I sat in was mustard too. Beyond these fixtures, there was a collection of deep-green plants populating one of two windowsills. Occasionally there were flowers on her desk, too rare to have been a self-indulgence, but rather bouquets that were gifted to her; infrequent enough that I didn't think they were from a lover, but frequent enough to make me wonder how many other patients she saw. I asked her that, once, and she'd questioned whether I spent much time wondering about that. It had seemed a strange response and on nights when I was reaching for something to busy my brain with – as though I didn't have enough within grabbing distance already – I sat with that answer like a dog staring into the pocket holes of a brain-training toy, determined to find the treat.

'Why did you pick this song?' She gestured to the speaker.

'Something about the title spoke to me.'

'Have you been making much time for music?'

She meant to ask whether I'd been making time for my thoughts. The answer to which was: No. Or whether I had kept so obsessively busy that there hadn't been space enough for the things I was trying to outrun. The answer, of course, being: Yes. The two ran in tandem now, though, like a mutated virus that could infect someone with as many as two strains at once. Busyness no longer stopped me from thinking; it only gave me static.

'Not as much time as I should,' I admitted, 'not with music.'

'You've been busy?'

'I'm tipped as a bestseller. Haven't you heard?' My tone was light, and she took the comment in jest. 'I haven't been able to stop, recently.'

'Because of work.'

Because of everything.

'How are you sleeping?' she asked, as though having heard my monologue.

'I'm managing five or so hours a night.'

'That isn't much, with everything happening.'

I turned to stare out of the window, and felt like a character from a film. I imagined her view of me in a perfect profile shot and whether, for cinematography's sake, the clock would be blurred out strategically behind me, creating a grey fade on the wall.

'I think it's *because* of everything that's happening.'

'Do you want to talk about that?'

I only laughed, and again Aster seemed to take the jest too.

'Or, perhaps, *can* we talk about that?' she said, amending the question.

The nightmares had started again. Which was a disingenuous thing to admit, because it implied there had been a period in my adult life when they had stopped. Which also wasn't true. There were only times when they ebbed low enough that I didn't remember them. Then, there were the times when they were ferocious, dragnetted by a full moon or an anniversary or a date that would have been important to Emma somehow, and they crashed, heaved themselves, even. They lashed at the seawall and spilled over its curve and I would wake howling-drowning like someone sucked under a current and Lena would be there to comfort me with the same soft noises my mother had once made, that Karin had once made, and I would shake and shudder and wide-eye stare into the black of the room before the grey outline of Emma rescinded.

'How often are you having the night terrors?'

'Night terrors makes them sound worse than they are.' I thought back over my seawall analogy. It was the writer in me now; I was always inclined to describe one thing in terms of something else, as though I had managed to professionalise avoidance strategies. *But isn't that exactly what you've done, Bestseller?* I blinked hard and swallowed back a voice that wasn't mine. It wasn't Emma's either, or anyone's I could place. But oh, it was there.

'How's Lena handling all of this? I take it she's being supportive, still.'

Lena hated my sessions with Aster, though she demanded them too. Whenever I had one – another thing that came in ebbs and flows according to the full-moon howl of my mental health in any given month – she would always tread around the borders of it when I arrived home. She made herself an unwelcome visitor step-toeing around the outer edge of a preened garden, asking things like, 'Did anything about us come up?' and 'Does she know much about me?' She never went as far as kicking the flowers, but there were times when I imagined a spiteful toddler sitting with arms folded in the well of her belly, desperate to hurl a foot.

Somewhat ironically, I'd mentioned that to Aster once too.

'She's being brilliant, always.'

'Are you managing much time together, before...'

I shrugged as she petered out. 'We have a day planned this weekend. A quiet day,' I said with a begrudging tilt.

Quiet was not a fellow I played well with, which was another problem both Aster and Lena tag-teamed in highlighting to me.

'You don't want quiet with her?'

'It isn't her,' I almost snapped, but held back, just. 'It's... the quiet of everything is loud.' I shook my head and closed my eyes and tried to find better words. 'I'm sorry, I know that doesn't make sense.'

I heard Aster shift in her seat, though I kept my eyes firmly shut.

'It does, actually.'

I smiled then, and blinked my eyes open to a narrow stare. 'You're saying that because I pay you to.'

Aster managed a laugh. 'Actually, telling you what I think you want to hear is the exact opposite of what I'm being paid to do here, Sally, and I think there's a sneaky clever part of you that knows it.' I resented the use of the word *sneaky*, even though she wasn't far wrong. 'I think you should make the most of the quiet you have with Lena, and Birdy, I assume?'

I nodded. 'Where I go, they... don't go.'

'The tour?'

'The tour.'

'You'd feel better if Lena was coming?'

I ran a hand through my hair and looked back at the window. 'I don't know whether I'd feel better, for my own reasons, if she was coming with me. As in, I don't want to be alone without her. Or whether I'd feel better for other reasons, as in, I don't want her to be alone here.'

When I glanced back I saw Aster had pursed her lips. She was squinting, as though inspecting the words. 'You're worried that something is going to happen to her?'

'Always.'

'Are the police still involved?' she asked, and I only nodded. 'And are the police concerned for Lena, or only you?'

'Me.' Everyone was always ever so concerned about little old me. 'She isn't staying at the apartment while I'm away, at least. I've asked her not to. She's staying at her own place.'

She seemed taken aback. 'Lena still hasn't got rid of her place?'

'Not yet.'

'And how do you feel about that?'

I imagined that she must have been dying to reach for a notebook by now. The next blow would send her hand twitching for something to scribble and scratch at.

'I'm the one who engineered it. I asked her not to.'

Aster's right hand shot up to her left forearm and she kneaded softly at the skin there. *Everyone has their ticks.* 'Is there a reason for that?'

'I don't want her to ever feel trapped.'

A beat of silence passed before she answered. 'Her, or you?'

'Either, or.' I shrugged again. But it was all for Lena's benefit really. I managed a tight smile to keep the chasing thought in my mouth, lest it leap right onto the pages of a manuscript or thesis that Aster might someday write about trauma survivors: *Me? I've been trapped somewhere for years.*

SIX

Birdy woke me by thundering into the room and straight into the leg of the coffee table in front of me. My eyes cracked open to sunlight, like venetian blinds slowly turned, and I blinked Lena into clear focus. She was setting a coffee on the table, black and steaming and rich; though the table was at an awkward angle now, and I wasn't sure I could reach the mug without uncurling from underneath the blanket fort I'd made for myself on the sofa. With her nurse's care she pushed damp hair away from my forehead – I must have been sweating on the dreamscape run through the woods – and kneeled between me and the table. She grabbed the coffee then, and blew across the lip of the mug to send steam rolling away the other side. She reminded me of a witch; the cup a small cauldron of something that would make me feel better. I tilted my head to look at the clock: 11am. There's no way she'd let me have something stronger until those hands had done another circuit. Instead, I pushed up onto my elbow and straightened myself enough to take the mug from her and sip. She touched my hair again, only the loose strands that were left behind from her first contact.

'Nightmares?'

'I couldn't sleep.' I handed the mug back to her and dropped flat onto my back. Birdy was curled into a ball on my stomach; the closest I would get to a creature in the womb, and I savoured the warmth of her already working through the blankets. I spoke to the ceiling then. 'I got chilly out here–'

'With the window open?'

I braced for a reprimand but when I turned I could see that she was smirking.

'Are you going to tell on me for smoking?' I cocked an eyebrow at her.

'So help me, Pober,' she poked softly at my ribs through the fleece linings around me, 'all I'm trying to do is keep you alive for a few more years.'

'Oh,' I laughed, 'and you think the smoking is going to be the deal-breaker?'

'I'm not stacking any odds against it.' She leaned forward and kissed my damp forehead. 'What do you want for breakfast? Brunch, whatever. I'll make us something.'

I thought back to what Aster had said about the quiet, the rest, something new-age and gentle about letting it take a seat at our table and exist with us for a while. I had rolled my eyes at the time and I had to swallow back the urge to recreate the reaction now. But still, it sounded like something Lena would be thankful for. And I owed her one for the smoking...

'Why don't we go out for brunch somewhere?'

The fact that she looked surprised was nearly hurtful, but I could understand.

'We're *actually* going to have a quiet day?'

I smiled. 'Unless you keep giving me sass and then we're going to have a *loud* argument.' I held out a hand for her to take, and I squeezed her fingers softly. 'An actual quiet day. You, me and Bird. A walk in the park, brunch, or more likely lunch by then, and then, you know,' I shrugged from under my folds, 'wild monkey sex followed by eating noodles straight from Chinese takeout boxes in the kitchen.'

She groaned. 'Well, if you're going to get all romantic on me...'

I didn't do romance well, of course. But I'd seen enough made-for-television films to try now and then.

It must have been National Dog Walking Day without either of us realising it. When we got to the park – which I imagined to be quiet, comforting – there was an influx of noise and animals and–

'Why are there so many fucking kids?' Lena came to a stop under a metal archway that marked the side entrance to the parkland and playing fields. It was one of the things that bonded us; our distinct lack of maternal desires or instincts – unless Birdy was making her small dog noises during a nightmare, at which time either one of us would leap to save her from whatever imagined beast might be chasing her through a dreamscape. 'Jesus, Sal, there... there are just fucking loads of them.'

Despite her terror – and her intermittent protestations that she lacked the maternal gene, if such a thing existed – I knew there was something in Lena that cared. It mightn't have been a maternal gene, per se. But she'd been a nurse in a private psychiatric clinic for the entire time I'd known her, predominantly caring for eating-disorder patients in need of residential care and assistance. That wasn't the sort of shit you could do for a living unless there was a care gene somewhere in the well of you – especially with some of the horror stories that she'd brought home on her worst days, nights, hours in the job.

'Do you want to go?'

'No! No, not at all.' She looped her arm through mine. 'Come on, Bird, lead the way.'

Birdy had come to a stop in front of us too; equally horrified, perhaps. She wasn't the sort of dog that would bite a child – or anyone, unless she thought they were a threat to me, such was her nature. But she also wasn't the sort of dog who would welcome a pat on the head from a child either. Tentatively, she took a few steps forward until she caught a smell enticing enough to pull me through the entryway and onto the path that snaked around the area. The further we walked, content in our personal bubble of quiet, the more the scene unfolded with an explanation. There were face-painting booths and craft stands and one hundred and three different food vendors. There were also large pop-up posters advertising a fundraiser for a local school; something about a new gymnasium, I thought, from the glance that I'd managed before a tumbleweed of children obscured my view again.

'Couldn't they have done it somewhere else?'

I laughed. 'You're so grumpy when kids are concerned but when you're at work–'

'That's different. Those kids need help, and besides which, they're not all kids.'

'Well, these kids need help.'

Four children chased by, one after the other in front of us, forcing us to make an abrupt stop to avoid a collision. Birdy let out a strangled moan.

'These kids need a butterfly net is what they need,' Lena answered, before steering me. 'Come on, this way looks quieter.'

And it was. We walked the path edged with fresh flowers and slowly the sound of chatter faded to a greyscale sound in the background of our bubble. Birdy moved at a steady pace and paused at regular intervals to sniff – and on one occasion to try to cock her leg up something, which was a quirk I'd come to sincerely admire in her. Lena laughed lightly when she spotted the action, and the sound of that alone sent a slow ripple of calm over me. I wished someone could bottle the feeling, so that I could pack it in with my hand luggage for the upcoming weeks. But instead I only shut my eyes for a second, pulled in a hearty deep breath and–

'Are you still with us?' Lena bumped against me.

'I am. I'm just enjoying,' I gestured with my hand, lifting Birdy's lead slightly in the process, 'I'm just enjoying all of this, you know? Quiet isn't always so bad, it turns out.'

'Ha, I'll remind you of that the next time you tell me you can't make space for it in your calendar.'

'Oh come on...' I left a beat for her to fill and when she didn't my calm stomach sagged a little. 'Have things really been that bad?'

'Sweetheart, I'm not going to lie to you.'

Three, four, five seconds of silence followed and a laugh hiccupped out of me. 'Is there more to that sentence?'

I turned and caught her expression; her mouth

bunched up to one side as though she were really putting thought into her answer, and then, 'No, I don't think there is.' Though she was smiling when she said it, it hurt me to think that Lena had felt neglected – had *been* – neglected – in the last weeks, maybe even months. She had been here for the entirety of my writing time, which had been hideous and angry and loud – on the best of days. Then, she'd been there for the letters and the sample chapters and the agents. Then–

'Christ, how have you stuck it out?' I asked, as the lists continued to grow on my mental abacus.

'I'm just in it for the fame and glory of shacking up with a famous writer.'

'I'm not a famous writer,' I snapped.

'I'll remind you of that the next time we drive past a bus stop and there's a whopping great picture of your book plastered to the end of it.' She pulled at my arm to turn me. 'Tea?'

'Nice house brick you've just thrown in there.'

'I'm nothing if not opportunistic. Tea? Or hot chocolate?'

I gasped. 'I'll push the boat out with a hot chocolate. What are you having? I'll get them.' We slowed to a stop at the edge of the counter for the drinks stand; a compact but modified camper-van that looked every bit the hipster watering hole. I pulled my phone out and thumbed into my wallet to pull up my e-card.

'Go on, I'll have a hot chocolate too.' Lena took Birdy's lead from me to free my hand. 'We'll go and perch. There's a free bench just behind you.' She kissed my cheek just as the woman serving turned around to face us – and I saw her eyes narrow.

I'm not buying hot chocolate from a homophobe, was my immediate reaction but–

'Oh my God, it's you.'

Lena and I swapped a look and I frowned, shrugged. I didn't recognise her at all, and I couldn't place a time when Birdy and I had been here on our own even, ordering tea and making polite conversation. There was nothing familiar about the woman or the scene she belonged to and yet...

She laughed – a nervous, awkward sound. 'I'm sorry, obviously you don't know me.' I tried to swap out my frown for a smile and I imagined my expression was a clumsy one. 'I saw you, you were on that talk show, the lunchtime one.' She started to click her fingers as though searching for a name. I couldn't even help her; there were at least three shows that she might have been referring to. Duke had pulled all the strings several times to arrange them. 'Christ, I can't remember. But I saw you, on the television, and I just...' A sigh fell out that sounded almost like love, but my logic prevailed and I realised it was more likely misguided admiration.

'I didn't offend you, did I?' I tried to joke, to break the act.

'Oh, no, no, not at all,' she said with hurried gestures. She struck me as the sort of person who might be rendered mute if their hands were chopped off, and I tried not to linger on the idea for too long. 'God, you just– I know this is weird, I'm making it weird now,' she made another clunky noise and quickened the pace of her speech, 'I was just so overwhelmed with respect and... awe!' She leaned too heavy on the word, making it a shout instead; it would have been written in italics. But she seemed relieved to have isolated the right feelings at last.

'Absolute awe, and utter respect. I think you're so, so brave for writing this story, and sharing it, and just, everything. Honestly, it was fucking dreadful what happened to you.'

My mouth bobbed open as though physiologically I was ready to reply; mentally, there was only dead air or static crawling about, moving from one ear to the other. *You don't even know me*, was the only thought I could clamber together. But Duke had warned me that people did, or they would. 'They'll *think* they do,' I'd snapped back when he first said it. 'Which is basically the same,' he'd replied. So instead of unhinging my jaws and taking the woman's head clean from her shoulders like an angered beast, I smiled; a toothy wide and accidental celebrity smile, even though that's absolutely not what I was, not what I was becoming.

'She's a brave one, isn't she?' Lena said then, and I was beyond glad.

'Sorry,' I finally found something to say, 'this is my partner, Lena.'

'Nice to meet you.'

'It's just *so* nice to meet you, both of you.' She wiped her hands clean of something on her short apron. 'What are you having? On me, on the house.'

'That's so kind of you,' I started to protest, 'but really–'

'Honestly, I'd like to.'

I side-eyed Lena who gave me a look of encouragement.

'How about I strike a deal with you: We'll take two hot chocolates, and I'll bring you a copy of the book when it's out?'

The woman looked as though I'd just offered her my

firstborn. Though in many ways, I suppose I had. She clasped her hands together and nodded with childlike enthusiasm. 'That would be... amazing, beyond amazing. Two hot chocolates?'

I nodded. 'Please.'

'Go, sit, I'll bring them to you.'

With that she turned and set about making what I suspected would be the best bloody hot chocolate she'd made in her young life. Lena, Birdy and I made for the bench. It was conveniently positioned in a patch of sunlight and I was thankful for the warmth. Somehow, despite the kindness of the woman, her recognition had chilled me too. I closed my eyes and tipped my head back as though basking in Cypriot rays rather than mild British heat.

'Do you think that will happen a lot?' I asked Lena.

'God, I hope so,' she answered and I shot round to face her. 'I told you, babe,' she tucked an arm behind me, 'I'm in it for the fame.'

'You're in it for the free shit,' I joked back.

She shrugged. 'The free shit doesn't hurt.'

SEVEN

After it happened – after Emma didn't come out of the woods – her parents moved. Their new house – occupied by her father alone, now – was a two-hour drive from my own home, and it bore no signs of their lost daughter. I spent the majority of the drive there in silence, bar the occasional traffic report that erupted from my speaker system like a keen child asking if we were there yet. It was an automatic feature that Lena wouldn't let me turn off; that was the precautionist in her – a word she told me didn't exist, though I told her it did, now, and that it was creative licence (and always used in an appropriate context). There was a diversion in place that meant the two-hour journey gained an unplanned for thirty-two minutes on the road, and it was somewhere in the sixteenth minute, when I finally rounded the corner onto a street I recognised, that I realised I was nervous. It wasn't a superficial nervous, either, but rather one that sat somewhere in the core of me; lower than my stomach, somehow, the feeling was distended in my pelvis as though held in place by precarious membranes and tissues, a cat's cradle of something growing. I pressed the button for the driver-side window to drop and I drank air in, in hungry mouthfuls, as though there hadn't been any at all in the car for me to draw from and I was only just now feeling it. Those heaving breaths helped me through until I arrived in viewing distance of the front door – a bottle-green, nearly; close to the colour of the free glasses case that an optician might provide as complementary with a new pair – and when I pulled up at the end of the driveway, I spotted Peter in the living-room window.

He was standing, arms folded across his chest with a stare fixed straight ahead. The posture reminded me of times when Emma had broken curfew, and I'd gone home with her in the vain hope that it might soften the wrath of her father. It hadn't done, typically. Instead he'd often bollocked the both of us for staying out later than he thought girls our age should. My own parents had always taken more of a high-road approach, realising while I was young that anything they told me not to do, I was statistically more likely to go ahead and try. Peter had always had a firmer hand, and though it hadn't unsettled the teenaged version of me, at this age it certainly held a weight to see him braced and ready.

I clambered free from the car and clicked it locked behind me, then made my way along the path to the door. The immaculate state of his front garden spoke volumes as to the time he had on his hands these days. And there, pride of place just outside the front door, taking up its rightful share of earth, was the rose bush he'd planted when his wife died. The cat's cradle in my stomach tightened then, as I remembered the phone call: Peter's voice, a strangled thing down the line; the choked sobs; the heart attack that no one could have predicted or prevented. Rose had been dead by the time the paramedics arrived.

'Sally.' His voice caught me off guard. The lighting, or lack thereof, made a silhouette of him in the open doorway, and even that felt threatening. I couldn't get a good enough look at his face to judge his mood, and his tone of voice gave nothing away. But then he stepped into the light and smiled, his face wrinkling like a lost treasure map might. 'God, I am glad you could come before you left.' He made a noise that I thought was nearly a laugh. 'Terrible grammar there, I think, don't judge me too harshly for it.'

That was something else, since becoming a writer – given that that was the moniker I'd been dubbed with – there was an undercurrent assumption that wherever you went, and whatever you heard, you lingered in the background of every exchange, silently correcting people's grammar. Secretly, I wasn't especially opposed to terrible grammar, but I thought there must be something shameful in admitting so.

'I'm glad I could too,' I said and opted to let the grammar comment slide. 'You don't hate me?' I wanted to get the question out the way early. It was on the nose, but I wasn't prepared to go into battle unarmed given the realities of the war I might be fighting. But as his treasure-map face smoothed out following the question, I realised that, far from any confrontation, there was something soft in Peter instead. And I felt my own internal weight shift; the knots loosen. 'I was scared you'd hate me,' I added, to cut through the quiet he'd left.

'I couldn't.' He shrugged and lifted his arms lightly. 'How could I?' Peter stepped aside then and gestured me into the house. 'There's tea brewing and I made some biscuits. Because I bake now.'

There was almost something shameful in the admission. But all it did was sadden me, and remind me again how much time Peter must juggle every day. Last year he'd spoken of going back to work, but to date he'd still only accepted freelance roles: odds and ends that could be done remotely, so he could stay rooted in this shrine to his wife. I glanced along the pictures that punctuated the hallway and felt selfishly grateful for the lack of Emma. Though not at all surprised to find that pictures of Rose, at various stages of their happy marriage, were still pride of place wherever I turned.

'Baking is good, baking means biscuits.' I came to a stop at the kitchen/dining-room table and waited for him to invite me to sit, which he did. The grate of wood against tiling made my shoulders bunch but they slackened when I sat down. While Peter busied himself with tea, mugs, a plate for the biscuits, I looked around the kitchen and tried to place what was different. 'Did you paint in here?'

'I did.' He joined me then and set a mug for each of us on the table. He padded back to retrieve the biscuits. 'Sometimes you just need a change of scenery, don't you? Though I suppose you'd know, or you'll know all about that, with all the travelling coming up. They're fruit and oat crunchies, you'll have to let me know what you think.' Everything came out conjoined as though the kitchen colour, the book tour, and the baking endeavours were part of a single thought.

I took a biscuit largely to keep my mouth busy. But when I snapped, chewed and swallowed, a pronounced, 'Mm,' fell out of me without even thinking.

'Jesus, Peter, these are good!'

He laughed then, a bashful one that set a shade of pink appearing out from his sideburns. 'I've had *a lot* of practice at those ones in particular. I think they would have been her favourite.' He took a biscuit for himself and in a single mouthful he cleared half of it, then chewed. I didn't ask which one of them he was referring to.

'So, we've already mentioned the tour...' I said, eager to kick the hive.

He covered his mouth while he chewed and spoke; a rude gesture for someone who had insisted on such strict manners for his daughter. 'Of course, I read the book.'

When Duke asked whether I had readers in mind for proof copies, I immediately rattled off the names of everyone close to me in the writing – the ones I'd firmly shut out of the room as I wrote. 'Of course, of course, central characters should get copies,' he'd answered, and something red and violent had flared in me at his use of 'characters'. I never corrected him on it, though, and I still thought about that sometimes.

Peter had received his copy by courier. While my parents' and Harry's were hand-delivered, I hadn't quite believed I could look Peter in the eye for long enough to give him a bound version of how his daughter spent her final days – and of course, what those final days had led to.

When he'd finished chewing he reached across the table and set his empty palm upright. I recognised the gesture as a plea for contact, though I couldn't easily marry it with the man offering it. I brushed my fingers free of biscuit crumbs before I reached out, and there was a shock of something like static when the soft of my hand rubbed against the rough of his. He squeezed, and smiled at me.

'You got Emma just right.'

And as though the feelings had always been there, teetering on the brink of breaking through, I found that I doubled over right there on the table. My forehead pressed against the cool of the wood, while my eyes filled and burst and leaked onto the veneer in a steady drip-drip-drip, answering my rushed blinks. Peter was still holding my hand, but with his other he must have reached up because I soon felt him sweep a palm across the back of my head, as though wanting to comfort me but feeling unsure of how to – which was an awkwardness I found easier to marry with him. I struggled upright after that and sank back into my chair, and I took ownership of my hand again, too, using both palms to force my hair away from my face. I cupped around the back of my neck and tried for a steady exhale. Then I realised I was still crying.

'I'm sorry,' I said, 'I don't know where that came from.'

'Please, I cry all the time.' Which was another sentiment I couldn't marry to the man. 'Perhaps not all the time,' he corrected himself, 'but certainly sometimes.' Peter took another biscuit, but this one he only held between the fingertips of each hand and turned and turned it over. 'There were times, reading back over the days before it, you know, when you got her just so...' He held an index finger and thumb pressed together as though making an A-okay gesture. 'Just so,' he repeated.

Whatever panicked creature had been living inside me until then, it settled. It curled its tail around itself, balled up tightly and found a corner in which to doze, letting out a contented sigh as it did so. And I found that once my breathing had steadied from the tears, I emulated that contentment.

Peter watched me. 'Have another biscuit,' he said. 'Do you want to take some for the road?'

'No, no,' I held a hand up, 'honestly. I'll have one now, though, thanks.'

He waited until I was shovelling food into my mouth before he asked, 'How do your parents feel about the book?'

In the days that had passed since seeing them, I'd decided that – contrary to my first thoughts – it had irked me that Dad hadn't read it. Too painful, he'd said; not something to live through a second time over, he'd said. It had always felt like a strand of narcissism when people narrated their second-hand struggles as though they took precedence over first-hand encounters of something. It must be very hard to *listen to* the things I lived through; that was the thought chasing its own tail around – another stray creature camping inside me – since I'd left Mum and Dad's. It must be very hard to know that horrible things happen in the world; that your own daughter shared a bunker space with those horrible things, for days, and–

'Sally?' Peter brought me back in. 'Are you okay?'

It was only then I realised that, far from the tears having ebbed, I'd started to cry again. I dabbed at my eyes with the sleeve of my cardigan. 'God, I'm so sorry, I don't know where all this feeling is bubbling up from.'

He reached forward, grabbed my mug and faced back into the kitchen. 'Why don't I make us some more tea? Or would you prefer coffee?' He opened the fridge. 'I think

I've got some orange juice in here somewhere, if you'd like something cold?'

He was too much the host. I wondered then how often Peter had visitors. Were there people in his life, still, or had the most important – only people – been culled in these last years? When he turned, expectant for an answer, I managed to smile back and say that more tea would be fine, please and thank you and yes, my parents were very supportive of the book. Duke had fenced my immediate reaction to Dad not having read it – 'Mum thinks it's fine, Dad parroted reviews.' – and he'd warned me that people would probably ask, on the tour. We'd decided then, that a safe and neutral response would be: 'They're both really supportive, they were, through everything, and they still are now, with the book.' Peter nodded along while the kettle boiled, wearing a thin-lipped expression that made me wonder whether he believed me. I would need to practise this lie.

'Sally, don't think me nosy,' he paused and let out a loose laugh, 'or do, I really don't mind you thinking that. But this tour, is it safe? Is it going to be safe, while you're away? The police...'

I only managed a shrug and a soft smile. 'It's as safe as it can be, I think.' Though there were options for additional protection available still, I was trying to be The Brave Woman who didn't need or want them. I didn't know how long that would last when faced off against cities I didn't know, rooms full of people I didn't recognise, Duke, who would no doubt leave me unattended despite his intermittent promises to Lena that he wouldn't dream of doing such a thing...

'Maybe when you're home, back in the city, maybe we could meet up again?'

The needy optimism in his voice near on crippled me. 'Why don't we go for dinner somewhere?'

'I can cook!'

I tapped the half-empty plate of biscuits. 'That much I can see, but wouldn't it be nice if you didn't have to? We'll find somewhere for dinner and I can tell you everything about the tour, all the juicy bits.' I tried to feign excitement rather than nerves; though nerves wasn't quite right either. Still, anything that didn't give away a deep-rooted sensation of shitting oneself would do. 'Does that sound...' I started again when he didn't answer, borrowing from his own needy tone. He was faced away from me by then, too, adding teabags, pouring water.

'Do you know, our Em used to say...'

I felt my breath catch at her name. I hadn't been braced for it.

'She used to say when I'm a proper grown-up, I'll come home and I'll treat *you* to a nice dinner somewhere.' He turned and made an unsteady walk back to the table with tea in each hand. 'I used to try to take her out every month or so. I was working so much when she was younger,' a huff of air escaped, 'you probably remember that.' I did. In our younger-younger years Emma used to hate the amount of time Peter spent away. In our older-younger years, she used to hate the amount of time he spent trying to make up for it – father-daughter dinners included, though I'd always wondered whether she was bluffing about her distaste for them. 'The older she got, the more of a chore it was for her, I'm sure. But she used to say, when I'm a grown-up...' The end of the sentence died out somewhere, dribbled the wrong route like verbal backwash.

'Well,' I cupped my hands around my mug and

focused only on the drink, 'I'm a proper grown-up, and I'd like to take you to dinner.' *Once I've survived the tour*, I thought but didn't say, because Lena had told me it wasn't a well-received line. And I wasn't altogether sure I was joking.

EIGHT

I wondered how many pieces a heart could feasibly break into. Would it be four? Would it fracture clean into left, right, upper and lower? And if that were the case, I wondered then, which part would I be leaving at home in my apartment? Though it wouldn't stay there for long. It would leave when Birdy did; when Lena wrapped her brilliant blue lead around her and hustled her from my home and back to her own, which she was due to do later in the day, once Birdy had accepted I wasn't coming back. But when I'd finished scouting around the rooms for the dog, and eventually found her sitting alongside my stuffed suitcase, I thought I would be leaving at least a single atrium behind wherever she was. *Will you carry it in your mouth?* I asked her, as though through the sheer force of our connection she might understand – and she tilted her head to the left, then the right. *Upper and lower*, I thought again, as my knees jerked and I napkin-folded myself onto the floor of the hallway. She took tentative steps, uncertain about leaving her post, but eventually made it all the way to me. Birdy had always been a small dog, my bag of flour, and I scooped her up tight like a child winning a plush animal in a fairground. I rubbed my nose into the smell of her neck and swallowed whole the grass and the dew and–

'Why do you smell like ham?' She stared up at me with answering eyes. 'Did Lena give you ham?'

'I was trying to build a rapport with her,' Lena answered from somewhere behind me. 'That, and trying to lure her away from your bag.' She soft-trod up the hallway behind me and crouched down on the floor to where we sat. 'Should I be sad that you're going away on a book tour and you're definitely going to miss that dog more than you're going to miss me?'

'I can FaceTime you.'

Lena huffed. 'I'm under no disillusions about the fact you'll be on FaceTime for her.' She reached forward and scratched the spot behind Birdy's right ear; the sweet spot, and I was warmed that Lena had remembered. 'We're going to take good care of each other, aren't we, Bird?'

'You'll be okay for the early walks?'

Lena groaned. 'Six in the morning is offensively early by anyone's standards but yes, I'll be okay for the early walks.' She leaned across and kissed the side of my temple, and Birdy made a high whine. 'I'm going to miss her too, madam, I'm allowed some time,' Lena answered her. 'Do you have everything you need?'

'Mm-hm.' I let Birdy go and she immediately hurried back to the bag by the door, and I felt another atrium break away. *Maybe I'll leave my entire heart here.* 'Everything is packed and ready. I've got my proof, I've got my notes.' I struggled up from the floor and brushed away the dust from my jeans.

'The office is all locked up?'

There were only two keys to the room. One I carried on a sixteen-inch chain around my neck; the other I kept in my purse. I was 'suspiciously protective' of the space; that's how Lena referred to it, on many an occasion. The only time when she had been allowed in was when I was already in there, pacing the floors during the ugly hours of the morning to get a scene right; to find the memory I was missing. I had found Lena unaccompanied in there, once, and it had been perhaps the worst argument we'd ever had. Since then she'd maintained a respectful distance; she knew which buttons to push and which ones to leave covered by protective plexiglass. I felt at my neck for the key before I answered her.

'You don't want me to...' She let the sentence die out when she saw my expression. *No, I don't want you to keep a spare.* I flashed a tight smile at her then went to do one final sweep of the kitchen, living room, bedroom windows. Lena followed me everywhere I went. 'I was only trying to be helpful. In case there's something in there you decide you need?'

'I've got everything I need.' I yanked at the living-room window – the one I always perched in when I "wasn't smoking" – but couldn't shift it, even with a measure of strength behind the manoeuvre. 'But thank you.'

'And Duke is collecting you?'

I checked my watch. 'In about twenty minutes. I'm meeting him up on Tailor's Way. The roadworks out there are still fucking up access to the street. Look,' I ran both hands through my hair and let them rest at the back of my neck, my fingers clasped together to make a brace, 'you're sure you're going to be okay?'

'Sally.' Lena crossed the room to me and motioned for my hands; I placed my palms against hers. 'Me and Bird are going to be fine. I'm more worried about you than anything.' She leaned forward to set a gentle kiss against my forehead. 'Try to enjoy this trip, okay? This is huge and you've worked so hard and– You deserve everything that's coming to you, Sal, you really do.'

And although it was a soft sentiment, something about it made my stomach turn. Still, I managed a smile and a forceful kiss and–

'We'll do something when I get back? Something big and fun and celebratory.'

'You bet your ass we will.' She tapped that very same ass as I stepped around her to head for the door. 'I'm going to finish packing my stuff and have a cup of tea here, then Birdy and I will head out too. Let me know when you get where you're going,' I turned to face her as she added, 'and I'll let you know when we get where we're going,' before I could even ask.

'I love you both.'

Birdy let out another whine from behind me and I shut my eyes against the sound.

'She'll be fine,' Lena said again, 'and we love you too.'

I felt the precursor to tears as soon as I heard the main door shut behind me but I swallowed it down. I'd never been one for crying in public – not even when I had to leave my dog/heart behind me for a lengthy period of time, though that pushed me close. I trudged the walk from my own neighbourhood into the next and rounded into Tailor's Way after only a few minutes, making me early. Duke was chronically late. It was part of his charm, he said, but when I was anxious and lingering and playing host to hornets in the bottom-back portion of my brain, I could have done with some punctuality. There was an empty taxi rank there for me to wait by, as agreed, and the only other patron was an older woman who kept checking her watch. *Your ride is late too*, I thought as I wheeled my bag to a standstill behind her. Alongside the rank there was a scrolling advertisement board that kept catching her attention. Whenever the image changed, her head would twitch; a cat watching for magpies out of an upper-floor window, she would stare for a beat as though assessing prey before accepting the unlikelihood of a catch. Then she went back to staring at the road.

I was checking my phone when the woman braved contact. It wasn't a conventional hello though. Instead, she made such a pronounced tutting sound that the nosy part of my brain couldn't help but make my head jerk. I fought the urge to look up until she tutted a second time and then, only seconds later, she added, 'Disgusting, that, isn't it?'

'I'm sorry?' I asked before my head was raised enough to see what she was referring to. But then I spotted it: My book cover. It was bold and threatening and dark, all of the things a true crime book is meant to be. My name was plastered across the top, the title of the book across the bottom, with horror-film woodland occupying the space between the two: *One woman's story of survival against the odds...*

I felt bile rise in my throat and I had to force out a slow breath. I was convinced I might upchuck right there on the pavement.

The woman turned then and said, 'Imagine, watching

a close friend going through something like that and doing nothing?'

I will not cry. I parroted it like an affirmation. *I will not fucking cry.*

'And then writing a book about it. Christ.' She tutted again and then went back to looking for her taxi. *I will not cry.* I guessed that she was my mother's age, maybe slightly older. Her hair was greying, long and pinned into a perfect bun that made her look every bit the firm nanny figure. She was wearing loose-fit jeans; loose-fit from years of wear, though, not loose-fit by design. The jeans were paired with a long knit jumper, a similar shade of grey to her hair but with strands of silver pulled through the weave. When she shifted suddenly, the fabric caught the sun. *I will not cry.* I didn't think she was my ideal reader; the one who had stood in the corner of the room with their arms folded, peering over my shoulder during note-taking, tapping their watch and pacing the floor while I wrote. This woman had definitely not been allowed in the room with me. But still, in a world where more and more people were recognising you, it probably did something worthwhile for the ego to be reminded by a complete stranger that you were, are, in fact, a fucking nobody.

'Hey, you getting in or what?' Duke's voice pulled me around. 'I tooted like three times on my way up the road.'

'That doesn't make you any different from *any* other taxi driver on this street,' I joked through the open passenger window. 'Pop the boot, I'll throw my bag in.'

'Okay but there's a surprise in there for you, so don't go rooting.'

When you'd been subjected to a violent attack, surprises tended to lose their thrill. Even though Duke had, historically, been good at giving me treats – to make an obedient dog of me, one who might sit still and tilt their head and smile for a camera, with a wagging tail and all. So when I threw my bag into the boot of his car, I couldn't help but part the lips on a fabric bag that was thrown in there, too, alongside what was clearly Duke's own travel bag. Stashed in the fabric, there were envelopes on envelopes and I needed a closer look before I could understand but–

'Hey, what did I say about not looking?'

'Fine, fine.' I slammed the boot and climbed into the passenger seat of the car. 'Do you know, when you said there was a treat back there for me I was hoping for a bottle of chilled gin and a sleeve of cigarettes.'

'You can't drink while I'm driving. It will distract me.' He checked his mirrors, swapped lanes, swapped lanes again while he spoke. A beat of silence passed before he added, 'But now we're nearly at the motorway, you'll find a fresh twenty pack in the glove compartment.'

I gasped. 'A whole twenty?'

'What happens on tour stays on tour.'

'You're setting a dangerous precedent there,' I was already fumbling with the cellophane of the packet, 'but if it means that I can smoke and drink as much as I want then I'm not going to complain.'

'I promised Lena I wouldn't let you get smashed every night.'

'And I'd wager there was an implicit promise that you wouldn't let me smoke either.' I paused, tactically, to spark up a cigarette and took a long and greedy inhale before saying, 'Yet here we are.' Smoke rushed out of me like warm water had just hit the dry ice of my lungs.

Duke waved his hand around to clear the smog. 'At

least open the window, would you? Christ, you're an animal.'

I let the comment slide, and Duke let the silence between us hang for a junction before he cleared his throat with obvious purpose. 'So...'

'What do you want?' I stayed fixed to the window, counting sheep and anything else my blurred eyes could find.

'Why do you assume that I want something?'

Seventy-two sheep; thirty-one cows; hundreds of–

'Okay, I do want something,' he added, when my non-response had lasted long enough to make him uncomfortable. Duke had always been one of those people for whom dead air was a lethal thing. 'We're recording with the podcast people tonight, which I know you already know. But, when I was talking to them about extracts, they asked whether you'd mind reading a part– Look, you have autonomy over this, Sal, right? Because you're the creative and who am I and who is anyone to– But they'd really like to hear you talk about, and hear you read about...'

There was only one thing that ever made him – ever made anyone – this uncomfortable. It was like listening to a feral creature caught in a trap built for a bear, and the merciful part of me opted to put him out of his misery. *Seventeen wild horses.* 'Emma, they want to hear me read about Emma.'

He took a sharp intake as though the name had stung him. 'Yes.'

FROM THE WOODS

I don't know how old I was when I met Emma. Of course, I know from photographic evidence that we were young. I was still in a phase of only wearing dresses. Meanwhile, Emma was in a phase of only wearing clothes that had some reference to Barbie on them. There were photographs that my mother enjoyed rolling out periodically; the proud parent showing off her children's snapshots. She loved to remind us of those days and in truth I think Emma and I both loved to see them. It may have been a narcissistic thing. We could legitimise cooing over ourselves and commenting, 'Look how cute we are in this one...' and no one seemed to mind. So I know that the friendship was far-reaching into the recesses of childhood – which is different to remembering it, but still. When I say that I don't know how old I was when I met her, I suppose what I implicitly mean there is that I cannot picture a time in my life when Emma wasn't in it. While many people might trace their earliest memories to family members or beloved pets, for me, it was her. She had always been there, like a limb or other essential.

When I was ten years old I remember sitting Emma down and asking what would happen when we got older. She thought I meant, 'What will we do for a living?' or even, 'Where do you think we'll go to university?' But I clarified for her that what I was really asking was, 'Do you think we'll separate, or will we still be friends?' Separate was the exact word I used too. There had been a spate of separations around our classroom. Parents were breaking apart at their cores and sending their fractured remains of children in to try to concentrate through maths and literacy skills, only for them to inevitably become disruptive midway through a school day. 'Don't mind Clara, she's going through some things; her parents are separating.' The teachers never said it to us, only among themselves – but walls have small ears, and the news spread. Soon, it stretched beyond parents. There were small factions of girls around our classroom who had been friends for as long as Emma and I and they, too, started to break away into small huddles. Like messy boulders breaking clean away from a larger rockface, what was once a classroom united by solid comradeship soon became a relationship – or rather, break-up of relationships – pandemic. I was convinced that Emma and I were only ever moments away from the argument that would chip one of us away from the other and send us cascading into a landscape of unknown waves below.

'Of course we'll be friends. Why are you being an idiot?'

'Don't call me an idiot!'

'Don't be one, then!'

Emma had collapsed into laughter and I soon followed. That was the moment that I realised, I think, that we were going to be okay. Or at least, that was the

moment when I believed it most. That belief was steadfast for years after, through actual break-ups and arguments with parents and mock examinations and–
Even into the woods, even *in* the woods, I believed for a while that we were going to be okay. Emma had that effect. She could always make me believe the utmost unbelievable things. She could always tether me to the rockface.

NINE

Duke and I only checked into the hotel once the podcast recording was done. I'd told him that I wanted to get the business out of the way, so I could comfortably lounge and wallow and plan for the days ahead. I stood outside the reception door caning through a cigarette, one drag after another after– Duke struggled to get my bag, his own, and whatever the sack of envelopes were out of the boot and balanced in a single trip. But he'd told me that I didn't need to help him, and I was apt to take the man at his word. When he thumped everything down to a stop in front of me I cocked an eyebrow before I turned to dub my cigarette on the ashtray that was fixed to the wall. He was panting, a full wheeze trailing through parted lips like the least healthy kid in a school relay.

'Light me up one of those, will you?' he asked.

I laughed and fumbled the packet free from my coat pocket. 'Sure, because it sounds like that's what you need.'

'We should get dinner after this, after we're settled.' Duke took the lit cigarette from me and inhaled like it was medicinal. 'Do you want to know what's in the bag?' He nodded to the fabric sack and I had an unexpected step back in time to when I was – *how old would I have been?* – and I caught Santa in our living room. My father had always taken precautions against me catching him in the act of delivering presents and, because of that, every Christmas until I was old enough to know better he would slink down our stairs wearing a full Santa attire. It paid off, too, given that one year I heard Santa and decided to sneak down. He ho-ho-ho'ed and laughed along with my semi-serious question about where the reindeer were parked and then he said, with a wink, 'Do you want to know what's in there?' Then he nodded to the bag of presents he'd brought with him. It had taken me a long time – or certainly, what felt like a long time – to say no, no, thank you. Santa had patted me on the head and told me what a good kid I was. The following morning, in slippers and a fleece dressing gown, Dad let me sit on his lap and tell him all about how I'd met Santa the night before. It wasn't until years later that I found it had been him all a–

Duke snapped his fingers in front of my face. 'Don't zone out, Sal, come back.'

For once I hadn't gone anywhere bad, and I resented him pulling me away from that luxury. 'If you're about to tell me that that bag is full of appearance requests then I don't know that I'm going to thank you for it.' I was an ungrateful client, sometimes, but Duke was making enough money by association to put up with it. That was my cynical reasoning for it. I'd voiced something similar to Lena once, too, though she'd been saddened by the idea.

'You don't think Duke likes you a little bit?' she'd asked, and I'd shaken my head. I couldn't see why anyone would.

Duke exhaled a plume of smoke and shook his head. 'Not everything is work, work, work. Sometimes it's pleasure.' He nudged the bag towards me with his foot. 'In that bag, is your fan mail.'

My stomach rollercoaster dropped. 'My...'

'Fan mail!' Duke's own smile was Cheshire Cat wide enough for the both of us. 'If you needed a sign that the interviews and the readings and the recordings were worth it, this is it, Sal. People love you already.' This was another unexpected bump in the rollercoaster track of my new life and my stomach dipped again. 'Why do you look like I've just given you homework?' he asked then, his voice singed with disappointment at the edges; a cigarette paper burning up his words. 'This was meant to be a good thing. I thought...' He paused, inhaled hard and said through smoke again, 'I thought it would be a kind thing for you to have, you know, in between visits and driving and all the rest of it.'

I forced a smile. 'It is a kind thing. I'm sorry.' And I used my best I'm sorry voice for the apology too. 'I just wasn't expecting something like that so... well, so soon, I guess. The book isn't even out.'

Duke seemed to think hard before he answered. I imagined him carefully weighing each word; planting one on one side of the scale, then the other, then... to make sure the sentence was perfectly balanced and therefore less likely to throw me off. I think I felt a flicker of pity for him then. 'Sally, I know this may come as something of a shock,' I felt my core muscles tense, 'but people actually like you.' He reached across to give my upper arm a squeeze. 'I know the story is big and horrible, kiddo, but you've told it now, you're telling it; you don't have to carry bad feeling *all* the time. You're allowed some good.'

My eyes started to sting with– *It's the cigarette smoke*, I told myself. 'You're allowed some good too,' I answered with a thin smile. 'Don't you have other clients, more grateful, less emotionally volatile ones, that you could be spending your time with sometimes?'

He laughed and leaned forward to dab out his own smoke. 'None that are going to make me the money that you will, doll.'

I laughed too. But the comment was bee-sting sharp.

Despite suggesting dinner, Duke had wanted to rest, too, before we went to eat. I was too restless for an early evening lie-down, though, and I told him I was going for a walk instead. He seemed hesitant, as though letting me out on my own might mean he'd never see me again; an untrustworthy dog unclipped from their lead in an endless field. I promised him that letting me off the leash wouldn't come to anything bad and he agreed to it then, answering as though I'd been seeking approval. I told him I wanted to find the bookshop for tomorrow's signing, that it would give me purpose in moving through the city with an end goal, and that seemed to help his nerves too. 'They're a late night one so you'll probably catch them open,' he said, his head already buried in a pillow. I keyed directions into my phone and left, and when I was two steps free of the hotel I called Lena.

The phone rang out three, four, five times and– 'Hi,

it's Lena, I can't get to the phone right now but if you'd like to leave me a message, I'll get back to you.'

'Hi, Lena, it's... it's just me.' I disconnected then. I hadn't called to say anything; I'd only called for the sake of it. She'd like the sentimentality of that. She was good at seeing feeling even when I was a total dunce at communicating it. Though I knew there would also be a part of her that would assume I'd called to check on Birdy – and that was a fair belief too.

It only took eleven minutes to walk to the bookshop, and even that was me taking my time. I stopped to survey shops on my travels; their doors were mostly closed for the day, bar the occasional niche establishment: a cupcake store that hadn't quite run out; a hairdressers that still had customers lingering by the door, observing an old *'Two customers at a time'* sign. The shop I was searching for was wedged between a butchers and a bar, and it was a beautiful brick building befitting of books. But the window display made me cross the street to create a safer distance from it. From the opposite side of the road, I surveyed a space that had been entirely overtaken by my book. The cover was blown up to an intimidating size – easily the same height as me – and there were early release copies of it stacked and stacked. There were, I thought, more copies than any single bookshop could have possibly had access to yet either. The entire point of touring the book before its release was the exclusivity of the events and yet, the shop looked ready to stock a hundred people or more. I wondered, then, whether the stacks were even all mine! Or whether some clever shop assistant had decided to stack any old hardbacks together and strategically position copies of my own work in front. *Am I being paranoid right now?* My head snapped around when I caught someone in my peripheral vision and the speed of that reaction felt like an answer. But on my way back from that glance I saw the part of the window display that was most offensive of all. So offensive, that I wanted to huff and puff and blow the whole thing apart.

'I'd like that removed.' The shop was nearly empty but I raised my voice all the same. 'In the window, I'd like that removed.'

'I'm sorry, can I ask who–'

'I'm Sally Pober.' I pointed to the window again then, to the offending object. 'And I'd like that removed.'

An older woman appeared alongside the young assistant that I'd launched my demand at. She said something to the younger woman, who then moved from behind the counter. I'd expected her to follow my finger, go immediately to their window display and snatch the cardboard cut-out from where it lingered. Only she didn't. Instead, the young woman flashed me an awkward smile and then disappeared to the opposite end of the shop and–

'I don't understand *how* in God's green anyone could think that's appropriate,' I continued to the older saleswoman as though I'd been talking to her all along. I assumed she'd heard the first waves of my demand anyway. 'I don't know who decided this, who you agreed or didn't agree to it with, but I'm not having it there, and if you don't remove it, I'm going to remove it myself.'

'Miss Pober, let me start by apologising–'

'Apology accepted,' I cut across her, 'now move it.'

The woman took heed of the tone. She apologised again before moving out from behind the counter and going to the window. She handled it awkwardly, as though this were her first time touching it, and I wondered who'd put it there to begin with. The woman shoved and pushed and manoeuvred until the life-size cardboard came free, taking a small stack of paperbacks along with it as the woman tumbled backwards with the character in her arms. She was holding it in front of her when she turned, as though making a human shield of the prop, but when faced off with it at a closer distance I found that it repelled me rather than spurred me on. I backstepped until I was pressed against the counter but even that didn't feel like distance enough. The woman set it down to lean against the wall before she closed the space between us, her hands knotted together, working themselves over like fresh nervous dough. She said something else; she might have apologised again. But I couldn't hear her through the hornet storm in my ears. I could only look just behind her to where the black cardboard cut-out of a man was standing still; the arms of the figure were bent up, as though holding something at the core of itself. And there, printed and taped, was a picture of my book.

So this is him, I thought, all the while still trying to push my airways open, let my stomach expand, feel my ribs shift and close– *So this is him*. 'Miss Pober, I really must apologise again...' When I half heard her I knew some of the hornets must be dissipating; fleeing back to the hive, but still– *So this is him*, I heard again and again until the thought rolled into another one: *So this must be the man who took us*.

And things became a kaleidoscope then. There was a lot of noise and the ground was hard and my breathing was loud. And I was trying to explain but nothing was emerging but then something did and it was childlike garble and then I don't remember asking, I couldn't have possibly asked but someone–

'Sally? Sal, doll, it's me.'

–someone must have called Duke. Duke must have come to help.

TEN

It was the morning after the panic attack. Duke and I were sitting in the hotel beer garden with the solemn faces of two people who may have simultaneously realised their marriage is in trouble, just before going on a family holiday with their closest relatives. Though I was grateful that, at least, my closest relatives were in fact an unknown distance away, and I didn't have to face-off against the worried expressions and the half-said questions and the quiet, gentle, implied, 'Are you sure you're ready for this, Sally?' propositions that would come under the guise of care. I swallowed the dregs of my orange juice and sparked up another cigarette. It was my third smoke of the day, but Duke hadn't said anything. After my display in the bookshop the previous evening, I guessed that he was only happy I was still alive – and not hospitalised with acute heart failure. 'It was genuinely like you were having a heart attack,' he'd said, his arm round my waist as he guided me back towards the hotel. 'I nearly called Lena, do you know that? I nearly called to ask what the bloody fuck I should be doing, doll, and what the bloody fuck should I have done, is this right?' he'd asked, his arm having shifted to fit snuggly around my shoulders which meant that he felt my half-arsed attempt at a shrug in response to his flurry of questions. When we got back to the room I collapsed onto the bed and buried my tired head in the cloud of a pillow and then said, 'Lena is the wrong kind of nurse for it,' before passing out, fully clothed and with a full face of slap still on, though most of that had deposited itself on the white cotton pillowcase covering by the time I woke up. After seven solid hours of sleep I clambered into a sitting position and scanned the room, and found Duke sitting in the armchair in the corner, quietly watching me. He'd smiled when he saw I was awake.

'You're being a bit creepy, you know,' I'd tried to joke as I turned over to face him easier. 'I'm not sure it's okay, to watch women while they're sleeping.'

'It is if you're keeping a lookout for signs of a pulse.'

Duke had held a strong silence while I showered and repainted my smile in place; though my hair I left to spring into its natural curl, with a loose promise to myself that I would straighten it neat later on in the day, before the event. In the bathroom I'd set a palm flat against my forehead and let a small groan tumble out, and somehow Duke had heard it from his sit-point in the room. That's when he'd suggested cigarettes and pastries and–

'Do you want more orange juice?'

I turned and squinted. The sun was rising at an awkward angle over the garden we were in, and it was making it impossible to look Duke in the eye – as was the rising shame of my behaviour from the evening before.

'I'm okay, thank you.'

'I read online that you need to keep your blood sugar up.'

I huffed. 'I don't know that that has much to do with a panic attack.'

He shook his head and reached forward to grab his own box of cigarettes. We were on a box apiece already by then; such was the stress of the first day away from my usual keeper and home. 'It's not for the panic attack as such, doll, it's just the energy expenditure that your body goes through during it. See–'

'Please stop.' I punctuated the plea with a flick of my lighter. He reached forward to meet the flame. 'If it makes you feel better, you can get me some more orange juice.' I dropped the lighter on the table, fell back in my chair and broke my clumsy eye contact with him.

There was a long pause before he said, 'I wasn't *offering* to get it.'

Duke's comment caught me so off guard that a grunt of a laugh hiccupped out of me, with such a scratch along my throat that I found I was soon coughing out my amusement too.

'Jesus, doll, it wasn't that funny.' He rested his cigarette in the ashtray. 'Do you want anything else while I'm going in?'

'Oh, Duke, really, sit down–'

'Nothing?'

I smiled. 'No, nothing, thank you.'

Even so, when he reappeared a short time later – a third of his cigarette had burnt down in the tray – he was holding half a pint of orange juice and another raspberry crown. I took both and smiled; it wasn't worth fighting him on this, I decided. Duke was drowning. I pulled a thirsty inhale of smoke and fostered a vision of him as an out-of-his-depth father who'd agreed to take his wayward teen on holiday without her mother. I hated that that was the part Lena must be expected to play. Instead of arguing my case any further, I decided it would be easier to down three mouthfuls of the orange juice and pick at the pastry instead. It was my second of the morning, coupled with three pieces of jam on toast, and I was one more hit of sugar away from either bouncing around the free lawn space that surrounded us or needing a nap; maybe one then the other. But at least either or both would keep me out of Duke's way for a while, which I thought he probably deserved. That said, though, he wasn't likely to let me off the leash any time soon without supervision, so finding ways to keep busy was going to be a necessity – for us both.

'What do you want to do today?' he asked then, and my head shot up.

'I didn't think we had anything booked until tonight?' He didn't say anything in response to that, and it took me longer than it should have to realise that I hadn't answered his question. 'We can just stay in the hotel, rest, whatever.' I knew he hadn't slept much; there might have been snatched moments, during his night-watch of me, but there can't have been much in the way of substantial rest. And he'd only had one pastry too. I thought about pushing what was left of my raspberry crown over to his side of the table.

'You're not on lockdown, Sal, we can do stuff. I'm just...'

He petered out and I watched as his face scrunched. He was looking for the right words, I knew, but I also knew there weren't any. Duke was worried. But I was a loose cannon now, which meant he was right to be.

'Why don't we have an hour, and you can sleep and I can read, and we'll go from there?' I suggested, with my sunniest tone.

Duke gave me a tired sigh. 'You don't want to write?'

I laughed. 'About what, last night? It doesn't have the same edge as my previous story does.' I thought about winking, as though underscoring the humour, but I wasn't sure the 'joke' had been good enough to deserve it. 'No, I don't want to write. But time to read would be great. I have some stuff that I'm endorsing.'

Duke made an 'Ooo' noise and smoke poured out of him like a peak on a train. 'Look at you, endorsing things.'

'I know,' I stood up then, 'good job people don't know what a raving nutcase I am or they wouldn't trust me with their work at all.' He moved to stand, too, but I put a hand on his shoulder as I reached him. 'I promise to get up to the room without having a panic attack or accusing someone of blind insensitivity, unless I think they really deserve it.'

He looked up at me, wearing the same squint I'd brandished earlier. 'It was insensitive for them to do what they did, with that cut-out.'

'I guess that's the trouble when you sell your life as a storybook.' I squeezed the ball of his shoulder and forced a smile before I walked away. *People are always forgetting the story is real.*

There was an ugly heat in the room. It was the type of stifling atmosphere reserved for school assemblies and village hall meetings where the air can't find an escape route, so it could only circulate its warmth and be added to with every lap of the space. I drew the line at fanning myself with a copy of my own book, but it was something I was seriously considering while Diane – the woman who I had screamed at the day before – was doing a dash around the room with a microphone in hand, to reach a woman at the back who was trying to wave a question at me. She could have shouted. The bookshop, while packed to its shelves on either side of the space, wasn't big enough to warrant a sound system in order that people might hear each other. Respectful quiet and enunciation would have done the trick. But at least while Diane was clambering over people on the back two rows, it meant I bought myself a second of silence and two sips of water. As I placed my glass back down on the ground I took a strategic scan around for Duke, who was leaning against shelves at the back of the space, out of the way, with his arms folded and neutral expression – until he saw me looking. Then he winked and held up an A-okay gesture of approval, and the mucus nerves that had been stretched between the edges of my stomach gave way to a real and physical relief. By the time the woman at the back of the room was actually asking her question, I found I was even smiling.

'Was it a therapeutic thing to do, to write this book, Sally?' she asked, smiling, and I struggled to marry the question with the light expression she wore.

I opted for a light answer to start with though. 'I think that depends on which of my counsellors you ask.' There was a low rumble of nervous laughter around the room then; a gentle wave, hesitant about reaching me. People were never sure how much humour they could find in my life's work. 'It was, in lots of ways. There are things in this book that I honestly don't think I knew, or remembered, until I wrote them down. And, even though I say this very much as a layperson,' I set a hand flat against my chest plate then, as though to underscore my modesty, 'I do wholeheartedly believe that one way or another those things need... they needed to come out, and the book was the way to do that.'

'Okay, thank you. And–'

'Oh, dear, I'm so sorry, one question per audience member, please,' Diane said as she snatched the mouthpiece away from the woman, 'we've got a lot of people to get through. Yes, there,' she clicked to get the attention of a member of staff, 'that gentleman at the front, please.'

I hadn't stipulated that the questions could only come from women. I thought that was probably a demand I wasn't allowed to make – unless I wanted to kiss my career goodbye before it had even launched. But when the microphone was handed over to the man – mid-forties, hair greying at the sides, reading glasses perched on the end of his nose even though he wasn't holding a book – I found myself wondering whether that's what The Man looked like. *Is that the kind of neutral, insignificant face you might wear?* I tried to match his smile as he stood up to speak to me.

'Firstly, Sally, I think you read *exceptionally* well from this, especially considering the content.' He paused then, as though anticipating a response, but I only smiled and ducked my head slightly, as if to graciously accept the praise. 'Secondly, do you think this book is the start of something for you, something big, I mean, or...'

I don't know what expression my face fell into, but it made the man laugh.

'I'm not being clear.' He pinched the bridge of his

nose and made a show of thinking. *No, you're not.* I let the dead air hang between us but I was secretly hoping, too, that Diane might snatch the airtime away from him soon. 'I think what I mean to say is, do you think this is the start of a career in true crime?'

From the corner of my eye I saw Duke straighten, push himself away from the supporting shelves as though he might intervene. But there wasn't a need. It was an inevitable question; one that Duke and I had talked about even. Though given that I was writing from lived experience, it seemed a strange question too. The only way I could answer was with stark honesty and, with what I hoped, was at least a humorous tone:

'Well, if it is I certainly hope I can write the next book without being kidnapped beforehand.'

'Next question from literally anyone else, please!' Diane clucked as though the humour hadn't quite landed with her. But there were small pockets of laughter around the room at my answer and the man, too, was laughing as he sat down. Then I glanced at Duke again, to find him beaming and half laughing and making that same A-okay gesture, and suddenly I was a child performing at a school talent show: I had hit the high note; I had kept my underwear covered; I had remembered all my lines. And I got through the whole evening without anyone dying or disappearing and that, I thought, as I drifted into a creeping sleep later in the night, must be the sign of something good.

ELEVEN

Lena had missed three calls from me and I was beginning to nurse a swarm of starving bees in my belly over it. Duke and I were meant to be having a day off together – somewhere between Manchester and Leeds, which were the cities we were bouncing between by then – but I couldn't focus. We had both promised each other an easy day and we had managed it, to an extent. Neither of us had made a move to roll free from our respective beds until 10.30am; a decision that was very much spurred on by the fact that the hotel we were staying in had a better room-service breakfast than they did a buffet. We'd made piglets of ourselves, both ordering stacked pancakes that were loaded with bacon and blueberries and an American measuring of syrup. Duke had said he would smoke and then shower, and I used the time to call Lena twice: the first to say a late good morning; the second, because I assumed she was busy rushing around, such was Lena's way, which was why she'd missed the first of the calls. But she answered neither. 'Give the woman a break,' Duke had encouraged me, 'she'll call back when she's free.' And I did manage to 'give her a break' – until nearly lunchtime. Duke went into a local eatery to scout out whether there was anything worth ordering, and whether they had an outdoor area big enough and sunny enough for us to park ourselves in. I stayed out the front of the restaurant on the pretence of smoking but really– 'Hi, you've reached Lena's phone.'

'So their outdoor area looks pretty rammed but– Sally!'

He found me, phone pressed to ear and fingers indenting into my forehead. I cut the call off before the answer machine asked me to speak. *Has she changed her outgoing message?* I suddenly wondered, which seemed a strange worry to stitch together but still, there it was.

'Do you know if she was on a night shift last night?' he asked then, as his tone moved from irritated to consoling at too quick a pace.

I tried to think. 'Fuck me, what day is it?'

'Wednesday.'

I thought and thought and thought and– 'Yes!' The relief of the realisation coursed through me like the second orgasm in a Sunday afternoon cluster. 'Yes, she'll have been on a night shift at work. Fuck, Duke, you're an absolute– Christ, come here.' I pulled him into a hug. It may have been the most human contact either of us had had since this jaunt started; unless he'd got lucky when I wasn't looking. Which, admittedly, wouldn't have surprised me.

He tapped softly at the spot between my shoulder blades. 'There, there. Now,' Duke pushed me away and held me by the balls of my shoulders, 'outdoor area, afternoon pint, or bottle of vino or– Hell, whatever you want, doll. Let's treat ourselves.'

The rumble of nerves gave way to a rumble of hunger then, and I nodded along. 'Everything you've just said sounds...' And I borrowed Duke's A-okay gesture, one he'd flashed me every night, at every book reading, at least once. He led the way in, weaving a path through the busy dining hall and out into the back patio. And even though I dutifully followed, I found myself reaching to check my phone one last time all the same.

The outdoor area was a cute one, lit by fairy lights and powered by lunchtime joy. Though it was surprisingly busy, too, given that we were in the middle of the day, in the middle of the week. Each table was punctuated by empty and half-empty pint and wine glasses. But as I took my seat – in the corner with my back to the wall and a clear view of anyone entering or leaving – I spotted a table full of empty cocktail glasses, populated by a group of giggling skirt-suits who were flushed with Sex on the Beach and Pornstar Martinis. There were half-eaten chunks of passion fruit piled in their ashtray. I hadn't realised I was staring so intently at them until Duke started to click his fingers in front of my face. My head snapped back at the sound of the gesture and I met his eyes.

'Did you zone out, are you judging them, or do you think one of them is cute?'

I looked around him and back to the women. 'I guess I zoned out.'

He snorted a laugh. 'Do you know something, Sally Pober, they say that women have a hard time with men but if you're an indicator of the time they have with women, then...' Duke petered out and turned his attention to the menu in front of him, which I quickly snatched away.

'Did you zone out or did you just decide that finishing that sentence was stupid?' I asked, my eyebrow cocked and the one menu now held hostage on my side of the table. 'I'll take a glass of red and a tuna sub.' I handed the menu back to him. 'And I'm not judgemental of women, generally. I'm judgemental of lunchtime drinking.' He opened his mouth with a rebuttal but I pre-empted what was coming. '*Excessive* lunchtime drinking.'

Duke nodded and excused himself. 'Now, was that a small glass of red or...' He didn't wait for an answer. And once he was gone, I went back to part-staring at the women across the way from me. They were beautiful, all of them; which only made me think of Lena, who was the next word up from beautiful. I was sure they hadn't invented one yet; no single adjective that could capture beautiful and decent and patient and...

'Wasting her life on a piece of shit like me,' I said to no one as I leaned back from the table and dropped hard against my seat. I took my phone out again, but instead of flicking into my call records or my WhatsApp, I opted for my emails. Duke's office was emailing us both twice daily with news and updates about the book, and the closest I'd got to reading any of it was through the light-bite versions that Duke gave me when we got back to the hotel room each night, as though waiting until I was a captive audience. In the seclusion of the corner, though, I decided to click into the first of the links that had been sent out earlier that day, and I held my breath while the internet browser loaded.

"*Sally Pober's true crime debut is an unashamedly honest expression of trauma and survival—*"

'From a writer with a promising career ahead of her.' Duke autocompleted the tagline as he leaned over and put a large glass of red in front of me. 'Apparently you have a bright future ahead of you and people are excited to see what you do. No pressure.' He winked then, and leaned over to lock my phone. 'You hate reading that stuff. What's going on?'

'I don't hate it.' I took a large glug from my glass and winced. 'I just find it...'

'Too flattering?'

'Something like that.'

Duke rested his forearms across the table to lean in closer. 'You know something, doll, I've worked with *a lot* of writers in my time, and they're normally pretty fucking excited when the world thinks the sun is lodged between their cheeks. Like, it's a good thing.' He said the last part slowly as though trying to underscore or italicise it. 'Look, I know something that'll cheer you up.' He paused to take a generous swig from his pint then slapped his lips together before finishing. 'How about we have this drink and have our food and then crack into that Santa's sack of fan mail that we brought with us?'

That you *brought with us*, I corrected him. But I took another sip of wine to stop the thought from spilling out. Duke had hauled the bag into every hotel with us so far, and it hadn't gone unnoticed that he was markedly more excited than I was at the prospect of opening it.

'If that's what you want to do,' I said, lukewarm, with another mouthful of red.

'It is.' Duke pulled his own phone out then. 'Come on, I'll give you the bite-size versions of the morning's headlines...'

I hated that he seemed to be tired by my petulance already, and that only made me miss Lena that bit more.

'It's a *good* thing that you have fan mail!' I could hear Lena moving around down the phone line: smashing up food for Birdy; setting the bowl on the ground; going back to the microwave. I imagined every movement along with her taking it. Duke was right; she had been working a night shift the evening before, which meant she had slept through all four of my calls (because of course I made another one when Duke took a bathroom break in the afternoon). When she'd eventually woken up, she'd called me in such a worry that I felt a pang of guilt for having called her so many times. Followed by a second pang of guilt when she rushed to reassure me that Birdy was fine, as though that would have been the sole cause for my concern. 'Don't you think it might boost you up a little to read it all?'

'*All?* I've agreed to five letters, to keep Duke quiet.'

Lena laughed. 'You're a funny creature, Sally.'

'Which I assume is why you're with me.'

'That and the free shit.'

I felt a tug of longing. 'Go, get your food. Call me later?'

'Text me pictures of any juicy ones!'

Duke seemed to think that every letter we opened was a juicy one. He parroted out snippets about me being an inspiration; about me spinning a good yarn; about how horrible it was for me to have lost Emma, as though I misplaced her somewhere in among the gnomes. I nodded along with him and only read out something from every other letter I opened, to make him feel matched. The five that I'd agreed to had somehow spiralled until nearly two thirds of the bag was spread out across our beds and partially over the hotel floor too. It was too much, and I felt as though a crow or some other almighty bird was trying to bat its wings inside my chest, only to find it was constantly knocking up against mucous and tissue and bone. I took periodic deep breaths that I managed to disguise as being overwhelmed or touched, which sated Duke further. But the reality of it was that bit less comfortable, and far from leaving me hungry for the bottle of wine that was sitting on my nightstand already, it left me wondering what the odds were that there was some Rescue Remedy left in the side pocket of my bag. Or failing that, whether I could quietly disappear to buy some.

'Okay, dig deep and this'll be our last one because you look knackered, doll.'

A great puff of relief erupted out of me as I reached my hand to the bottom of the bag; a child hungry for the best share of a lucky dip. The envelope I pulled up looked different to the others.

'I'm going to take one last dip too,' Duke said, while I studied the writing.

Everything else so far had been addressed to Duke or to Duke's office, FAO Sally Pober. But this one only said my name across the front, written in long and looping cursive script that reminded me too much of the scrawl Emma had perfected during our early teens. She had spent hours watching tutorials on how to get the writing just so. I wedged a fingernail underneath the lip and tore the paper open, then hurried to pull the contents free. The letter itself was a white A4 sheet, scored into three sections. When I unfolded it there was only writing on the middle portion, though, and the message was noted in that same cursive font.

'This is more of the same,' Duke said, folding his final letter back into its envelope. His words were singed with disappointment, as though he'd been hoping that someone might have discussed their adoration of me in a more inventive format than outright saying it. He had already started to collect up the letters that were dotted around us when he asked, 'How about yours? Anything juicy?'

The same winged creature as before was thrashing itself against my ribcage now, causing knocks of pain as though beating out the contents of the letter in Morse code, shouting it for the whole fucking world to hear. Still, I managed to shake my head and when I looked at Duke I hoped my terror might appear as tiredness. 'No,' I shook my head, 'nothing special in this last one either.'

'Hey ho,' he answered, his back to me, which afforded me the cover I needed to read the letter again and again and again, before folding it back into its envelope and then folding that into my back pocket. But still I saw the scrawl; long and looping and accusatory:

What will you do when they find out it's fiction?

BEFORE THE WOODS

TWELVE

The music was too loud and the room too busy and the people too drunk. But it was an unwritten law of being a teenager in a small-town setting that if someone's parents were away – and your own weren't paying attention – it called for a house party and some terrible decision-making. The fact that Sarah and Sharon were necking onto each other in the corner while a Blackpool Illumination chorus of phone screens hovered around them, recording every second of their drunken error, spoke volumes to how behind Emma and I were. It had taken us thirty minutes to convince her dad that she was coming to my house for pizza and a film and that, for safety's sake, it didn't seem right for her to walk home alone later in the evening. 'No, my parents won't be able to give her a lift; they're having a dinner party, you see, that's why I can get away with takeout pizza,' I'd told Peter, in my sweetest, no-I'm-not-horse-shitting-you-around voice. We already knew, too, that neither Peter nor Rose would be able to give Emma a lift, on account of them having plans that kept them out of the house for most of the evening as well. It had all lined up perfectly. And frankly, Peter should have been glad that Emma was going to fuck around at someone else's house for the evening rather than dragging trouble into her own empty one – which she absolutely had wanted to, right up until me telling her what a poor idea that was. 'You don't shit where you eat,' I'd told her while I ran a lick of black eyeliner across her left lid, 'it's just sensible to shit elsewhere.'

And people were indeed shitting. The queue for the bathroom was snaked along Sid's hallway and out into her parents' garden where, at a glance, I could see at least three boys peeing into her mum's pristine daisy beds.

'Do you think they'll kill the flowers?' she asked when she came to a stop next to me. 'I don't know what I'll tell Mum if they do.'

I snorted a laugh. 'As long as it isn't the truth, you'll be fine.'

'Fuck my life.' She ran a hand through her cropped hair. 'Boys are shit.'

'Preaching to the queer choir.' I held out a balled fist for her to bump and she promptly did. 'Gotta go, I've misplaced my Emma.'

'She's in the kitchen with James,' Sid shouted after me.

'Of course she fucking is.' I pushed through the floating bodies, knocking one into another into another, as though in place of our childhood party games we were making pinballs, piñatas and playing cards of ourselves – though the literal playing cards had been relegated to a corner table where people looked to be playing Ring of Fire with them. Forcing through the doorway into the kitchen was like being birthed, such was the tight squeeze past the people lingering, waiting for drinks. And I got there just in time to see James lifting Emma onto the work surface, angling her into the corner space so her legs were widened around his hips. She looked at me over his shoulder with a 'What?' gesture then winked.

Emma and I were middle-tier popular, which wasn't a bad place to be. People knew we existed, they knew we were smart, and they knew we weren't to be fucked with. That was enough for us – or it had been. But James was top-tier popular. That was a whole different breed of popular. With their underage tattoos and their plans every weekend and their 'No, I don't care what happens in life after school' attitude. For the first three months of sixth form James had been squeezing another top tier – Jennifer Something-Or-Other – but somewhere around November, he'd taken a liking to Emma – and she loved it. If I'd been so inclined, I would have loved it too. I came out at fifteen but even I could see the attraction in James; tall as an oak and stacked like a rugby player. He had both palms flat against the work surface, one either side of Emma, as though forming a barrier around her. I couldn't see his expression but hers looked happy enough.

'Do you think they'll regret it in the morning?'

I turned around and faced off with Sid again. When I followed her stare, I saw she was focused in on Sarah and Sharon who were *still* necking for an audience, though numbers had diminished since I last looked. Apparently the novelty of straight girls getting drunk and getting off really did have a limit. But there were one or two looking on still, one or two phone screens floating.

'They can't even deny it.'

'Not with that many phones. Besides which,' Sid fidgeted to get her phone free from her front pocket and after a few fast movements held it up to me, 'it's already online.' Sarah and Sharon were trapped in an Instagram square. 'That isn't even the only account with it on, either.'

'Been tracking it all down, have you?' I smirked.

'Piss off, Pober. I wanted to see whether you can tell it's my house.' She pocketed the phone. 'If their parents complain, school gets involved, school wants to know where the party was, my parents hear–'

'Anyone ever tell you that you think too much, Sid?'

She tucked an arm around my shoulder and stared into the room of bodies. 'Someone says it at least once a day.'

There was the sudden pressure of someone forcing their way between us. Sid's arm gave way to make space and I stepped aside too. Emma appeared in the room we'd made. 'I'm done with James. Sid, do you have any wine?'

'Because you're cultured?'

'Why are you done with James?'

Sid and I asked in synchronicity but Sid clicked her fingers and pointed to me. 'That's more important. Em, why are you done with James?'

She shrugged. 'Top tier isn't all it's cracked up to be.'

Sid and I swapped a look, but neither of us said anything more about it. Instead, she turned and led the way through her party. Emma looped arms with me then and dragged me along with her in the search for more cultured booze.

'Why are we done with James?' I asked, when it was just the two of us in earshot.

'Everyone is remembered for something from their time in school, right?' she asked, as we walked past Sarah and Sharon who were trying to right their clothes and their hair, both of which being equally tousled.

'Apparently so.'

'I'm not going to have my thing be that I had sex on the countertop in Sid's parents' kitchen.'

Jesus. I nodded and tried to keep my face neutral. 'I think that's a really smart decision, Em.' We came to a stop when we saw Sid reaching into a cupboard and pulling free a bottle of warm white wine. 'Much smarter than this is about to get...'

THIRTEEN

Mum tapped on the door and waited until she heard me shout before she came in. She was holding a tray with two massive mugs of steaming tea, and when she trod a little closer I saw that there were two portions of jam on toast too. She leaned over to set the tray down on the bed between me and Emma, who promptly shoved an entire half a round of toast into her mouth.

'So you're not hungover then,' Mum said with a laugh.

'Not in the least bit, Mrs Pober–' Mum held up her hand to pause Emma. 'Lucy,' she corrected herself. 'My throat thinks my stomach's been cut, mind you.'

Mum and I swapped a look before falling over ourselves in laughter.

'What?' Emma glanced between us. 'What? That's an actual phrase.'

'No, love, it isn't.' Mum reached over to give Emma's hair a ruffle. 'Sal, I'll let you explain. I'm going to put another two rounds in for Emma's poor throat.' She left the room chuckling to herself still, and pulled the door closed behind her.

'It *is* a phrase,' Emma protested.

'The phrase is, my stomach thinks my throat's been cut.'

Emma landed hard against the two pillows that were propped up behind her, with a half a round of jam on toast in hand too. She took small mouthfuls, as though chewing over what I'd said to her, and her forehead creased like it did whenever she'd been in a Business Studies double-period. 'Do you know,' she gestured with the toast as she spoke, 'that *does* make more sense.'

'Mad that,' I said, reaching for my own piece. 'It's almost like I'm right.'

'Hm, almost.' She wiped her palms together and sent crumbs flying into the folds of my bedsheets. 'What's the plan for today?'

'We've got that career development–'

'Bollocks.'

'I know, but we promised we'd do it.'

'Oh, fucking hell, Sal. Do you really want to be remembered for being reliable?'

I thought over the idea for a second, because it did seem like a fair question. But still, 'I'm not sure I want to be remembered for being *un*reliable. Is there a middle-ground?'

'The middle-ground would be not signing me up for volunteer days at school on a Saturday, after a Friday-night party.' She threw back the bedsheets and made to move. 'You don't want to be remembered for dragging friends into hare-brained ideas with you either, you know, Pober.'

'No?' I chewed the last of my toast. 'It doesn't seem to bother you.'

'*Nothing* that I suggest is hare-brained.'

'Let's agree to disagree.'

'That's what Dad says to Mum when he thinks she's talking shit.' She jumped on the spot, tugging her skinny jeans a fraction higher with each drop. 'Have we become our parents already?'

'Pah,' I threw back my own share of the bedcovers, 'we're definitely not going to be remembered for *that*, Em, I can promise you that much.' I was on the hunt across my floordrobe for clothes by then, looking through the dregs of the week to see what had made it out of school alive. 'But I'm probably never going to be unreliable either, I may as well get that out there right now.'

When I looked up I caught her smiling. 'There are probably worse qualities to have in a best friend, now that I think of it.'

Jean Trippier stood at the front of the room, bright-eyed and beaming in a way that no one should, ever, in school, on a weekend. But still, she was the kindest member of staff going. Her hair was tied up in a neat bun, precariously balanced on the top of her head, and her glasses were perched on the end of her nose as though she were already prepped to read whatever she expected us to be writing down throughout the session. She wasn't a teacher, not a proper one, which is probably what made her so much nicer too – and it's why she told us to call her Jean, 'Never Miss Trippier, thank you very much,' she'd say whenever she was correcting a student who had made the error for the first time. She nodded her count tally as she moved around the room, mentally checking us all off the list of expected attendees, I guessed, then when she reached the front of the room and the last of the students, she checked her watch. I wondered how many of us were missing. As sixth formers, we'd been encouraged to take part in the day as an 'extracurricular write-off' that we could put on our UCAS forms if nothing else, but apparently some people simply couldn't be arsed with the Brownie points – and Jean obviously took a similar attitude, given that she grabbed a pen and turned to start writing on the board, rather than holding up the session.

'This is bullshit,' Emma muttered next to me, her voice low and grumpy.

I sighed. 'Then leave.'

'Well I can't now I'm here, can I?'

'You never know,' I snapped back as Jean underlined her first instructions, 'you might actually decide on what you want to do with your life while you're here.'

'Wise words, Miss Pober.' My eyes widened and my head shot up to meet Jean's stare, but her face softened into a smile. 'I realise people have better things to be doing on a Saturday morning, nursing hangovers for one, by the looks of some of you young things. But I promise this session will be of benefit, one way or another.' She paused as though giving people a chance to respond. Jean pointed to the board behind her then. 'First exercise, in your pairs, or groups, I want you all to note down quickly what you wanted to be when you were a kid. The very first job you can think of. Just take a minute.'

Around the room there were echoes of 'Lollipop Lady' and 'Astronaut'. Though I was sure I heard someone say 'A dealer', but I couldn't work out whose voice it had been. I let a second roll by before nudging my elbow into Emma's.

'I wanted to be a hairdresser.'

'You did not!' she answered, and she seemed sincerely shocked.

'Honest to fuck, I genuinely did.'

'I'd never let you near my hair.'

'You don't seem to mind when I'm holding it out the way of the loo.'

'Yeah well,' she slumped lower in her seat, 'that's different.'

'Come on, Em, Christ, just get involved.' I felt my patience starting to fray then. I didn't know whether it was tiredness or some delayed hangover kicking in, but I definitely didn't have the patience that Jean did when it came to grumpy teenagers. 'What did you want to be when you were a kid?'

She tipped her head back and stared hard into the ceiling. 'Famous.'

FOURTEEN

I passed the last of the dirty plates to Dad, who dunked them into the bowl with a splash. Mum tutted from behind us at the kitchen table. She'd done the Sunday dinner so it was only right that we cleaned up from it; though Dad seemed to object to the household chore balance. He was rinsing off the remains of his beef drippings into the sink while I started to wipe down the kitchen countertops.

'You're a good kid,' Mum said, her head already buried in a clothing catalogue.

'It's only fair,' I answered and I deliberately bumped into Dad as I said it. I imagined him glaring down at me in a quiet grump but I didn't care enough to look and check. 'Dinner was bloody lovely, mind you, Mum.'

'It was, Luce,' he chimed in then, 'cracking stuff.'

'You two.' She licked her finger and turned a page. 'You could have invited Emma.' A deep groan fell out of me before I had the chance to censor it, like an emotional kick to the back of the knees, and I knew Mum wouldn't be able to let it pass. 'Oh no, trouble in paradise?'

'Lucy, she's told us it isn't like that,' Dad snapped, too eager to come to my defence. 'Right, Sal?'

'Right, Dad.' I stood alongside him and gave him an awkward squeeze. 'But I think Mum was probably just using it as, you know, a phrase.'

'Oh.' He grabbed another plate. 'Oh.'

'Come on,' Mum beckoned me, 'your dad can manage a second. Come and tell me what's going on.' I thought I heard the early signs of a protest from Dad but it didn't materialise. So I dropped my duties and lowered myself into the chair that Mum had pushed out for me. 'You two seemed all right yesterday morning? Nothing happened at the party, did it?'

'No, nothing like that.' I fidgeted with a napkin that hadn't been cleared away yet. 'Honestly, Mum, I think all the talk of university and, you know, life, I think it's got her feeling a bit funny. She hasn't said anything, but...'

'Something isn't right?'

'Exactly.'

'Maybe she's just having a wee panic?' Dad offered.

'Maybe. But she's always been so excited for uni, not least because it gets her out from under Peter's feet.' I rolled my eyes; another involuntary gesture that happened from time to time, when Emma's dad came up. He was a nice enough man on the surface of it, but when it came to his daughter he ran too tight a ship and Em wasn't built for it. 'Unless she's changed her mind about uni altogether. Who friggin' knows at this point with her.'

'Things are that bad?' Mum's frown deepened then, the seriousness of the situation properly settling on her.

'Like I said, she hasn't said anything. But she's talking a lot about stuff like, I don't know, what she wants to be remembered for? Really random sh– stuff, just random stuff like that.' Neither of them would have told me off for swearing, but it didn't feel right at the table still. 'She asked yesterday if I wanted to be remembered for being reliable, like it's just a bad thing.'

'And what did you say?' Dad ruffled the crown of my hair.

'I said I didn't want to be remembered for being unreliable.'

'Good answer, kid. Lucy,' he spoke over my head then, 'pudding?'

I saw Mum shift her glance to the washing board where plates were draining.

'That's my job,' I said, answering a comment she hadn't even made. But I could read Mum as well as she could read me. 'I'll dry up in a second.'

'There's a Victoria sponge in the fridge,' she answered Dad. 'Love, do you think she's... I mean, you don't think she's having stupid thoughts?'

'No more stupid than the thoughts every other seventeen-year-old in our school is having.' I shrugged and shook my head. But the motion must have shifted something loose, because I suddenly realised what Mum was really asking. 'Oh, Jesus, no, she doesn't want– Christ, Emma doesn't want to die!' I made the announcement with such gusto that I lifted out of my seat slightly before dropping right back against it. 'Jesus, Mum, no. Sorry, if that's the impression...'

'Not at all, Sal, not at all.' She reached across and gave my hand a squeeze. 'It's a stressful time for you all, though, and you can't be too careful. We can't be too careful, us parents,' she squeezed again, 'and we get some silly worries ourselves sometimes, that's all.'

Dad reached around me to set a slice of cake in front

of me, then placed one on the table for Mum too. While he was walking back to get his own he asked, 'So what, Emma is thinking about what her legacy in life might be? Or her legacy in school?'

I thought for a second before answering. 'Both?'

'Bloody hell.' He sat back in his place with a slice of cake notably bigger than mine and Mum's. 'Remember when we were kids and we were just worried about getting ratted every weekend?'

'No, I was never like that.' Mum winked at me. 'If you're worried, love, if it's becoming a problem I mean, why don't you try talking to her about it?'

'Honestly,' I waved the idea away, 'it's just me getting a bit... irritated with it all. There's nothing *actually* wrong, apart from me not having as much patience as I need. If it gets any worse then I'll talk to her,' I said with a level of conviction that I definitely didn't feel, before shoving a forkful of cake into my mouth.

'So how was the development thing?' Dad asked then, already chewing through his second mouthful. 'Helpful?'

'Yes and no? I still think English is the way to go for uni.'

'To teach?' Mum asked.

I shrugged. 'What else do you do with an English degree?'

'Write,' Dad suggested, though it sounded more like a question than a serious career prospect. 'Mind, I don't know that you can make a proper job of being a writer. I don't mean *you*, I mean, the royal you. Who *writes* for a living?'

'Besides which I don't think I've got a good enough story in me.'

'Doesn't everyone?' Mum asked. 'They say that, don't they? That everyone has a story in them.'

I didn't know who 'they' were, but I was getting more and more advice from them the closer I got to leaving school, starting university, and abandoning life as I knew it, and I was getting more and more desperate to know what their source of information was. I ate the rest of my cake in silence while Mum and Dad talked over my head about writing, and English, and teaching, and–

'You wanted to be a hairdresser when you were a nipper,' Dad said, his voice burnt with nostalgia around the edges, 'you could always swing back to that.'

'What, the hairdresser thing, or being a nipper?' I joked.

'We'd be happy with either, Lucy, wouldn't we?'

'No,' Mum answered in a level tone, 'she's far less trouble at this age than she was then.' She winked at me over a forkful of cake, then spoke around it as she chewed. 'Honestly, Sal, you know that your dad and I don't care what you do as long as you're happy while you're at it. That's all it comes down to, that's all either of you should be aiming for.' She knocked toes with me under the table then dropped her attention back to her cake. But I thought I caught the glisten of a tear before she looked away.

FIFTEEN

Emma was lying with her arse wedged against her pillow and her legs upright against the wall. She was flicking through an old edition of one of her Dad's *True Crime Now* magazines, thumbing through it like a catalogue of inspiration for something. Meanwhile, I was on my third draft of a personal statement that was still succeeding in making me sound like I'd done fuck all with my life – which as a seventeen-year-old from a small town, was bang on the money. Emma had been reading out snippets of the odd story while I'd been working, too, which definitely hadn't helped. I'd come over so we could work on our statements together, but as soon as her parents had gone out for the afternoon she'd thrown her notepad to the opposite side of the room and pulled the magazine out instead. She'd had it stashed beneath her pillow like contraband. 'Dad is weirdly protective over them,' she'd explained, before licking her thumb and skimming to another page.

'Do you remember when Heather disappeared with her boyfriend for literally like, one night, and everyone lost their shit that something terrible had happened to her? Do you remember that? People *still* talk about that sometimes.'

I paused my writing and wracked my brain for a memory that had anything to do with what she'd just said. 'Who the fuck is Heather?'

She lowered her magazine and craned around to look at me from her awkward angle. 'You're shitting me.'

'I'm really not.' I crossed out another three words and went back to counting the characters in the sentence. 'Seriously, Heather who?'

'Heather who was like, two years above us in school? She finished last year, went off with her boyfriend somewhere to start a new life away from...' Emma let the sentence trail off and only waved her free hand around, as though that explained it all. 'There's no way that you don't remember her, Sal, think, woman, think.' She went back to looking through the magazine then. 'She was gorgeous. Blonde hair, blue eyes, the lot.'

'Why do you know so much about this woman?' I managed a laugh.

'Because she's a local legend!'

'Which is exactly what you're aspiring to be these days, right?'

She slammed the magazine down with enough force to crease the pages and I knew my tone had been too hard-edged. 'I'm just trying to make something of myself.'

'Then write your personal statement!'

Emma struggled to get upright on the bed then, and she let the magazine fall open between us. 'Sal, what if I try, right, hear me out,' she set a hand on my writing arm to stop my scribbling, 'what if I try *really* hard to make something of myself, like you will, and I don't get there.

What if I fuck up, and let everyone down, and let my *Dad* down, Christ, can you imagine?'

And just like that, the messy jigsaw of my best friend tumbled into place; all the awkward and odd angles formed to build a picture of a young woman who, like the rest of us, was in fact just shitting herself at the prospect of getting it all wrong. I dropped my notebook and pen and pulled her into a tight hug that seemed to catch her off guard.

'You're a fucking idiot.'

'Thanks, Sal,' she said into my hair, 'but that's not really the encouragement I was looking for.' I let her go free and she picked up her reading material then, as though the conversation were over. But added, 'I just think maybe there are alternative routes to making something of yourself, ones that we're not being taught about at school.'

'Like disappearing with your boyfriend for a night and letting everyone worry sick that something had happened to you?'

'Say what you like, but everyone remembers Heather.'

Apart from me, apparently, I thought, but I managed to keep the comment in. Instead I said, 'You're a terrible host. I haven't had a brew in like, nearly two hours.'

'You know where the kettle is.' Emma wriggled back into the same awkward position as before and let her legs rest against the wall. 'While you're there, make me one.' She blew me a kiss before burying herself in the folds of paper, and I went without a word – for fear, still, of what might come out.

The kettle took years to boil. While I was waiting for the whistle of it, I browsed along the hall of fame that was Emma's parents' hallway; at least, that's what I called it whenever I wanted to wind Emma up. It was a catalogue of accomplishments, each framed picture forming part of a timeline that started with Emma's earliest stars of the week and ending in a wide-smiled photograph of her that I could remember being taken on our GCSE results day. She'd still got the envelope in her hand and, if I looked hard enough, I was sure I could see the brilliant bright pink of the floral blouse that my own mum had been wearing, just out of shot. *Is this why you're panicking, Em?* I thought, as I eyed the spaces that had been left at the end of the wall. *Has your Dad already got the frames ready for A levels, and undergrad?*

The longer I stood in the hallway the more I found myself empathising with Emma's total fear of what was happening, not happening, about to happen, not about to happen in her life. It was a fucking relief when the kettle whistled to a boil, and I could disappear back into the kitchen to make us both tea. We'd always treated each other's homes like our own, so I went ferreting through the sweet cupboard, too, until I landed on a packet of chocolate digestives that was hidden right at the back. I wedged the biscuits under my arm and trod back upstairs with a mug of tea in each hand. But when I walked in Emma was frantically scribbling something in my notepad and I was so stunned at the turnaround that I nearly dropped the teas. I crept in quietly, worried that any slight disturbance in the air might throw her off writing her statement, which is what I thought she *must* be doing by now.

I set a tea on her bedside table before creeping round to my own side. I clambered onto the bed with my mug, and wedged it between my knees while I tried to perform the impossible: opening a plastic packet of something without making an offensive amount of noise. I'd just managed to tear the perforation free and find the thin ribbon snaked on the inside of the packet when Emma's head snapped up. *Bollocks*. I smiled.

'I'm so sorry, I didn't mean to throw you off.' I waved the biscuits at her. 'It's okay for us to open these, right?'

Emma didn't answer straight away. She only narrowed her eyes, as though inspecting me for something, and I thought it likely didn't have anything to do with the digestives. She glanced down again at the page in front of her and crossed through a few of the things she'd written, before looking back at me, like we were making a collaborative effort of whatever was noted there.

'But seriously, Em, these biscuits...' I started again when she didn't answer – and her stare had gone on for so long that it was starting to get uncomfortable.

'Sal, I've got an idea. It's fucking mental. But...' She looked back at the plans in front of her. 'I think it could also be fucking brilliant.'

SIXTEEN

It was the longest I'd gone without talking to Emma, ever. But I couldn't bring myself to, no matter how many times she called; no matter the notes that were slipped under my locker door at school. I bunked off our shared classes, I took a different cycle route in the morning. I didn't know her anymore, and it had been the fastest dislocation I'd ever known; paralleled only by the sensation of my kneecap twisting out of place during a football match when I was ten years old. The pains of each were similar, though, that lingering ache even when the joint looked to be patched back in place. My hurt over Emma ran so deep that I wondered whether it was observable to anyone else; whether there was a subtle limp people would notice if they watched me for long enough. Two days in, people started to make comments around school.

'Where's your twin?' Cat asked me while we were queueing to get into the swimming pool changing rooms. 'Doesn't she usually tag along and cheer you on?'

I forced a laugh. 'She has a thing on, I think. I'm not

sure.' I stared at the tiled wall in front of me. Though I had many skills in life, I'd never been especially confident that bullshitting people was one of them. So I thought I could at least have the decency not to look at the woman while I was trying to lie to her. We shuffled along a couple of inches. 'You know what timetables are like at the minute with all the career-planning stuff they're forcing down us.'

Cat grumbled. 'What do you want to be when you grow up?' she asked in a mock tone. 'Christ, I'm sick of it.' She turned around then, and dropped her back against the wall, tipped her head back to stare at the ceiling. 'Do you and Emma know where you're going to uni yet?'

My stomach turned with an audible cry. I hated the implication, that *of course* we'd be going to university together, as though there were no other option. 'I think Emma is actually thinking of giving university a miss.'

Cat huffed. 'That's as likely as you giving university a miss.'

'Ah well, you've got me there. English Lit. God willing.'

'You'll crush it,' she turned her head to smile at me, 'both of you will. You're a good team, you and Emma.'

The queue started to move again then, and I felt a swell of gratitude for it.

Three days on, and the weekend made it impossible to hide the problems. In the space of a week Emma and I had somehow become the married couple that struggles on with each workday, only to find they can't stomach the thought of a prolonged stretch of time with each other at the weekend, as though it were impossible to fill that much dead air. But in place of dead air, I'd created physical space. She and I often went to town together on a Saturday afternoon, so I deliberately went in the morning; she and I would bring a takeaway back to her place or mine, so I suggested dinner out with Mum and Dad. The two went along with it so easily, too, that it almost didn't even feel like a ploy but rather a masterplan that had worked out nicely for all involved – especially Dad, who was inhaling a steak the size of a toilet seat. That's literally how it was marketed on the menu, and I wondered who the hell thought that comparison was an appetising one. But when Dad threw down his napkin, dropped back against his chair, and sighed with a hearty satisfaction, I thought: *Well, it obviously works for some people.*

'So what's happened with Emma?' Mum asked, like it was nothing, before she threw another piece of wholetail scampi into her mouth.

'What makes you think something has happened with Emma?' I kept my head ducked towards my plate, and pushed a tomato from one side to the other as though dribbling a small football, the bed of abandoned salad my pitch. 'She's just busy this weekend.'

'With what?' Dad asked, as he picked up his fork again. It had looked, for a second, like he was ready to admit defeat. But apparently he'd changed his mind. He threw a piece of steak into his open mouth, a small gristly lump that made a grinding noise as he chewed. 'Christ, sorry,' he said, the food still in his mouth as he spoke, and everything about the scene made me want to upchuck the goat's cheese tart that I'd just managed to force down.

'Jesus, Vince, you're not half an animal sometimes,'

Mum said, already reaching over to dab at a dribble of something that was creeping out the side of his mouth. 'Go on, sorry, Sal, you were telling us about Emma.'

'I don't know that I was, actually.' I flashed Mum a tight smile and tried to change the subject. 'Are you going to visit Aunt Liz tomorrow?'

Dad rolled his eyes and Mum slapped his arm for it. 'Yes,' she used an especially curt tone, 'we are, aren't we, Vince?' He murmured in agreement but kept chewing and reloading as though to keep his mouth busy. 'The woman's just lost her husband, Vince, the least we can do is support her through it how we can.'

'She didn't lose Stu, Luce, he just came to his senses.' Dad's eyes burst wide when he finished speaking, as though he was also surprised by the comment. 'But yes, we're going to see your Aunt Liz. What are your plans?' he tried to steer.

'I was actually going to ask whether I could come with you?'

I saw them swap a look and I prayed, *prayed*, that neither of them would be bolshy enough to say anything. I was convinced I saw Mum shake her head slightly. Then Dad answered for them both. 'Of course, we'll be leaving at about 11am.'

'Great, chance for a bit of a lie-in then too.' I smiled a more authentic smile and went back to the last outer crust edges of my tart. All the while thinking: *And that's Sunday taken care of.*

I managed to avoid their interrogations for the rest of the meal out, too, and between that and the run I went for when we got home, and the long bath I took after the run, the evening scarpered away from me before anyone had a chance to pin me down for questions. Until–

'Sal, can I come in?' Mum poked a hand through the door to knock on the inside wall. She came in without waiting for an answer, as parents are wont to do, and I rolled my eyes and smiled, as kids are wont to do. 'I know, I know, why do I ask,' she joked as she perched on the corner of my bed. 'Put the book down a second, love, will you? I just want a minute.'

I dog-eared the page I was partway through reading. 'What's up?'

'Emma–'

'Mum...'

'I know something has happened between the two of you.' She ducked into my line of vision; I'd been avoiding her stare until then. 'And I know it's not boy trouble.' I managed a laugh then at least, which broke some of the chill between us. 'You're a good kid and you'll talk to us when you're ready, or when you need to. But I'm going to say one thing, without even knowing what's happened between you.' My mouth dropped open to snap back but she set a hand up to stop me. 'One thing?' And I reluctantly nodded in agreement. 'You've been friends *forever*, and whatever it is now won't even matter in ten years.' She leaned forward to give my hand a squeeze, and pull my gaze back to her. 'I promise.'

I managed a smile then. 'I hope you're right, Mum. I really do.'

SEVENTEEN

Emma and I managed another week of shared custody, whereby whenever one of us was likely to be at one thing, the other looked set to avoid it. It ran counter to the missed calls I was still getting, though, and I wondered whether she'd decided that a phone call would be easier to panic her way through than a full-frontal confrontation. That was assuming she had the decency to feel panic at all. Her social media feed made it look as though life was spinning on as normal – she was an active user, which made it that bit easier to keep an eye on things – but there was a Sally-shaped hole in the daily proceedings that I could see with every click. Still, the space felt necessary; something like a safe distance, something like deniability. And the plan of that was working just fine until Emma decided to channel her inner Shakespearean anti-hero and turn up at the house one night in the early hours of the morning, before dawn had even started to yawn awake, and I wondered why – when I stumbled from bed with watercolour vision and aching limbs – she had decided *this* was an appropriate time to make an announcement that my parents and neighbours alike were likely to overhear. Not only the announcement, of course, but the small shower of pebbles knock-knock-knocking in the minutes before the announcement too. She couldn't have called, like a modern-day villain. Instead she'd managed to seek out the bibbles in the back garden and launch them in a small but effective scattering against my bedroom window.

'Thank fuck,' she said when I appeared, 'I was almost out of bricks.'

'I'm just going to leave that sentence for a second so you can gauge the full weight of crazy.' I balanced myself on my window ledge and looked down at her. 'Assuming you have any gauge for what that is anymore.'

'Oh, come on, Sal,' she flung her arms up and dropped them again in frustration, 'haven't you punished me enough?'

'This isn't about punishing you,' I bit. 'It was about giving you time to come to your senses and realise what a fucking *mental* thing you suggested to me the other week. Which given that you're here, I'm assuming has finally happened.' She bunched her lips up to one side in an expression that looked sceptical. 'Oh fuck me, Em, you haven't come to your senses? You *actually* think this is a good idea?'

'I believe that I agreed it was a mental idea.'

I let a pause stretch out between us before I said again, 'I'm just going to leave that sentence for a second so you can–'

'Sally!' she snapped in a whisper. 'Jesus, you're my best friend. You're meant to be my ride or die.'

'I'm not sure that extends to committing a crime.'

'Oh shush,' she seemed to mock the phrasing, 'it isn't a *crime.*'

'Actually I think you'll find it is.'

'Whatever, it isn't a crime like murder.'

I couldn't argue with her like this. Every rebuttal felt like a small pebble dropped in my stomach, forcing acid to splash about in short-sharp, splashes-sploshes. I set my palm flat against my abdomen as though I could settle the movement but there was a physical grinding, a tension I couldn't knead out.

'Hey, you okay?' Emma's tone was one of genuine concern then, and I was too easily reminded of all the reasons why we were friends: she was kind; loyal; fiercely protective; determined; hilarious– *A real ride or die*, I thought with a swell of feeling that immediately overflowed through both eyes, sending a tear down each cheek. 'Shit, Sal, should I come up? Do you need me to wake your mum?' She moved closer to the wall as she spoke, as though she might scale up to me if an emergency should unfold. She was standing so close then, that I had to dangle out uncomfortably just to see her face.

'The spare key to the back door is under the dahlia pot. Come in,' I said and then I went back to bed to wait for her.

Emma arrived with small, cartoon character steps, as though she were Shaggy or Scooby trying to creep out of a haunted mansion. There were a lot of mixed messages in the comparison that I didn't have the energy to unpick. She lifted the duvet and crawled into bed next to me, like we were about to have a normal sleepover. I felt the cold of outside clinging to her clothes still, knocking against my bare legs as she moved closer. Neither of us said anything for what felt like a long time.

'Do you honestly think I'm mad?' she asked eventually.

'Yes.'

'But, Sal, listen,' she angled herself to face me then, 'it's a victimless crime. We disappear for a day or two, three days maximum, and I've got the whole story worked out for when we get back. I've even found somewhere in the woods that—'

'Emma, listen to yourself!' I was curt with her but all too aware that my parents were sleeping two rooms away too. It was hard to be outraged with someone in a whisper, but I was giving it a damn good go. 'You're planning a *fake* kidnapping so we can be famous for a while? You hear that, right? You hear that that's your plan.'

'Look, you don't have to go along with it, Sally, but...' She hesitated over whatever was coming next. 'I'd rather do it with you than with someone else, that's all I'm going to say. And if you want in, then I've got everything all planned, and you don't even need to do anything. You just need to be... complicit.'

'You'd rather do it with me?'

She nodded. 'Obviously, you're my best friend.'

'Meaning, you'll do it with someone else if you have to?' She hesitated again but I was too tense to wait for a response. I found that I was grabbing her wrist, tightening my fingers until I felt her skin pinch. 'Emma, have you spoken to someone else about this?'

'Please, I'm not *that* mental. I mentioned Heather to one or two people, I wanted to see how remembered she is. It turns out, *very*.'

'So you've been talking to people about a girl who's town famous for being "kidnapped" for the night by her own boyfriend, and now you're going to go ahead and get "kidnapped"? You don't think people will connect those things, like, *at all?*'

Emma's eyes were trapped-animal wide and I wondered whether a bag of pennies had just dropped; a two-pence pusher when a hurricane of coins falls off the edge and into the tray at the bottom. But instead of panic she broke into a smile. 'Does that mean you're going to do it with me?'

I shook my head. 'I can't go along with this, Emma.' I moved away from her then, distanced myself from her physically in the bed and tipped my head back against the wall behind us. 'If you do it, I won't tell anyone. But I can't go along with this. Fucking hell, can't you just take your exams like the rest of us?'

Emma matched my positioning and tipped her head back too. There were the remains of glow-in-the-dark stars on my ceiling; fixed in place with superglue because Emma and I hadn't known any better. We'd told Mum and Dad we didn't need help fixing them in place. I could remember the day so clearly.

'I'll take my exams after.'

'With extenuating circumstances no doubt,' I answered, my tone flat.

'I hadn't even thought of that.' She tapped my arm. 'See, you're the brains of the operation, Sal. I *need* you.'

And with those three simple words, I felt my resolve tug. The small smudge in the bottom corner of my determination as I realised yes, yes, I would do this. I would take some convincing, but I would do it, because *fuck*, I sighed, *I'll always do anything you ask me to.*

EIGHTEEN

When I kissed Mum goodbye the morning I was going to be kidnapped, there was a small and ridiculous part of me that honestly thought I mightn't see her again. I held her closer than I had in years and breathed in the smell of her, cherished the feeling of her arms tightening around me and the firm plant of her lips on the top of my head too. She enjoyed the hug as much as I did, I think. Though she looked at me suspiciously when she let me go; held me at arm's length and narrowed her eyes as though searching for the reason behind the affection. Part of me hoped she would find it. Instead, she only smiled, gave my shoulders a second squeeze and let me go. She was busying herself in the kitchen while I struggled into my backpack. There were packed sandwiches in there: two ham; two tuna. The latter of which seemed like a mistake given that there was no way they'd keep long enough; Emma and I would have to eat those first. It was the strangest teddy bears' picnic I had ever made.

'I am glad you and Emma worked things out, Sal,'

Mum said as she filled the kettle with water. When she set it back on the stand the noise of it made me flinch. 'Friends like her are hard to find.'

'Hey, friends like me are hard to find too,' I answered, and I was surprised at how light my tone was. 'But yeah, we worked stuff out all right. We'll be fine.' I flashed Mum a tight smile as she turned to me. 'We always are.'

'Do you know your plans for the day? Off anywhere exciting?'

The cover story was that we were going for a hike through the nearby woods. It wasn't unusual for us to spend a Saturday exercising somewhere, though it would usually be a run or a swim, followed by a weekend's worth of food and a movie. Only this time, it was a hike and a horror story – one that we'd be the stars of. I told Mum that we were heading in the opposite direction to where we were actually aiming for. But it was the same body of woodland; close enough to a truth. Despite Emma's lean towards dramatic storytelling, I'd managed to convince her that keeping as close to the truth as possible was going to be the only way through this. Although the thought seemed a little laughable too; the idea of there being any way through this at all.

'Well,' Mum carried on making her tea, 'be careful and have fun.'

'I love you, Mum,' I said from the doorway.

'Love you too, Sal. See you both later.'

Only you won't. I sighed, smiled and set off – before I could change my mind.

'What the fuck is with all these gnomes?' I was following the path that Emma trod. She obviously knew where she was going, though she hadn't given me specifics. 'A spot in the woods' was as much as I knew and I had gone along with it, all the while thinking that the less I knew about the madness the better. But I wondered all the same whether this was a spot she'd found or one she'd made, in her mad scientist planning of the whole event. 'Em, seriously, don't you find this weird?'

She laughed from up ahead. 'No weirder than the rest of this.'

There was a confidence to her in those moments that I almost didn't recognise. She trod the path as though she were overly familiar with it, and I wondered how many times she must have visited here in the planning of this. Had she been coming here alone for days, hours at a time, slipping off the grid to imagine what it would be like to— *Slip off the grid*, I thought as we walked through another huddle of gnomes. I'd never been to these parts of the woods before; why would I have been? So I couldn't work out exactly why the place looked like the crossover of a children's story and a horror scene, but something about the collapse of those two things felt right. I'd always naively thought that losing my virginity would have been the intersection between childhood and adulthood. But it turned out that staging my own kidnapping, alongside my best friend, would actually be the point when everything turned.

'And we're here!' She gestured towards the opening to a muddied, sodden underground bunker that looked to have no door to it, other than the makeshift one made by nature, formed of leaves and moss and other shit we'd have to force our way through to make it fully inside. 'I know it's not The Ritz, but think it'll do?'

'I mean,' I crouched to look in, 'we're going to freeze to death long before anyone finds us as kidnapping victims.' Emma cocked an eyebrow at me and folded her arms in a confrontational pose. 'But then think how famous we'll be when we've died together in a woodland bunker, with no explanation as to why we were there.'

'Fucking hell, Mary Sue, you can always go home if you're that worried.'

'I'm worried about the fact that it's *winter*,' I underscored the season in case she'd forgotten, 'but whatever, I brought blankets, and sandwiches, so we'll make do. It'll be...' I lingered, searching for the right word, as though there was one, 'authentic, when we're found shivering and hypothermic.'

'Is that a word?'

'Is that your main concern right now? Whether I just made a word up?'

Emma was struggling to free something from her bag. When she shook the item loose, I saw it was a waterproof lining, a picnic blanket almost. She struggled her way into the hideout, smudging her knees with the first christenings of mud, and laid it out as close to flat as she could manage in the cramped space.

'And before you say anything, about why the kidnapper would have lined the bunker, I've already thought way ahead of you.' She sat cross-legged, pulled her bag into her lap, and tapped the space next to her to welcome me in. 'Anything we don't want them to find, we can just burn on our way out of the woods.' She shrugged. 'Or if we start to get cold I guess we could burn shit too.'

'Except if people see a fire in the woods, there's a real

possibility they'll come to see where it's coming from.' I matched her pose and crossed my own legs but sat opposite her rather than alongside her. I needed a view of her face; it was the only thing likely to remind me of why the fuck I was crazy enough to be doing this. 'But apart from that, fine plan.'

'Sally, why did you come? All you're doing is shitting on my ideas,' she asked, in a tone that sounded truly exasperated and altogether fed up – and it stung. 'Seriously, you could have let me do this alone, or with someone else...'

Emma carried on talking after that but I missed the majority of what was said. The mention of her doing this with someone else sent a swarm of something batting from one ear to another, swelling to fit the empty crevices in my head. At times like these, I realised I loved Emma too much – but I was never sure whether it was as a sibling or something altogether different, or worse still, whether it was somehow both. But whichever justification it was, I wouldn't admit to either aloud – especially not while we were hunkering down for three days together in a woodland bunker with barely enough food to last us a day, never mind the three we were planning on staying. I'd told her that too much food would look suspicious; we needed signs of starvation, dehydration. She told me I'd thought of everything. Though now, that seemed more of a problem than it did a perk.

'Are you even listening to me?' she said, snapping me back.

'No, I was thinking about that episode of *Friends* where Rachel makes trifle but with half a pie filling instead. Do you remember that?' It was the first thing I'd been able to think of, and from her expression I could see it had thrown her. But at least it was a subject change.

'That's a terrible episode. None of them come out good in that.' She shifted herself to lie back against me, her legs bunched up at awkward angles and her head in my lap, like we might have done if we were at one of our homes, in one of our beds, binging on everything: food and television shows alike. 'I much prefer the earlier seasons to those later ones anyway.'

'Because you love the Ross and Rachel drama.'

'He's her–'

'Lobster,' I interrupted her, 'I'm only too aware.'

'I reckon you're mine, you know?' she said then, and I felt my stomach drop out of me and fall through the soil. 'In a friend way,' she added and I made a show of being relieved, though I couldn't decide whether I was. 'You don't have to look so thankful about that, you cheeky cow.'

I leaned forward to kiss her on the forehead. 'You're my lobster, too, Em, in a friend way.' That seemed to appease her long enough for her to relax into my lap again. She closed her eyes as though ready for sleep already. Whereas sleep couldn't have been further from my mind. I dropped my head back against the cold wet wall behind me and felt the early soak of it through my hair. *No point in being squeamish now, Sal,* I thought as I resisted the urge to move away. *This is only the start.*

NINETEEN

Emma was shoving things into her bag with the fury of a girl who'd found her boyfriend in bed with someone else. There was a spite to every action, as though I'd personally affronted her somehow; as though I'd been anything but supportive with this fucking madness. But now we were two nights in and Emma was tired of the cold; she was hungry and agitated and– 'I just want to fucking leave, Sally!' And she just wanted to go home. All I wanted, in exchange for that, was for her to explain to me in advance what the fuck we were going to say to our parents who had no doubt been flipping their absolute shit for the last two days solid while we'd been playing True Crime Victims in the woods.

'We can still go along with the plan, if you want, whatever.' She waved my question away. 'I don't care. Maybe we just come clean and tell them what we did, maybe that's the easiest way out of this.'

'You're actually fucking mad.'

'Stop fucking saying that!' She waved her hands then, waved each, either side of her head, let her bag fall to the floor and her feet stomp, like a child denied their favourite sweets. And it did nothing to dissuade me from thinking that Emma was in fact a bit mental – but then, I was hardly in a position to judge. 'You keep fucking calling me that, Sally, and I'm tired of it. Totally fucking tired of it.' She grabbed her bag and started to struggle with the plastic blanket – the one she was going to burn on her way out, according to the plan of two days ago – but given that I was standing on the corner of it still, she didn't get far with moving it. She dropped her bag again, and I wondered whether I was about to face off against another foot-stomping tantrum. I'd never seen her like this, and I hated it. 'First you didn't want to come, now you don't want to fucking leave. Move your fucking foot.'

'Stop swearing at me.' It was all I could say, even though it sounded like a weak plea. 'Stop swearing and just talk to me. I'm not saying we *can't* leave, I'm just saying we need a plan for when we do.'

She ran a muddied hand through muddied hair; she looked every bit the woman in dishevelled warpaint. 'I think we just come clean.'

I nodded slowly. 'And that's what we'll be famous for then? The girls who tried to stage a kidnapping then gave up two days in and decided to admit to what their plan was all along. That's what we'll have follow us around?'

Emma's eyes burnt with a fury but she looked close to tears too. She bounced gently on the spot once, twice, three times without answering my questions. Then without any further word she launched herself, shoved her hands hard into the balls of my shoulders so I was thrown off balance and knocked against the wall behind me. And when I righted myself, she did it again.

'Fuck you, Sally. We both know the reason you went

along with this to start with, but don't pretend you didn't come into this with your eyes open.'

My eyes were narrowed then, though, inspecting her words for the cracks where a light-bulb moment might shine through. 'Why did I go along with this exactly?'

'Please,' she spat back, her tone mocking and cruel and hard-edged. It was one she'd always reserved for other people – lower-tier popular people, maybe, but never for me. 'Don't act like you don't know that you *love* me.' She leaned hard on the word in a way that made it sound like an insult. 'You have for years, and we've always ignored it, but now it's bubbling away at you, isn't it? Is that why you don't *really* want to leave early, because we're getting *all* this time together?'

In truth, the time with Emma had been horrible. For two days she had moaned about the cold, the hunger, as though she were a criminal of war trapped in conditions that were of someone else's making, rather than her own. If there had been any doubt about my feelings for her – *okay, there* was *doubt about my feelings for her,* I admitted – any lingering doubts from when we'd arrived had been clarified by this Christ-awful crash course in what it was like not to breathe and have a break from her; what it was like to see her thrown into the wilderness and asked to survive. Whatever it was that helped a human to grapple with the wilds of inhospitable conditions, Emma didn't have it – and some primal, angry, tired, hungry part of me *hated* that about her.

It must have been the same primal, angry, tired and hungry part that decided not to proffer Emma's comment with an answer at all. Because instead of forming a fully-fledged sentence, I could only laugh. A harsh burp of a noise that erupted out of me and left us both equally surprised, I think, because in synchronicity with feeling my own shocked eyes spread wide, I saw the same expression take over Emma's face. There wasn't a chance to say anything then, before she found a single sliver of primal. She must have dug deep for it. And before I could answer, try to answer, even, she closed what small gap there was between us, raised her right palm and slapped me with the fury of a disappointed mother. I felt the burn of her skin against my own and it lingered there for seconds longer, even after her hand was removed, so much that I could have been forgiven for thinking her hot palm was there still, cupping my cheek. But it wasn't. Instead, it had dropped back to her side and while I cradled my face I noticed that Emma was fidgeting the hand that she'd slapped me with, and I wondered whether her skin was stung from mine. *It would serve you right*, I thought as I slowly managed to gather myself.

But still, I couldn't find an answer. *What the fuck do I say to any of this?* There was something defeatist in me, as though the tired and hungry parts had had a talk while I wasn't listening, perhaps, and between them they'd decided that maybe it didn't matter at all what happened next anymore. It didn't matter whether Emma wanted to leave, whether she wanted to come clean, whether anything. Because too much blood had been spilled in the bunker already, and I knew, *knew*, there was only so much any friendship could come back from.

'Going home isn't an option,' the angry part of me managed to say.

'So you're *actually* going to kidnap me, force me to stay here?'

I didn't use my palm. Instead, I brought the back of my right hand to strike her right cheek and in the process

I sent her stumbling backwards too. She lost her footing and landed hard on the frozen earth underneath us. Emma held her cheek for a second longer but when I crouched level with her she buried both hands in the grime then, and used each palm to gain leverage in pushing herself away from me, as though she hadn't been the first one to throw a slap. And with those thoughts I found I was swallowing down the bile of another laugh that was forming. I fixed a hand on her knee to stop her pushing away any further and she froze. She looked truly afraid then, and I remember thinking how glad I was.

'Going home isn't an option.'

'Sally, you're taking this too far now. Now *you're* being mental with it.'

I felt a twitch at the corner of my mouth; a knee-jerk twinge that might become a smile if I left it unchecked. 'Yeah, Em, *you're* the one that wanted to stage a kidnapping, *you're* the one that planned it all, *you're* the one who coerced–'

'I didn't coerce–'

I slammed my hand across her mouth to trap her mock outrage there. 'You're the one who coerced me into doing this. And now *I'm* the one who's mental for not wanting *everyone* we know to know what little fuck-ups we both are?' I found I was putting more pressure against her mouth then, as though not only was I trying to keep words trapped, but maybe force them back down her throat altogether. The pressure was such that her head was pressed hard against the edge of the bunker but I kept pushing, kept pushing. 'Just like you've always pushed,' I said aloud then, even though I knew it was out of link with the rest of the conversation. Emma looked at me befittingly for that too. But again all I could manage to say was, 'You've always pushed, Emma, you've *always* pushed.'

And then I pushed back. Hand against mouth. Fingertips pinching nose. Knees against upper arms. Buttocks against stomach. *Don't leave a bruise*, I remember thinking, *don't leave them with a single trace.*

NOW

FROM THE WOODS

They scoured the bunker from base to brim trying to find something – anything. The only trace contact there showed that Emma and I had both been there, which wasn't exactly information the police didn't already have. I'd told them how when he visited us – which he did, often, even bringing sandwiches down to us once or twice too – he was plastic-wrapped from head to foot. I never saw his face, only the slip of eyes that showed through the headgear he was wearing. He wouldn't have been out of place as a team member in a forensics department. 'It looked like he should be on a television drama,' was how I described him to the police. The outfit he wore was brilliant white and loud when he struggled into the space, his adult male body fitting awkwardly inside the guts of the earth; a space that was hardly big enough for two teenage girls to fit in. He would crinkle and crack and sit with us and just – watch. There were occasional slips of conversation. 'Are you scared?' he'd asked once, and looked from me to Emma and back again, waiting for an answer. I think I'd managed to nod. I hadn't been brave enough to look across at Emma to see whether she'd mustered her own response though.

The man was never brilliant white when he left. He always took slips of the earth's crust with him; leaves and prints and smudges coated to his plastic outer. I have since wondered where he went home to, after those fleeting meetings with us. Did he strip off and get into his car? Was he close enough to walk home? Did he climb into the shower, in the suit, when he arrived there? Or did he hose himself off in his large garden, affixed to the back of his detached house that he shared with his wife and children? The fact that we didn't know the answers is what kept us fixed there, I think. Emma only mentioned running once, and I never had the courage to suggest the idea aloud; though I found that in the moments of snatched sleep, it was the only thing I could dream of.

'We should make a run for it, Sal. What have we got to lose?'

I remember giving her a hooded look. I didn't want to say it. But she understood. We had no way of knowing how close he was to us at any given moment, and that's why we stayed, uncomfortably locked in the bowels of the earth for a little while longer, to see what the strange man in the white suit might do next. Now, it seems odd to me that we waited. I remember us being such buxom, raucous teenagers; two girls who always had an opinion on everything and a mouth with which to share it and yet, and yet...

I think the police took buckets of soil and sand and shit back to the station with them while they were looking for signs of the man in that godforsaken space. Still, he'd left nothing behind. In the end, he was only the anonymous killer of a young girl and the ghost that haunted her best friend. Left to be exercised, exorcised in these very pages, all these many years later.

TWENTY

It made the six o'clock news. There was a reporter with blonde hair so bright that you seldom see it on anyone over the age of three years old, but there she was, with fairy-tale hair curled and flicked, and far too neat for the landscape that formed her backdrop. The woman was wearing a navy-blue raincoat and holding the microphone so tight her knuckles were pushing through her pale skin like she was about to punch a man, and I remembered Emma's slap. I sat fixed to the edge of the sofa with the note burning a hole in my back pocket. The remote was a stress-ease that I tightened my grip around. The newswoman must have been freezing, stranded with her team in the middle of the woods as she was at this time of night. I had a less obvious excuse for the pull of skin and judder of breath and heartbeat that couldn't quite steady. I was glad Lena wasn't home yet, though Birdy was, and she could tell something was unsettled in the place. She lay balled at my feet while I watched the report, but every now and then small wisps of upset escaped her; a slight whimper that gave voice to my own discomfort.

'Since the beginning of Sally Pober's book tour, fans have been holding vigils here each evening...'

Did Duke know that? Did Lena?

Behind her there were still clusters of candles, I could see. But there was also a bloodshed of broken crockery: red hats and white faces; fishing rods and miniature coats that had been flung from the bodies of the gnomes. I knew the police had taken some at the time of the kidnapping, though maybe not all. *Or maybe they took them all and someone replaced them*, I thought then, before shaking the idea away and trying to reoccupy the space with a thought that actually fucking mattered.

'But sometime during last night, there was a disruption in the area so pronounced that local residents were privy to the noise. In fact, it was a local farming couple just one mile away that reported the incident...'

I thought of the poor Olssons. From memory, I couldn't place another house that would have been within howling distance of the bunker. Not that there was a bunker left; that much was apparent. Behind the nameless woman, the woodland was all shape. With enough time, I might have been able to hand-hold someone to the area where Emma and I had hidden – *were held*, I corrected the slip. But from this angle, it was many trees in an ocean of forest where someone had thrown candles and gnomes around as though staging a surrealist art exhibition.

My phone hummed on the table in front of me, and I managed to drag my eyes away from the television long enough to see the name: Worsley. I didn't answer. Because she should have called me hours ago. It was terrible practice on her part. But when the phone hummed a second time, hardly a minute later, it was a different name that appeared: Harry.

'Is she sitting next to you?'

There was a long pause before he said, 'You're on speakerphone.'

I matched the stretch of silence before saying, 'Okay.'

'Sally, I'm so sorry that I didn't get to you before the news broke,' Worsley started, and I felt my jaw tighten; my top and lower teeth pressed together like I was struggling with tough meat. 'I told one of my juniors to get in touch with you, because I was attending the scene itself and– Not that it matters now but they obviously didn't call.' She left a pause, as though for me to fill the space with confirmation or denial but I didn't give her either. Instead, I let my eyes flit back to the television screen – Allison Tilly, the reporter's name, was floating across the bottom of the report now – before I awkwardly shifted forward to reach into my back pocket.

'Stuff like this was bound to start happening, Sally.' Harry had picked up the task of talking me down. Though the truth of it was that I didn't need either of them to. The most harrowing part of this whole incident was that complete strangers had been lighting candles in the woods for a young woman they didn't know. The fact that complete strangers had then gone ahead and trashed those displays, and the horror-show house of gnomes that had somehow managed to survive in the local area, actually came as no surprise. People were hideous; of course someone wanted to trash an outpouring of mourning. And of course someone wanted to make Emma a martyr of misspent youth and misfortune. At least while they were looking at her, at the bunker, they weren't looking at me. Though I was sorely tempted then, to ask

Harry whether there were any new or existing suspects in the case off the back of all this – and if so, could they get handwriting samples.

I spread the note out flat on the coffee table in front of me. Or rather, as flat as something can be spread after days on end quartered into someone's rear pocket. Birdy, as though sensing the extent of the intrusion caused by the mere slip of paper, stood up then, and balanced her small paws on the edge of the table. She sniffed at the note, her nose bumping lightly against the corner before she abruptly shook her head; in the same way she does when someone blows on her.

'The bottom line is,' Harry carried on, and it was only then that I realised he'd been reassuring me this whole time, while I'd been handling my evidence, 'we'll protect you however we need to, but you need to let us.'

'Lena is the only person I'm worried about,' I answered then, fingering at the corner of the paper, touching it softly as though it were a love note – rather than a hand-delivered threat that could unfold into something that might ruin my entire fucking life.

'Okay, well we have no reason to believe that you or Lena are at any direct risk at the moment. If that were to change for some reason, then we'd have to consider options–'

'Like?' I cut across Worsley.

'Like surveillance of some description, at home, and certainly when you're out and about doing your book readings. I'm led to believe that Duke has follow-up dates scheduled for you, now the book has been released properly?'

Of course he's told her. 'That's my understanding of things. But this–'

'Shouldn't change anything for you, Sally. You have to live your life.'

Harry's sentiment was appropriately punctuated by the sound of the doorbell. There were very few people who could have got to that point in the building without needing to be buzzed through.

'I have to go. Thank you both for calling.' *Eventually*, I thought but held back on saying. I was already disconnecting the phone, fumbling with the note; folding it neatly across its scored lines and slipping it back into my pocket.

There was a physical heat to it, I felt sure. But it was something that I'd started to get used to, after so much time having it stashed on my person. I couldn't risk Duke finding it, or anyone else. Nor could I bring myself to throw it away, though I wasn't altogether sure why. Instead, I chose my outfits based on my ability to carry the contraband anywhere, everywhere I went, like I was the martyr, not Emma, with a cross that no one could see, but I could feel with every step.

Birdy skidded past me along the hallway, racing to meet the intruder. There were three locks pulled across the door and I looked hard through the spyhole before I thought about undoing any of them. My vision of the visitor was obscured though, blocked out by a ridiculous bunch of flowers that looked large enough to swallow whole any vase that might have been available in the flat.

'Knock-knock, doll,' Duke's voice came from behind the bouquet and I could have cried a silent tear of joy. I pressed my palms flat against the door-spread and inhaled, exhaled, inhaled hard until my hands felt steady enough to unbolt. One, two, three and then out Birdy went, scattering around his feet with too much excitement, as though the flowers were for her – or, more realistically, as though the flowers were made from meat treats. 'Sweets, move it along,' Duke said to her, moving his feet this way then that to try to avoid the clutter of her small paws dancing around him. 'These are obviously for you,' he handed the flowers across to me then, 'and you holding those seems to drastically reduce my odds of being killed by your dog, so if you please.' He made a show of stepping round Birdy another two times before giving up entirely and scooping her up into a tight hug. 'I have clients that are exactly like you.'

'Of which I hope I'm not one of them.' I kicked the door closed behind us both but, sans hands, I rushed to set the flowers on the nearest level surface so I could triple-lock us all into safety.

'So that's where we're at.' I turned around to catch a cocked eye from Duke, who now had Birdy comfortably wedged under his right arm. 'Mummy doesn't feel safe, baby, even with a guard dog like you.' He used a talking-to-a-child voice that I hated on him.

'Have you seen the news?'

'Of course I have.'

They both followed me into the kitchen, where I soon started opening, closing, opening cupboards to find an outlandish vase for the outlandish flowers.

'Sweets, this was bound to start happening,' he said softly, as he set Birdy back down to ground level. 'You must have known the book would draw out crazies? We talked about this, Harry talked to you about this and–'

'I know.' I ran two hands through my tangled mess of hair. 'I know it all, but it doesn't stop me from feeling unnerved by the whole fucking thing, Duke.'

'I get that, sweets, I do.' He walked around to the side

of the kitchen island that I was leaning against, and dropped back to lean against the counter himself, leaving only a small gap between us. 'You can't let this ruin the things you have planned for this, the things this book will bring you.'

I huffed. That's what it came down to with him now: he was all commissions and overexposure, as though I were a Polaroid print of some rare and beautiful thing to be tampered with and considered at length by the experts.

'Like ridiculous bunches of flowers?'

'Oh,' he gestured towards the bunch, 'they aren't from me.'

Something crawled the inner walls of my gut; small centipede feet. 'What?'

'They aren't from me. I was literally just about to buzz myself up when the delivery guy came to a stop and asked if this was the right address and–' I was already fumbling with the card that was fixed to a plastic stem. 'Well, who's the secret admirer?' he asked when I'd parted the lips of the message.

I forced a smile. 'Lena, obviously.' I made a show of smiling over the card before slipping it into my back pocket; the same back pocket where the other note was burning away, its edges singing at me whenever I moved, whenever I thought of it. 'Did you want a coffee?'

Duke pulled free a packet of cigarettes from his own back pocket. 'You smoke, I'll make the coffee. Fair deal?'

My smile was more genuine then, and the centipede feet stopped moving. 'That's a more than fair deal, I'd say.' I took the packet from him and crossed the open-plan space to perch in my usual spot. But when I leaned against the window I felt the bend of the thick card in my back pocket and felt the need to steady myself then, a sudden bout of vertigo kicking in – or maybe it was a fight or flight response that I was feeling. Either way, I had to hold one hand firm in place until I was three breaths into the cigarette and Duke was crossing the room with two mugs, at which point I realised that I needed to bring my new degree of panic down to a standard Sally degree of panic to hold a conversation with him, lest he realise something wasn't quite right.

'Things been okay with Lena since you got back?' he asked.

'Absolutely. I've been hard work, she's been a star.'

He huffed. 'You can't have been that hard, Sal.' I threw him a quizzical look and he nodded behind us. 'Flowers.'

'Oh.' I pulled a hard inhale and listened to the paper burn. 'Those.'

What will you do when they find out it's fiction?

TWENTY-ONE

The flower shop was offensive in both colour and scent. It was like walking into a literal watercolour where one bunch had no choice but to bleed into the next, such was the space limitation. There were two people in the queue in front of me and I bit back on the urge to pay both of them to either move, or simply leave. No one with money wants to be *that* person but I was learning there were situations that called for it. I shuffled from one foot to another and eyed the roses and the lilies and the carnations and the– I realised the man in front of me in the queue was watching me then, and I smiled, lowered my face, and prayed to whomever might be listening that he wasn't a true crime fan. *Not that you write true crime*, a voice that wasn't my own reminded me. I'd managed to convince myself it was Emma speaking, but that didn't seem right either. Maybe it was the person who wrote the note, sent the flowers; maybe I had made them real enough, rather than simply existing in the abstract where they could do whatever they wanted and I could... panic, panic was all I could do. *Panic and wait,* I thought then, in my own familiar and defeated and exhausted tone.

The first person in the queue moved along, allowing me and the man in front to shuffle. I overheard something about peonies, something about an anniversary, something about, 'Will they get there in time?' The young woman behind the counter rushed to assure him they would and he continued with his order while I tried to scour the place to find where in this watercolour mess the peonies might live, as though there was an expectation for them to have at least one of every flower on display. Though it gave me something to do until the man turned to leave.

'Sorry,' he said as he faced me again, 'Sally Pober, right?'

Fuck. I forced a smile. 'Right. Do I...'

'No, no,' he rushed to reassure me, his palms held up as though in defence, 'I saw an interview with you.'

I hated how often this happened now. It was testimony to the strength of true crime in written form that so many people knew who I was, but the same heathens could walk right past Jessie Burton in the street and not realise it. They didn't know what they were missing.

'I didn't get your name?' I did my best I'm-not-having-a-breakdown impression and offered the man my hand, which he accepted even though he seemed surprised the chance was there for it.

'Daniel.' He shook in firm sharp movements, and I realised Daniel must be a businessman. 'I'm here ordering flowers for my wife, it's our anniversary.' He started to over-explain in that way nervous people do. 'Rhianna,' he added, and I nodded along. 'In fact, she's a big fan too!' he said then, in a tone of mild surprise, as though he'd only just realised or remembered that his wife also liked my work.

'Well, that's always great to hear, Daniel. You tell Rhianna I said a happy anniversary to you both.' I made to move round him then, to get to my real destination. Though I realised the potential rudeness of that, so for bonus sociability points I added, 'Nice to meet you, Daniel, I'm glad you enjoyed the interview.' Then I was free to make my break to the counter, while Daniel muttered his I've-just-met-someone-I-perceive-to-be-famous goodbye.

'Hi there, I'm Kristen,' the florist said, with an American accent and a brightness that matched the tones of the shop. I wondered how many times she had to do this on the average day, and whether by the time she got home she was, in fact, the most miserable person in the fucking world. 'How can I help today?'

'Hi, Kristen. I got a delivery from here yesterday—'

'Oh no, is there something you're unhappy with?'

Only being interrupted, I thought but didn't say. Instead, I smiled and rushed to reassure her. I needed Kristen to be a friend. 'The flowers are actually *gorgeous*, like, so, so pretty.' She looked relieved; I was sure I saw a soft 'phew' escape her mouth too. 'But I actually wondered if there's any way to tell who ordered them? I know it's sneaky of me but...'

She smiled. 'Secret admirer?'

'Something like that.'

'Well, let me...' She started to move the computer mouse around on the stand-up desk between us. There were a series of clicks while Kristen bunched her mouth up at one side and tilted her head this way, then that. 'I really shouldn't be doing this,' she said then, though she was obviously halfway through doing *something* by then. *Go ahead*, the criminal in me wanted to encourage her, *what's a slight GDPR breach between new-found friends?* But then a better idea struck.

'Kristen,' I lowered my voice even though we were alone in the shop by then, 'can I level with you about something?' The poor girl nodded along with the wide-eyed excitement of someone about to be escorted into a secret. 'My first book has hit the shelves recently–'

'That's amazing!'

Whether it was her excitement, the interruption, or a medley of both, I felt my hand clench and release, clench and release under the counter. Above it, I only smiled. 'It's pretty cool, right? It's *nearly* a bestseller, we're getting there. It's all super wild,' I used my best American-high-school-girl energy, 'but since all of the interviews and blah-blah that comes with it, I've been having some security issues.' And though I didn't think the gesture possible, Kristen's eyes spread wider still. 'The flowers, they didn't have a note,' I lied, 'so, even though I don't need huge details or anything, because I absolutely get you wouldn't be able to do that, I was just wondering if there was any way to...'

'Understood.' She flashed me a tight smile. 'It's a shame that some men have to go ahead and shit on a woman's success like that, isn't it?' Her tone had changed at breakneck speed; I felt myself jerk back at the severity of it, even. Kristen was post-#MeToo. These women took no shit. And the series of clicks and whirs started again from her computer screen. 'Now, for the sake of my livelihood I can't exactly go around giving out customers' details. But I can tell you it was a cash sale, and that the name on the receipt is Blackburn.'

I thought back to the many bugs of the bunker. The ways in which woodlice would ball themselves up and make a game of the space's curved edges, before burrowing back into the ground, crawling through and starting again like children at an outlandish party. There had been a beetle once, too, sitting on Emma's knee when she'd woken up from a restless nap. She went mental, flailed her arms and squealed and thrashed about in what limited space there was. We didn't know what happened to it, where it went; whether it even survived her attack or died from the shock of a human howling at it. I imagined all of those bugs then, and the many generations of them that had spawned since: the slugs and the harvestmen and the millipedes, joining those centipede feet as they rushed from one side of my stunned body to the other.

'Blackburn?' I repeated, while wasps and bees fought for space in each ear.

'Mm-hm,' she confirmed, 'E. Blackburn.'

There was an angry earthquake shudder in the ground beneath and flower by flower I blinked out the colours. Black spots of judgement came in and out and my knees were weak and the wasps were loud. Kristen was touching me then, and someone else was touching me and–

'Sally, can you see how many fingers I'm holding up?'

There were only flowers and insects and things with small enough legs to scatter and noise-make like Birdy on wooden flooring but not as warming, not as nice. Then I remembered the peonies and I moved my slow head to one side then the other to find them but there was no colour only black spots and–

'Sally? Sally, can you hear me?'

'We're going to have to take her in.'

'Okay, let's get the love on a stretcher.'

'It was so nice to meet you!' the American girl shouted after me as the ceiling started to move and the flowers leaned and bowed and licked my cheeks goodbye and there was a voice I recognised and a name I knew and–

'Emma,' I managed to say then in a childlike splutter.

'You need us to call Emma, honey?' a woman said to me then, with a halo of light behind her head. 'Can I get Emma's surname? Is she in your phone somewhere?'

'No, no,' I tapped the side of my head. *Blackburn.* 'In here.'

'Okay.' She pushed a gloved hand over my forehead and I became aware of the dampness of my skin under her touch. 'Why don't you rest for me now, honey, and we'll call Emma when we get to the hospital? Does that sound okay?'

Nothing sounded okay. Nothing would be okay. The colours had gone then. The colours had gone and Emma was back. What did that mean?

My entire body was tucked into an Oodie. I was bunched up at one end of the sofa, my legs lifted up to my chest and soft fabric pulled around me, as though I had nested inside – as though I might never leave. Birdy was balled alongside me, her small body folded neatly around itself to form a comma on the seat; a reminder for me to pause and breathe, I thought. I snuck a hand out from under my covers to stroke her and she let out a contented sigh that warmed me. After that I went back to looking out the window, back to the not moving that I'd managed so successfully since I got home. But my attention was pulled away seconds later when Lena set a steaming mug on the coffee table for me. She disappeared again then, and came back with cigarettes, a lighter and a saucer that she balanced on the arm of the sofa. I looked up at her through a squint, as though I had spent too long inspecting the core of the sun. I considered shielding my eyes with a hand but that would mean moving too far from under the covers.

'What did I do to deserve cigarettes?'

Lena perched on the edge of the coffee table while she fumbled with the packet, pulled one free and handed it towards me. *That* I would move my hand for.

'I think the more pertinent question is where did I find them hidden?' she asked with a raised eyebrow, though her tone was light. 'Honestly, Sally, a panic attack? Darling, I had no idea your stress was getting so out of control.' She was holding the lighter hostage and I realised the only way to that, was through this conversation.

'Neither did I,' I lied, 'neither did I...'

TWENTY-TWO

Aster was unsettled which subsequently unsettled me – as though I hadn't been disturbed before calling her. She agreed to see me for an emergency appointment, though she warned me over the phone that her office situation was not what it usually was. I didn't know what to expect, exactly, given the anal uniformity that was normally observable in Aster's colourless space, designed with such obvious cleanliness in mind that, had she not been a therapist herself, someone may have felt inclined to diagnose her with a problem. I used it as a distraction technique on the journey there, imagining a plant pot out of place, or that a succulent had sprouted a brilliant pink flower stain in the otherwise plain room. Though by the time my journey was over, my ideas had become so outlandish – a rogue client had broken in overnight and Jackson Pollock-ed the back wall, whose main purpose had previously only been to reflect sunlight – that the reality was startlingly disappointing. Aster's office was being deep-cleaned. 'I get it done every month,' she explained. I smiled, thin-lipped, and thought, *Of course you fucking do.* Resultantly, though, that meant that our unscheduled appointment was taking place in one of Aster's colleague's rooms – and her distaste at that was apparent.

'I didn't mean to drag you in specifically,' I said as she saw me in. I wondered whether Aster had planned to have a day away from the office and the judder-shake of my voice down the line at 8am had managed to interrupt that. Or whether she had in fact known all along that she would be taking appointments in this office today – but she still couldn't fucking stand it. The more I thought, the more I found a shameful schoolgirl grin appearing over her discomfort, and I worked tremendously hard to stifle it on account of being a grown woman who should know better. But of course, that spiteful streak in me was precisely what had landed me in an emergency therapy appointment. That desire for discomfort, that desire to– *kill people.* A small strangled sound fell out of me and I thought the negative intrusion served me right.

'I know, it isn't to my taste either,' Aster said, misinterpreting the noise. 'Do you want the sofa, or the...' She waved in the direction of a beanbag in the corner of the room, positioned to give someone the vantage point of seeing through the main window. Aster had, I assumed, already shotgunned the large armchair as her own. By way of an answer, I lowered myself sheepishly down on one end of the sofa and then Aster took her seat too. 'No, I can't say it looks too tempting to me either.' She leaned forward to collect the recorder, set the tape going and then put it back on the table between us. 'So...'

'Doesn't this room give you a fucking headache?'

I surveyed the space. If pushed, this would have been *exactly* how I imagined the inside of a clown's mind. The furniture didn't match; all four walls were a different colour – different shades of the same colour, admittedly, but still! There were picture frames that punctuated every wall but, from experience, I knew it was bad practice to tell clients too much about one's life, so I craned my eyes to see each image and, lo and behold, they were generic snapshots of mountains, the ocean, a jungle landscape. One element at a time might have been enough to calm a person down. All of the elements together and it was enough to bring on–

My chest tightened and I kneaded at it with the butt of my hand.

'Are you okay, Sally?'

I looked back at Aster then, and caught a sincerely concerned expression.

'I've been having chest pains since I got home from...' I didn't know how to name the Before and After of this. 'All of the places Duke dragged me to. Too many to list. I can only assume my heart is growing.' I leaned forward to pull my water bottle free of my handbag, but before I took a sip another thought occurred to me: 'That, or it's shrinking.'

Aster smiled at the reference and I wondered whether that meant she had children. *Older children by now?* Or whether she was just a die-hard fan of Jim Carrey films. The latter option was my preferred explanation. I had never been able to imagine her as a mother. Caring though she was, she didn't strike me as the maternal sort; an assessment that I made without judgement. I didn't have it in me either.

'Do you need some air, I can...' Aster looked towards the window, but I rebuffed the offer. 'Okay then, so,' she looped her hands together and dropped them into the bowl of her lap, 'what is it that we're talking about today?'

I pulled in the deepest breath that I could muster while still feeling like a small cricket was making a xylophone of my chest cartilage. Was it my conscience causing me pain? Would it be assuaged, calmed, even, once I'd said–

'Aster, I killed Emma.'

And there it was: the confession that I had kept locked inside that same chest cartilage for years, prowling the spaces between my ribs, heart, and lungs, occasionally banging at the walls as though determined to get out. Now it finally had, and all Aster did was smile. Of course, this was a natural reaction for her, I supposed. It was hardly the first time I had unleashed the tiger of my guilt into her office – or rather, on this occasion, someone else's office. But I didn't think Aster would mind if it flexed its claws and left trail marks down the four shades of blue that made up the design scheme; it may even give the room an edge. Though it has to be said, I didn't feel any better for the admission. Like an 'I love you' said too many times by ignorant teenagers, I had confessed to this before; my words had lost their worth, despite the intention behind them having shifted so sharply.

Aster leaned further forwards in her seat then, and looked to put considerable thought into what she was about to say before letting anything come out. 'Sally, we've talked about survivor's guilt before...'

Air leaked out of me as though seeping from a puncture. I felt my whole body ease into the sofa and I tipped my head back to stare at the ceiling as I listened to her.

'I know what your feelings are about it all. But it isn't the crock that you think it is. It's a very real thing, and it makes sense that this, the book, everything that's happening around the book, it would bring on a kind of flare-up of these feelings. Which we also talked about before...'

So there was the reality. I couldn't confess now, even if I tried to. Or rather, I could; I just wouldn't be taken seriously when I did it. And I wondered whether the letter-writer, flower-sender would believe that; whether it would placate them at all to know that I'd tried. The only flaw with the plan being, of course, that I didn't know who the fuck they were, so had no means to tell them about my honourable attempt to confess my sins to my overpriced counsellor. And that's when another thought struck me, square in the centre of my forehead like a fingertip pressing down.

'Someone sent me flowers, from Emma,' I blurted out.

I'd lost track of what Aster had been saying, but that announcement stopped her in her tracks. She looked as though I'd leaned forward, open-palmed, and tapped her quiet.

'It's making me...' *Come on, Sally, what's the end of that sentence?* I heard in Emma's voice, though it had hardened around the edges since I'd last heard her as my antagonist. 'It's making me crazy, not knowing who sent them, where they came from, why.' All of that, at least, was the absolute truth of that matter too, and *that* it did feel good to confess to someone. I had kept the truth from Lena, Duke. Even if I had tried to explain, everything would have been greyscale and murky, and I was beyond the point of thinking that more lies would fix my lies – though I wagered, too, that at some point I would have no choice in using that ethos to fix the matters unfolding around me. So perhaps I was saving my lies for when I really needed them.

Aster was pensive, troubled. I could see it from the bottom half of her face, though her forehead stayed stock still and I'd never noticed that Botox vanity about her before. 'The flowers only had Emma's name on the card?'

I shook my head. 'No, her name wasn't on the card. I went to the florist, explained the situation. Crazy true crime fans, can't be too careful, blah-blah–'

'Which I think, given the circumstances, isn't exactly something you should brush off with such a blasé attitude anymore.'

She had a point.

'The florist gave me the name of the sender as an E. Blackburn.'

'Can the police find out anything more?'

I felt my forehead pull together, making a face that I imagined Aster couldn't even if she put concerted effort into it. 'I haven't told the police.'

'Sally, why the hell not?' Her hand shot up to her mouth then, as though she might be able to ram the outburst back in. 'Sorry, I–'

'It's all good,' I forced a smile, 'good to be reminded that I'm not making too big a deal out of this.'

Aster took a long time to think then. There were too many intricate details around the room for me to count as a distraction technique, without causing my already impaired cognitive functions even more damage. I imagined that my chronic headache would see a free upgrade to a migraine if I were to make a quiet tally of the picture frames, plants, and throw cushions. The list continued on, but even noting those early decorations had me kneading at my temples. I'd never been quite so glad to hear Aster speak.

'Sally, you should go to the police about this,' she said, and then halted me with a raised palm when I opened my mouth to dispute her comment. Despite my faux reluctance in attending these sessions, I had to admit that by now Aster knew me all too well. 'I'm not going to try to change your mind. I know a fruitless endeavour when I see one. But you need to be aware,' she paused, shook her head and then edited the sentence, 'you need to have this validated, you are *not* making too much of a thing about something that poses a very real threat to your safety. So, that said, I'm going to make you aware of two possibilities here. The first being one you've jovially admitted to yourself, that being, you have some super fan or another who's decided to reach out to you now the book is out there.'

I felt my forehead knit again. 'What's the second option?'

'Well...' She seemed hesitant to say it which only made me all the more curious. I leaned forward in my seat then, too, as though lessening the distance between us might pressure her into talking. 'In cases like these, it's someone you know.'

I huffed. 'I'd already entertained that idea. Some quack at Duke's office or–'

'I'm not talking about someone you know in passing, Sally. I'm talking about someone you *know*. Someone who knows you, or has known you. How else would they know just the right way to get under your skin?'

I resented the accusation. 'What makes you think they know how to get under my skin, exactly?'

Aster smiled, though it wasn't her usual smile. Instead, there was something like pity stained on the expression. I imagined I could see sympathy and mercy smudged on her teeth like cheap lipstick when she said, 'If they don't, then why are you here?'

TWENTY-THREE

'You can't just take off whenever you fucking feel like it, Sally!' Duke's voice bellowed through the speaker system of my car, so loud that it had me reaching for the volume dial. It was the second time I'd turned him down and yet somehow he persisted.

'That's awkward, Duke, because it sort of looks like I have.'

'Sally, I can't– You are– This is un-fucking-believable.'

Significantly, Duke wasn't annoyed that I'd taken off without giving him any advance notice. Duke was annoyed that I'd taken off without giving him advance notice on a day when I was meant to be showing up for a radio interview about the early reception to the book. It was sneaking up the bestseller charts across the board and everyone – apart from me, and Birdy who was also lukewarm about the news – was rapt with excitement about it. I had even caught Lena, unable to sleep in the early hours of that morning, refreshing the pages for one database and then another to see whether the rankings had shifted. I didn't need to be excited; other people were doing a fine job of it for me.

Apart from Duke, that is, who was merely pissed off.

'When are you coming home? How long have you taken off for, exactly?'

'Don't be so bloody dramatic, Duke. Jesus.'

'Well, how am I meant to know? You've taken the dog with you, you might *never* come back as far as I know.' Birdy grumbled in the passenger seat and I imagined her soft smug delight, at being the only thing I would care enough to take if I were ever to abscond from my daily living. 'Are you back tonight?'

I sighed. 'Yes, Jesus. I'm literally just going to my parents'.'

'That's what Lena said too!'

'Don't say it like it's a conspiracy, Duke, you sound mental.' I slowed down to exit the junction that would bring me onto the next A-road. 'I have some stuff that I need to collect from my mum's,' I admitted, and then I sweetened the admission further by adding, 'look, I didn't want to make a thing but there's this new project I've got in the works.'

There was a long pause on the other end of the line. 'What, like a new book?'

'It depends on whether I've got the materials for it.' *And whether I can track down the fucker who's sending me threats via fan mail.* There had been another letter, since the flowers. It was hand-delivered to Duke's office again, with no distinguishable features to make it any different from the outside to any other letter in the bag that Duke's assistant handed over to me. Yet, when I'd seen the handwriting on the envelope, I'd known:

What will you do when they find out it's fiction?

'Duke, are you still there?' I considered grabbing my empty Twix packet – the breakfast of champions – and crinkling it against the mouthpiece, as though that old trick might still work.

'Is it a sequel?' he eventually asked, and I huffed a laugh.

'What more is there to say about the Emma story, Duke?'

'So it's something entirely different?'

'I guess?'

'Jesus, Sally, you aren't giving me much.'

'Because I don't have much to give. Seriously, give me a day to get these things sorted at my parents' and I'll be able to tell you more. Is that a fair deal or is that a fair deal?' I reached across to stroke Birdy who was getting restless against the raised voices. I kneaded at the soft under-flesh of her folded ear, and I wasn't sure which one of us was more calmed by the action.

'It's a fair deal. I'll look forward to hearing all about it at the party.'

'About the party...' I started.

'Sally, don't you dare.'

Tipsters had wagered the book would hit at least one number one spot before the week was out. There were literally people betting on my book beating the latest romantic comedy to the highest ranking chart position. When he saw the interest, Duke immediately set about arranging a celebration; it was his answer to everything. 'And if I don't top the charts?' I'd asked at the time, and he'd only shrugged. 'Then it's a mixer for you to get acquainted with the industry.'

'Okay, I have another thing–'

'What other thing could there possibly be?' he snapped across me.

'No, no,' I hurried, 'it's nothing bad. It's just, could you get a guest book?'

'What, for people to sign in?'

'Sort of.' I swapped ears for Birdy and took a deep breath. 'For people to leave messages, you know, if they want to. It won't be mandatory, obviously. But I thought it would be a nice thing for me to have, as a keepsake.'

'Oh, Sal.' Something in him had softened from toffee brittle to warmed caramel. 'Of course, doll, of course. Hey, I hope you find what you're looking for today, okay? Call me when you're home.'

We both knew I wouldn't.

The rest of the journey took us another thirty-five minutes. Dad was out the front of the house when we pulled in, practising a leisurely pace from one side of the front garden to the other while he smoked his way through what I guessed would be a menthol cigarette.

'Caught you,' I said as I stepped out of the car. Birdy came rushing out soon after and bounded over to Dad, who was already dropping to his knees to greet her.

'Guilty as charged,' he said in a light-hearted tone while Birdy made a valiant effort at jumping high enough to lick his face. 'Guilty as charged,' he said over and again, 'Guilty as...' The sound was replaced by a humming noise in my ear, as though low static were being played behind my head somewhere, and I tensed, released, tensed, breathed, and tried to find equilibrium enough to speak.

'Where's Mum?'

'Ha,' he stood, 'Pilates.' He snubbed out what was left of his smoke and then crossed to a nearby plant pot. With his index finger he pressed down on the butt of the dead cigarette and pushed and pushed until– 'Honestly, if your mother ever took up gardening, I'd be in some real trouble.' He held an arm wide then, as though gesturing me close to him. 'Tea?'

'Please.' I was surprised at the immediate comfort I took from the contact. When he closed in around me, I found myself wedged between his soft side and his strong arm, and a part of me could have wept with something like relief. *It's all okay now*, a voice seemed to say, *Dad will fix things*. Even though, of course, that was unlikely to be the case. Though he may have found a beginning to fixing things. 'Did you manage to dig out the stuff I asked you to find?'

'I did. All boxed up and waiting to go,' he answered as he trod down the hallway ahead of me and Birdy. 'Interested to know what you want it for.'

'Another book that you won't read,' I said, though I kept the tone of it light. Dad turned and cocked an eyebrow at me. 'I mean, it was a sarcastic and at once very serious answer.' We arrived in the kitchen then, and there it was; a big, brown box of possibilities, precariously held together with parcel tape, sitting on the table as promised. 'It's seen better days,' I said.

'It's been a while since you... well, since you needed it.'

The last time had been for the last book. There wasn't much in there about Emma, exactly. So much of the information about her had come from diaries and newspaper reports and police documentation – and, of course, my imagination. But for this I needed the specifics of something. And the living memories I had of that time in our lives wouldn't be anywhere near detailed enough for–

'Biscuits?'

Dad snapped my attention back. 'I'm okay.'

'You look thin.'

'Biscuits would be great.' I landed hard on one of the chairs at the kitchen table and Birdy, as though having heard the promise of biscuits, promptly balanced on her back legs and rested her front paws on my knee. 'Come on up then, baby,' I said as I scooped her up and balanced her on my lap. There was a time when she would have fit there easily enough. Now, either she had grown or I had shrunk, or some medley of the two had taken place. She wobbled back and forth, finding her own balance, and by the time Dad turned around with a plate loaded full of biscuits the mutt had rested her head on the edge of the table to wait for him. I couldn't see her face, but I wagered that he was getting the same look Lena did when she was in Birdy's spot on the sofa.

'So tell me,' Dad started, pretending he hadn't even noticed the dog, 'what's the new book about?'

I broke off a piece of plain shortbread and held it in the palm of my hand for Birdy to sample from. Dad was faced away again, collecting full mugs of tea to bring over. 'I don't even know that it is a book yet, to be honest.' When he turned back around I saw a disbelieving look on him. 'Seriously, a lot of writers get cold feet when it comes to a second book.'

He pushed a mug towards me and then settled down opposite us with his own. 'Have a biscuit. Do you think there's more to say about the Emma– About what happened to Emma?'

The two statements had knocked together with such a force that I nearly jerked forwards from impact. Who could stand to eat a Bourbon in the face of this questioning? Yet, I persisted, and instead opted for a Rich Tea that I hoped I wouldn't vomit back up over the table. I couldn't remember when I'd last managed a full meal. *Guilt will do that though*, I thought then as I dunked.

'I don't know that the new book is about Emma.'

He nodded slowly. 'But it's about school?'

'It might be about school.'

Another nod. 'You're not going to tell me anything more?'

I laughed then, and fed the last third of a biscuit to Birdy. Once my hand was free, I grabbed my tea for the harsh warmth of the porcelain. 'I don't have any more to tell, Dad, honestly. I have this idea about someone we went to school with and I just wanted to quietly explore–'

'Sal, what I'm asking here is whether you're inviting any trouble your way,' he said, interrupting me. And I experienced what can only be described as a fracture of feeling, right through the core of my chest. 'If you've got a theory, if you've remembered something, if...' He waved away any other possible sentence-enders. 'Whatever the if, I just don't want– What I'm saying is that I couldn't stand–'

'I won't bring in any trouble,' I reassured him, using my softest voice. He didn't need to explain his worries; I knew well enough that, by now, Dad likely had images of The Man reappearing in our lives – or more specifically, in mine. It had been a concern throughout the entirety of writing the first book and it was clear that it would be an undercurrent one for any follow-ups I might haul together. Dad was good like that, in the ways that mattered.

He nodded and reached for a biscuit, then changed the subject at breakneck speed: something to do with Pilates and yoga and taking care of your body as it ages. I listened and nodded and laughed when it felt right, and I said nothing of trouble; nothing of how I had already invited trouble; pulled out a seat for it at the table; asked it how it liked to drink its tea.

TWENTY-FOUR

Lena got to the door before I did. It was Duke – she'd buzzed him in only a minute before – so I left the two of them to bitch about me while I finished getting ready for the party I didn't want to go to, to celebrate the book that may or may not be a bestseller. It had hit the number one spot in several e-reader charts but Duke was plugging for the big one – and their rankings would be emailed out to industry experts no later than 8pm. It timed perfectly for the party that wasn't to celebrate my book being a bestseller. But at least, if the worst should happen, there would be enough alcohol readily available to drown Duke's sorrows.

Over the day I had oscillated between a cocktail dress and a suit; such was the beauty of shitting on gender stereotyping. I'd eventually decided on the suit, though, and before venturing out into the (small) madding crowd I took another look in the floor-to-ceiling mirror that Lena had insisted we have fitted. I remember having hopes for reasoning far more adventurous than the realities that had unfolded since; it had turned out Lena really did just want an easier way of checking her entire outfit before leaving the house. When and if we broke up, I had already decided this would be the first thing I gave her custody of. In the harsh-looking glass, I loosened my tie another tug and played around with suit jacket buttoned, unbuttoned, buttoned. But I was wearing a white shirt and braces underneath so unbuttoned made more sense and– *How in the fuck can you care about this when you're about to rub elbows with the person who's threatening to out you?*

I forced out a long, slow breath and turned to kiss Birdy on the head. She was buried in the folds of my duvet behind me, staring out at my reflection. Since the trip to Dad's my behaviour had been so erratic that I think even the dog was grateful for some time away from me. She didn't even follow me out of the room. And from their chatter, it was clear that neither Lena nor Duke had heard me open the door and step out into the hallway.

'Honestly, is this what fame does to people or…'

'I've worked with some writers who have really gone off the deep end in their time.'

'Is that what you think is happening, you think she's going off–'

'I'm not a shrink, doll, I'm a literary agent.'

'I just don't know how worried I should be here, Duke. She isn't herself. She isn't herself at all.' Though I couldn't see her, in my mind's eye I could tell from her tone that Lena was running one hand through her straightened to perfection hair. 'I'll do what you said, I'll suggest going away.'

'It doesn't have to be right now,' Duke added, and I smiled. *Of course it doesn't, because I'm booked up to my ovaries in events.* 'But maybe when this string of events is done with, you can suggest it then? A good clean break,' he said firmly, 'once the events are out of the way.'

'Are you two ready?' I cut across them as I walked from hallway to kitchen where they'd tucked themselves, out of earshot, I thought they'd wagered. 'Also, could you be more beautiful if you tried?' I rested the palm of my hand flat against the bottom of Lena's back and leaned in to kiss her cheek. Her hair was dishevelled from all that panicking and plotting.

'Look at you,' Duke said, taking a step back and assessing me, 'could you be any more "Yes I'm a writer and queer" if you tried?'

'Oh Jesus, Duke, don't challenge her,' Lena joined. 'She's probably got a "trans lives matter" badge in her back pocket just waiting.'

'But they do matter!'

'I know they do, Sal, I know,' she put an arm around me, 'I'm just saying, maybe the badge doesn't go with every outfit.'

'Fucking up heteronormativity goes with *every* outfit,' Duke chimed and I clapped a quick applause. 'All the same, if everyone is good?' He looked from me to Lena and back again. I only nodded. 'Marvellous! Car already waiting. Let's go, go.'

Lena steered me towards the front door while I shouted a 'Bye Birdy' over my shoulder. I left Lena to alarm the flat; lock and double-lock the front door; check the locks twice over. She was the only one besides me who knew how to get it just so. Meanwhile, I wandered down the corridor, arm looped with my agent's, and for the briefest of seconds everything felt blissfully fucking normal. And I could have cried at the pre-emptive loss of that feeling.

By 7.48pm I had been introduced to as many as forty people I'd never seen before in my life. And I remembered a good twenty-nine per cent of the names I'd been given for each of those people. There was Ade from Millers' House Publishing and Fran from Warebrooks' Suppliers and there was Lin and Wendy and Kathryn and, and, and. The only person I had any true interest in was Lena, who somehow – after promising to stay right by my side throughout the entire event – had instead taken to lapping the room as though she were the star of the show, and I was only too happy to let her take the role. I spied her talking to someone who may have been called Steve – or Andrew, possibly even Matthew. And it gave me the perfect opportunity to find Duke, steal a cigarette and disappear into the smoking area of the venue.

'Doll, it's nearly time,' he said, double-checking his watch. Of course I knew what the time was. I'd been nervously checking throughout the night, too, but mostly because I knew the announcement would one way or another be the peak of the evening, and that would inevitably mean that we were on the downward slope to going home – back to my dog. I'd checked the home camera system no fewer than thirty times in the two hours that we'd been away and so far the most interesting thing I'd seen Birdy do was climb into the window seat that I usually shared with her and take a long stare out into the world, before clambering back onto the sofa. Still, it had been a comfort. 'Have this, take a hot five, be back in time?'

'Yes, sir.' I pocketed the smoke and disappeared

through the crowd, all the while wondering whether Lena would look up for long enough to notice.

'Hey, the big true crime hit,' someone said as soon as I stepped into the garden. It was a beautiful space, decorated with greenery and fairy lights, and if only Duke would have been kind enough to give me the entire packet of cigarettes, I could have blissfully spent the entire affair outside, alone. Apart from Smoky Joe in front of me now, who spoke through a veritable smog of what smelt like cigar. 'Having a good time, beautiful?'

I hated men who assumed and called me that. It was a peeve if ever there was one.

But I was the big true crime hit, I reminded myself, I was on my best behaviour. So I only smiled and said, 'I really am. Duke got a boatload of big shots together in there, didn't he?' I paused to spark up. 'Are you having fun?'

'I am, I am.' I was only too delighted to see him dab out his own bad habit into a nearby ashtray. 'I'd love to chat more but I'm a glass off being pissed and I want to sign that guestbook of yours before my handwriting becomes a doctor's.' He paused to laugh at his own jibe. 'Lovely idea by the way, the guestbook. Catch me inside, won't you? Be fab to chat more.'

Everything rolled out of him as though he were voicing a single thought rather than several stitched together. To add insult, as he scooted by me to get to the door he added a kiss on the cheek to his goodbye and still I could only smile. Now, I wagered that I deserved an entire packet of cigarettes for not having climbed onto my tampon-shaped soapbox and spouting something about space, something about– *You're looking for reasons to be angry*. The thought was an intrusive albeit accurate one. I found a wall to lean against and pulled in hard on the cigarette to calm whatever was rising in me. From this angle, I could glance straight through the cluttered room and watch the man in question sign something in the book that had been left in the entryway. People had caught me over the evening to say what a tender idea it was, a time capsule of a special night. Of course, none of them knew I was gathering evidence.

I had cleared the following day to lock myself in the office to research the new book that my agent, family and life partner now believed I was writing. In reality, I was planning to go through the book line by line to compare the handwriting samples with those of the notelets I'd received from Duke's office; both of which were firmly locked inside a drawer of my desk, firmly double-locked in the office itself. I exhaled a plume of smoke above me and by the time I looked back through the doorway the man had gone. He'd been replaced by Lena, though, who was rushing towards me with Christmas morning excitement.

'Babe,' she was out of puff and making a show of getting her breath back, 'Christ, I'm so– I need to work out more.'

I laughed, the most authentic laugh of the evening. 'Is that what you rushed out to tell me?'

'You need to come in,' she managed then. 'Duke is getting champagne. You need to come in.' She was still out of breath from having run the length of the room, but the excitement was blurring her breathing, too. Still, she persisted. 'The book did it, babe, you fucking did it.' Lena lunged forward into a forceful hug then, knocking into me with such clout that I nearly lost my balance. When she pulled away from the embrace she placed a hand either side of my face and kissed me square on the mouth. I could taste the sting of alcohol on her but not clearly enough to wonder what she'd been drinking. 'You're number fucking one.'

Everything after that was watercolour. I remember Lena dragging me to the bar, where Duke was ready with champagne. I remember the man from outside kissing my cheek again. Nearly one hundred per cent of the people I'd been introduced to earlier in the evening came to congratulate me and this time around I remembered even fewer of their names. Though I tried to take a mental imprint of the faces of people who didn't congratulate me: *Have I been introduced to you? Are you a welcome guest here?* But whenever I tried to catch Duke to ask who so-and-so was, he would only slap me on the back and give me a fresh glass of something boozy. By the fourth glass I remember trying to concentrate on Lena talking to someone by the guestbook; I didn't know his face, but she seemed familiar with him. And I was too drunk to disentangle worry from envy from panic from joy.

I'm number fucking one, I remember thinking around the sixth – seventh? – glass. *And you're a fucking fraud*, by the eighth...

FROM THE WOODS

I have especially vivid recollections of the memorial service. The school was determined to do something to mark Emma's passing. It became a calendar event, with comments swapped on social media asking whether this person was going, that person, another person. 'Do you think Sally will come?' was a comment that appeared on a loop. My school attendance had left something to be desired in the weeks after Emma died, understandably, not least because I was being hauled into police interview suites and carefully designed offices of counsellors almost alternately. Everyone wanted to know what I could remember, anything more, anything new. By the time the memorial was scheduled and police approved, my parents were deeply concerned that, psychologically and emotionally, I simply wouldn't be able to handle the event as a whole. They were right.

It was the first public panic attack that I had. In the years after they became commonplace. But on that unexpectedly sunny afternoon, while cohorts of children – because that's what we were, despite what we thought –

were marched into the school hall, I felt the rise of bile and panic and–

'I can't breathe,' I'd whispered to my mother. 'I don't think I can breathe.'

Mum tucked an arm around me and ushered me from the room as though it were a practised manoeuvre; maybe it was. I could imagine the ways in which her and Dad might have stayed up late one evening running through the operation of herding me from the room until it ran as smoothly as possible; until one or both of them were absolutely prepared for me to crack up just as soon as I saw an inflated version of Emma's most recent school photograph, fixed to a large easel at the front of the stage in case anyone were to forget why we were there. She rushed me past Harry – as I would come to know him later in the investigation – who gave a sombre nod, next to teachers who had lined up along the back of the room, level with the police presence.

'And why will the police need to be there, exactly?' Dad had asked Harry during one of many visits, where both men cradled their mugs of tea in our living room and discussed my well-being and safety. I listened from the doorway. 'Do you think she's at risk, in going to the memorial? Because if that's what you're saying–'

'That's not what I mean to imply, Vince.' They were on first-name terms by then. Despite the police maintaining a professional distance, by the time a teenager has wept in your arms over her dead best friend that you're yet to find the killer of, it becomes impossible that some latent paternal instinct wouldn't kick in. I knew that Harry was in my, our, life then. I knew it, too, from the frankness with which he and my father spoke to each other. Harry had a mug reserved for him; Harry took his tea with two sugars; Harry would be on our Christmas card list. 'We can't rule out that the killer is someone that the girls knew, and if it's someone the girls knew...'

'Then it could be someone at the girls' school.' Dad had completed the sentence, and a long pause rolled out in the seconds afterwards. 'She'll never be able to trust anyone ever again, will she?'

'She'll get there,' Harry had answered, too quickly; instinct, again. 'She'll get through this, and she'll make something of herself. She'll make something new.'

TWENTY-FIVE

Lena wasn't there when I woke up. I didn't even go to the trouble of checking the time. I assumed she was at work already. She was one of those strange creatures who had the innate ability to drink inordinate amounts of alcohol and then wake up the next morning feeling completely fine. I was no such creature. So before I unlocked the door to my home office, I made the strongest black coffee that the machine would allow for, without issuing a health warning across its display screen. Birdy followed me from point to point around the flat while I wandered. I allowed us both the luxury of ten minutes sitting at the window while my coffee cooled and the fumes of it soothed me. But then I trod back to the bedroom to find the key I needed for the office door. This room – that would have been a spare bedroom for anyone else – was always colder than the others. Its position in the flat layout meant that it never saw the light of day until much later in the afternoon. So that morning, an unwelcome chill poured out when I pushed the door open; though something about it was refreshing, given the watercolour edges of my cognitions still, laboured from whatever champagne was left in my system – which was probably a lot, the way Duke had been pouring drinks.

The box from my parents' house was on the floor – where my best work always happened – waiting for me. Lena had only seen it for a second when I'd carried it into the flat days earlier. 'Research,' I'd said, answering a question she hadn't yet asked, and I reasoned it was a truth, of sorts. I clambered to ground level and took great care in keeping the coffee steady as I moved. When I was cross-legged with the mug next to me, Birdy took up her rightful spot: curled up into a tight ball and pressed hard against my left thigh, where she would stay until she inevitably became too warm. I kneaded her soft curls and took a generous mouthful of my drink before I attacked the box. The strips of tape had been administered without rhyme or reason, by the looks of it, and I tried to remember whether I had sealed these memories or whether I'd only asked Dad to. It occurred to me, as I yanked the third strip of brown tape away, I might be pulling the box apart completely.

'Everything might come spilling out entirely,' I said to Birdy then, as I finally managed to lift the left lip of the cardboard.

Emma's face was the first thing I saw waiting for me inside and I physically recoiled at the sight. It wasn't often you got to look your victim in the eye years after you'd killed her. These days, though, it felt like I was carrying her wherever I went. In the lifeless hours of the early mornings now, it even sometimes crossed my mind that I mightn't have killed her at all. Perhaps my life had become a psychological thriller, a blockbuster where the alleged murder victim had somehow escaped, put a deformed and hard-to-identify body in their place and lived out their life in secret, only to return years later to wreak vengeance on the person who'd 'killed' them – that would be the part I had to play. Though of course this was optimism; the product of an overactive imagination that had decided if it were Emma sending notes, having flowers delivered, that, somehow, I could handle it. It would be easier than the lingering spectre of No One: the real culprit behind it all.

'At least if it were you,' I said, speaking then to Emma's neat school portrait, 'I'd be able to kill you again.'

The box was a time capsule of better days. Or rather, the idealised images of better days. Photographs where Emma and I both looked our best, having scrubbed up especially well for school photographs. Then, there were the photographs where we looked especially terrible, one of us having stretched an arm out to capture visual evidence of the hangover we happened to be suffering at the time of the picture being caught. There were old notes, scribbled and thrown to each other from one side of the room to the other, and there were the notes signed by other people entirely: Colette, the French exchange student who insisted on signing every note 'Cx'. She and I had had a five-minute dalliance somewhere between those notes, too, which I wagered was how they wound up in the box. There were notes from other people to other people, and I remembered a time when these paper exchanges offered us ripe opportunities to endlessly tease and/or blackmail each other, if only we could intercept them before they arrived at their intended destination, which would probably explain the crumpled note from Luke, about how fit he thought our substitute teacher was. I gave up on reading the notes eventually, only skimmed them for signs of Emma's involvement and then discarded them in a wild pile next to me. It wasn't until I paused to sip my coffee – now cold – that I realised how long the minor endeavour had taken. After that, there came the photographs.

I was one cold coffee and two contraband cigarettes into the sorting process when I found the thing I hadn't known I was looking for: Emma, with James' arm slung around her, his mouth pressed close to her ear and her smile schoolgirl wide, feeling the hot breath of the boy she loved close by. It had been years since I'd thought of him. But there was a time when he and Emma had been so close that I wagered she might well have told him anything. So I set the image to one side and kept sorting through further snaps. There were so many pictures that didn't feature Emma at all, though I still spent time searching for signs of her in them, and it was in those moments that it occurred to me how, even now, life tended to revolve a little bit around Emma Blackburn. Or at least, a significant portion of my life did.

'Though a significant portion of life also now revolves around–'

'Babe?'

A cold and uncomfortable feeling shot up my spine causing it to straighten. *How the fuck is she home?* I struggled upright from the floor but left everything else where it was. I was slumped in the doorway by the time Lena found me. She was soaked through in her running gear, meanwhile I was trying my utmost to act casual, as though there wasn't a chilled bead of sweat travelling out from under my hairline and over the rise of my left shoulder blade. This was the closest she'd come to being in this room for so long. But both Birdy – who was now lingering around my feet – and I were steadfast guards in ensuring no one, not even Lena, got close to the small house of horrors that doubled as my writing space. There were far too many ghosts in the room; far too many truths. And yet, despite my standoffish posture, Lena tried to peer over my shoulder as she stilled in front of me.

'Nothing I can see?' she asked with a smirk.

'Nothing to see.' I leaned forward and soft-kissed her on the edge of her mouth. 'I thought you were working.'

'Sal.' The single syllable was weighted with disappointment and I immediately knew that I'd done something wrong – but I couldn't set my fingertip on what. 'I told you, I booked today off so we could spend time together after the party, because you're number fucking one,' she grabbed me by the balls of my shoulder and gently tried to shake some enthusiasm into me, 'remember? Ringing any bells?'

I ran a hand through my hair. My scalp was damp with panic. 'Le, I really–'

'No.' Lena's tone was firmer then, and from the corner of my eye I thought even Birdy's head snapped up at the sound. 'We've hardly seen each other, at all, since those wild book adventures that you and Duke went on. We have a day together, and we have something to celebrate.' She waved a hand towards the mess of the office behind me. 'Whatever top secret nonsense you're working on in there will still be there tomorrow, or in the late hours of this evening when you creep out of bed and do work behind my back.'

'You make it sound like I'm cheating on you.' I laughed.

'Yeah, well, sometimes it feels like you are.'

I didn't get a response out. Lena knew that it was a

parting shot she'd fired, and she wasn't going to let me undercut it with my writer's tongue. She criticised me once for using my 'superpower' – also known as my ability to stitch pathos into a sentence – against her, during arguments. There was nothing I could say to her last comment to turn sympathy around to me, though, was there? Please, don't criticise me, someone is threatening to out me for my having murdered my best friend and then financially capitalise on the incident. As pathos goes, it didn't exactly have potential. So I let her comment hang, mould spores filtering through the air to seed in respiratory problems that would lend me a panic attack later, and I stayed stock-still while she walked back along the hallway. The physical space gave me time to catch my breath – and lock the office.

'Lena, wait.' I went after her once I knew the door was double-locked and James' photograph secured. I rounded the corner in time to find her pouring a strawberry and cream frappuccino down the kitchen sink. 'Now come on,' I decided on the spot there was an opportunity for humour here, 'I know you're pissed at me, but there are lines you just don't cross.'

She turned around, drink in hand, but at least she wasn't pouring anymore. 'So help me, Pober, you aren't as cute as you think you are.' Lena put the drink down on the side then, and wiped her hands clean of spilled cream. 'Besides, it was mine, not yours.' She closed the distance between us. 'I would never, ever, be pissed enough to pour your favourite drink down the drain.' She huffed a laugh then. 'Second-favourite drink. I know gin will always be your first love.'

I pulled her to me, a loose hug to press her pelvis against my own. 'You are my first love.' I saw the beginnings of a laugh bubble up in her and I pulled her tighter towards me, to try to save the moment. 'No shit, no writer's tongue talking. Lena, *you* are my first love. Work,' I shrugged, 'it's going to be there tomorrow, tonight, whenever. What do *you* want to do today?'

Lena pushed my hair behind my ears to clear my face. I hadn't even showered yet, having tumbled straight from bed to work to panic. *I must look a fucking state*, I thought, suddenly embarrassed in a way I hadn't been around Lena since she and I first started seeing each other. I couldn't decide what it meant, whether this signalled a new phase in our relationship or some kind of lunar turn in me. But I was relieved when Lena countered it by resting a finger under my chin to lift my face back to her. She kissed my forehead, nose, mouth until I was smiling again.

'I want us to drink our drinks and eat our blueberry muffins while we watch old episodes of *Come Dine With Me* on Netflix. Then I want you to take a long bath, that I'll run for you,' I opened my mouth to dispute that part but she ploughed on all the same, 'and then we're going to go out for a nice dinner, and celebrate the fact that you're sitting pretty at the *top* of the *biggest* bestseller list in the country. Okay? Okay,' she said, without leaving breathing space enough for me to argue against any part of the plan. 'I love you, Sally Pober, top to toes, and I know work is everything.'

'But it shouldn't be.'

'But it is.'

And I wondered whether I'd said what I'd said, knowing exactly what she'd say back. 'I'm sorry.'

'Don't be.' She kissed me again then, softly on the corner of my mouth. 'Just try to remember that there's more to life than the people in those boxes. Some of us are still living and breathing and,' she sighed, 'desperate to watch terrible television with you.'

I managed a smile. 'Did you say something about blueberry muffins?'

'That she hears, Birdy,' she said to the small creature curled between our feet. '*That* she hears.' But I heard nothing more after; nothing but the background static of panic that was becoming so commonplace to me now, I recognised it like a pulse of blood, or a heartbeat.

TWENTY-SIX

Despite the nice day – and it was, admittedly, a nice day, even with my baseline panic – Lena still decided to sleep at her own place that night. And then again the night after that. When she told me I felt very much like I was being baited, encouraged into a longer, harder discussion than I was willing to have. Instead of concern, all I actually thought in the face of her announcement was, *Well thank God I can get to work earlier*. I kissed her goodbye at the doorway two nights running and managed a dejected sort of smile, as though implying a sadness without having to go through the motions of verbally communicating such a feeling. Then when I heard the downstairs security door slam shut – a noise that was deep enough to penetrate up to my level of the building, which had been another part of the place's appeal – I made coffee and went back to my office. I didn't want to trap Birdy in there with me, knowing she could comfortably have the run of the flat if she pleased. So I double-locked the front door and pulled the safety chain across too. Lena couldn't sneak up on me now even if she made a concerted effort to.

And from there began the slow and arduous task of trawling through the social media profiles of everyone I went to school with. On the first night working at it, I spent an inordinate amount of time typing James' full name into search engines but there was no return. It occurred to me then, that he might have changed his name, or changed surnames at least. *Maybe he's modern-day enough to have taken his partner's surname*, I thought as I pulled up the first of too many social media sites to try. I leaned into Instagram, on the premise that seeing his face, even all these years later, would be an easier spot. But on searching for James, Jay, J, and Jim through 'friends" profiles, I didn't find a jot. The only search results were for men I didn't recognise in the slightest and I hoped that a person couldn't change that much in such a time frame – though I couldn't rule out the concern/possibility altogether, either. Still, after staring longingly at Sid Stanton's grid for longer than absolutely necessary – she was a professional photographer now, it turned out, and a bloody good one if those small squares were anything to go by – I closed Instagram down entirely and went to the next in line: Facebook.

I took a window break while the site loaded. Birdy had been sprawled in the hallway but when she saw me pad into the kitchen she quickly followed suit. I set the kettle to boil and sourced her a treat. 'Take it in the window, baby,' I told her and she dutifully did. The kettle took too long to boil and by the time it whistled I was already smoking my first cigarette of breaktime. With no Lena to reprimand me, I reasoned I could get away with at least ten a day – or ten a night, given that it only seemed to be evening times when she couldn't stand to be around me any longer. I was sure, deep down, that that wasn't the reason for her leaving – or at least, I was optimistic that it wasn't. But I was also sure her leaving might have been some kind of quiet test, and in not stopping her, I had failed twice over. And yet, I still didn't call her, or even check my phone during the break. Instead, I made fresh, strong tea and perched with Birdy at the window while I finished one cigarette and then another. All the while wondering what had become of James.

Admittedly, I didn't make an effort to get to know him. I'm not sure Emma did either, unless a mutual interest in each other's genitals counts as a shared interest. *Nowadays it probably does*, I thought with a long exhale. He was a jock if ever there was one, though, and he was rumoured to be on the radar of some scout or another thanks to his prowess on the football field. I tried and tried to remember more, but I recall it all seeming distastefully American at the time and it didn't feel much different now.

I dabbed the cigarette on the outer wall of the building and went back to work. Birdy followed me in this time.

'If only you could talk, little Bird,' I said softly to her as she curled up in a ball under my chair. 'But given the secrets you know, maybe it isn't a bad thing.'

The first four profiles I checked were useless. The vain girls had grown into vain women, and all I could really determine from looking at any one of their profiles was a) how well they'd married and b) how many children they'd managed to force out. The general responses to both being well, and lots. In the end I had to Jenga my way through profiles, pulling out one that I was friends with to lead to ten that I wasn't. James had been in the year above us at school, which inevitably meant that my pool of friends was a lower tier of popularity to him, relegated as such, thanks to the years we were born. Emma briefly stepped into the higher circle of popularity – Dante's lesser-known level of Hell – but when her and James stopped sleeping together she was soon forced back into the category of people who moved seats in the common room to make room for those born in an earlier year bracket. Her and James stayed close, though, I could remember that much.

Sid's profile appeared again soon into the searching, though we weren't actually connected. Still, the page was open enough for me to see yet more images of the beach and sea and hillsides that left me longing for something beyond the cityscape, where it suddenly felt more dangerous than it did homely. I reached under the chair to gently pet at Birdy's back and said, 'We're out of here, babe, as soon as this fucktard is dealt with.' She grumbled, as though quietly agreeing to the plan. I soon realised, though, that nature scenery wasn't the only thing Sid had stockpiled on her very open profile. I assumed it was wide open because in many ways it was a portfolio of work for anyone who happened to be looking for someone skilled behind a lens. But the openness meant that anyone – namely me – could stride right into her photo albums and–

'Bingo.'

One album – titled 'Back in the day' – boasted photo after photo of us all. I was six clicks in when I found an awkward Polaroid of Emma kissing my cheek and my eyes stung at the sight. It can't have been tears, but there was certainly feeling. Another three clicks and I found a photograph captioned: 'Let's hear it for the boys'. And there the boys were, our homegrown athletes throwing arms around each other in what looked like a post-match celebration. They were muddied and dirtied and evidently delighted with themselves, and there James was, right in the centre of it all. I skimmed through the tagged names in search of his and drew a blank again, which left the only remaining option of trawling through the other names that were listed. Into every open friends list I typed the same goddamn name until eventually Luke Kendall's profile gave me exactly what I was looking for. But in a disappointing form.

A post from three months ago showed a young him next to a young James. They were holding beer that they were too young to be drinking and their smiles were the kind of watercolour smirk that comes with weed. The caption? 'Can't believe it's been four years, mate. Miss you even now. X'

'Fuck.' I scrolled through the comments, littered as they were with names I knew and names I didn't and– 'Fuck!'

I ran a hand through my hair, shot back from my desk – unnerving poor Birdy in the process – and paced the room.

'What sort of a fucking lead is this?'

There were materials all over the floor still, and it sent a sharp pain through my chest to think of going through them only to find more dead-ends.

'How the hell am I ever going to work this out, Bird?' I asked the dog as I looked from photograph to scrapbook to photograph to leaver's book to– 'Wait.' I hurried back to my desk and grabbed my mobile. There was one text from

Lena – from two hours ago, asking how work was going, but I reasoned that not answering was answer enough – and instead I clicked into my recent calls and hit Duke's name. He answered on the fourth ring and he sounded hazy in his greeting.

'What happened to the guestbook?' I asked.

'Wait, what? Sally?' There was the sound of shuffling in the background. 'Sally, do you have any idea what fucking time it is?'

I didn't. But a quick look at my laptop screen told me: 1.38am. 'Shit, Duke, I'm sorry,' I resumed pacing as I spoke as though the movement of it might slow or at least steady my thinking, 'but the guestbook, from the book party, the other–'

'I know when the party was, Sally.' He didn't expand. But there came more shuffling in the background and I played out a cinematic image of Duke stumbling from his bed, padding into his own home office, and holding up the guestbook in a style befitting of a eureka moment. But his reaction was understated by comparison. 'I've got it right here, okay? It's safe.'

'Okay, that's great, thank you. I can probably be there in, I don't know, about a quarter of an hour if that suits you.' I was powering down my laptop, pre-empting his agreement rather than his outrage.

'Sally, it's the middle of the goddamn night, what's the matter with you?'

'I need the guestbook. It's not like I'm asking you to come here.' I tried to match his tone. 'It's going to hold up my work if I don't have it, Duke.'

'And what work would that be?'

A long pause stretched out between us, during which time I eyed the documents and images that decorated the floor. Sans an explanation, Duke let out a hefty sigh instead.

'Lena is worried sick about you.'

I hated it when they talked; a sneaky secretive faction.

'I know. How about we talk about that when I come over?'

Another sigh. 'It's that important?'

I tried to steady my voice before I answered. 'It's that important.'

'I'll come to you.' I heard further commotion in the background. I had only seen Duke's home a handful of times but already I knew the space well enough to imagine him moving from one room to another as he spoke. 'I'll be there soon, okay?'

'Duke, seriously, I'm the one who needs it, I can come–'

'How much have you had to drink?' he asked flatly. I looked to my desk where my empty tea mug sat squat next to the laptop – alongside the empty whisky tumbler. 'I'll be there soon, okay.'

This time it wasn't a question. So I muttered my humble goodbye and left the phone on my desk before dragging myself back to the floor. It would take Duke around fifteen minutes to get to me, which meant I had a good ten minutes before I needed to get up, brush my teeth, and put the kettle to boil for us both. I used the time wisely to stare and stare at everything laid out before me – but I saw nothing at all.

TWENTY-SEVEN

I woke up five hours later with the kind of thick tongue that only comes from heavy drinking. The walls of my mouth were covered in lichen; each cheek a small, dehydrated organism that I prodded at with my tongue. I set my palm against my forehead and couldn't work out whether the dampness stemmed from hand or brow, but even that single movement had been enough somehow to turn my stomach over. I groaned, and Birdy matched the sound with a low grumble from somewhere beside and below me. I let my hand drop off the edge of the sofa to try to find her but only managed to catch the outer fringes of her coat. She didn't stand to lessen the distance between us, though, and I felt as though that may be her small way of kicking me into the dog house. It wasn't until I tried to turn over, to greet her, beg her forgiveness kindly for the fact that I'd gargled whisky like a demonstrator at a dental convention the night before, that I realised I wasn't on my own.

Duke was sitting in the armchair adjacent. He had one leg folded over the other but in the manly way: his foot balancing on his knee. But his head was tipped back at an awkward angle towards the ceiling and it wasn't until I stared harder that I realised he was dozing too. I thought of clearing my throat, deliberately loud, to wake him; that old move. But like a toddler's mosaic the sharpened pieces of the night before started to come together to form an odd shape, not entirely reminiscent of the original object – or rather, the real events – though accurate enough for me to get an image of it and remember. 'Shit.' I called Duke about the guestbook.

I struggled into an upright position that took far too much effort for someone of my age, and I vowed to pour the whisky away. *Just as soon as I can make it to the sink*, I thought with a hand clutched against my mouth. It would be an empty gesture, given the drinks' cupboard of wine, gin, vodka and other ghosts. At least this would give me something to tell Lena, though, a sign of something.

With my elbows balanced against my knees, I let my head drop between my legs; a half-arsed attempt at the recovery position. There, I took deep inhales and exhales to ready myself for the arduous process of standing up. Having lowered my head gave me a better view of Birdy, and I could see all too well her disapproving stare, mixed with what I thought looked like watered sadness in her eyes, too, and it was enough to stir an ill-feeling that wasn't even related to the booze.

'Baby, I'm sorry,' I said in a whisper, and the small mutt leaned forward to press her wet nose against my bare calf. I took it as a quiet forgiveness and managed to reach down to scratch her head softly.

'Ah, you're awake.'

My head snapped up and a wave of seasickness hit me.

'Easy. There are limits, doll, and while I don't mind mopping your sweaty brow while you sleep, I'm not mopping the floor after you've... You know.'

'I dragged you over here.'

'You did,' he said as he stood, stretched and moved out of my line of sight. 'I suspect you'll be needing a coffee?'

'Oh, Duke, I don't–'

'It wasn't a question.' He was already moving towards the kitchen. 'There are things you and I need to talk about, Sal, and we're both going to need coffee for this particular snowstorm of shit particles.'

I managed a laugh. 'I had no idea you were such a writer.'

'Well, what can I say, when I spend enough time around tortured types, it starts to bleed out of me.' I heard the percussion of his movements: the clunk of cupboards; the soft machinery knocking together as the coffee machine stirred to life. 'Go to the window seat and get some fresh air. There are smokes on the table if you want one.'

'Don't those two things contradict each other?'

There was a long pause before he said, 'Sally, do you want a cigarette or not?'

And that's when I saw it, lying there open on my coffee table like some display piece used to dress a scene in a catalogue. The cigarettes were on top of the open pages. There was no way I could reach for one without seeing the other, and I wondered whether that had been Duke's reason for suggesting a smoke in the first place. But I shook the thought away. *Is Duke that calculating?* But then, he'd said there was a shitstorm coming. While I oscillated between worries I managed to grab the cigarettes and heave myself free of the seat. On the walk from sofa to window I clutched my swollen stomach like an expectant mother and imagined the swill movement of booze beneath the skin. The thought alone was enough to bring bile rising but – Duke's wisdom having paid off – the blow of air that came in as soon as the window was open was the coolant that I needed, and swallowing back the urge to vomit everything up became *slightly* easier. By the time I was perched on the window seat with a cigarette between my lips, I had managed to convince myself I might get through this without vomiting. Unless, of course–

'Do you know who wrote it?'

'I'm sorry?' I squinted up at Duke who was holding out a coffee cup to me now. I didn't yet know what was in the guestbook. But I could guess. 'I don't know what you're ta–'

'Sally, don't. I've worked with drunks and liars my entire life and one way or another I always find them out. Do you know who wrote it?' He set the coffee down alongside me then, and took his own back into the centre of the room. I thought he planned to sit a safe distance from me and the stench of the previous evening's binge, but what he was actually doing was getting the goddamn book. Coffee in one hand, and guestbook awkwardly held open in the other, he thrust the open pages in front of my face like an outraged mother, having just found pornography in her youngest son's room.

What will you do when they find out it's fiction?

'Do you know who wrote it?'

I spoke from behind my hand. 'They were there.'

'You know who they are?'

I looked up at him and felt the sting of feeling watering my eyes. I could only shake my head. It hadn't occurred to me that the shock was coursing through me as aftershocks might until I tried to light my cigarette, and found that my hands were trembling at random intervals. In the end, Duke took pity on me. He turned around and threw the book on the sofa, placed his coffee on the edge of the table, then he held the lighter steady. I was on my second mouthful of much-needed nicotine by the time his own smoke was lit.

'This is why you've been acting like a crazy bitch.'

'Don't call me a crazy bitch.'

'Spade a spade.' He pulled in and exhaled a plume of smoke into the living room. He was sitting beside me at the window by then. 'This is why you wanted the guestbook there, to see whether they were there.'

'Sort of,' I managed. 'I didn't think they'd write *that*, exactly. But I thought if they were there, and they wrote something, then I'd be able to...' I petered out when I heard him soft-chuckle at my reasoning.

'You're a regular little Nancy Drew, aren't you?'

'Well, apparently not.'

I turned to the side and pulled my feet up onto the seat, with my spine pressed against the cool of the frame. Duke awkwardly matched the gesture which meant we could only look at each other now; or look longingly out of the window itself, into a city where no one knew whether I was a murderer or not.

My hand was shaking again when I took another drag. 'I'm sorry.'

'For what?'

'Causing a mess.'

'Oh, Sally.' I thought there'd be more, but he only went back to his smoking, as though having said enough for me to take up the mantle of talking. I didn't offer anything though; I was too nervous of incriminating myself further. 'What else have they,' he waved in the general direction of the book, 'what other attempts have they made to spook you?'

'Fan mail,' I managed, 'and flowers. Here.'

'They know where you live?' He seemed more concerned than he did outraged. I only nodded. 'Do they know where Lena lives?'

'She hasn't received anything, not that she's said, anyway.'

'No, well, we'll get to that mess in a minute. First to deal with this one. Can anyone prove anything?' he asked plainly, and though I don't know what expression my face fell into, it was enough to make Duke choke with laughter, sending an eruption of smoke out of him too. He waved the smog away. 'Don't look so fucking outraged, Sally.'

I didn't know how to answer his question other than with uncomfortable honesty. 'I have no idea whether they can prove anything. But I don't understand how they can.'

He nodded slowly. 'Okay, well, I say ride it out.'

Again, I waited for more. But instead he stretched out for his coffee and took two generous sips before making an 'Ahh' noise, that didn't look to signify any more meaning in the conversation.

'You aren't even going to ask?' I spat out in the end.

Duke shrugged and reached forward to pet Birdy who was sleeping between our feet. 'I'm not naïve to the realities of writing, Sal. Of course there's some fiction in that book. But your family have read it, Emma's family have read it, beyond that I haven't got any concerns. It's not the big deal you think it is, doll. Besides which, I'm a literary agent, not a defence barrister. There are some things I'm just best off not knowing.'

I was stunned dumb and silent. My cigarette had all but burnt out during the conversation, so I dropped it into the window-ledge ashtray and went back to cradling my coffee instead. I was three sips in and no less shaky when Duke handed me a cigarette that I hadn't even heard him light.

'Sweets, look at it this way. The book is a bestseller already. Can you imagine what would happen if someone accused it of being fiction?' When I didn't answer he pressed on with his enthusiasm, 'Do the words *In Cold Blood* mean anything to you?'

'No one accused Capote of being a murderer.'

'How are they accusing... Sally, listen, let's not get caught up in this. A lot of people thought Capote was a butcher by the end of his career too.' He leaned over and set his empty cup on the floor next to him. 'It's a hassle and a faff to deal with. But until they're *actually* threatening to out you for something, there's nothing to be done. Nancy Drew-ing your way through, well, whatever it is you've been doing– Is there even a second book?' he interrupted himself, as though realising the wider fiction at play.

I decided that after his kindness and patience – neither of which felt like things I deserved – I at least had to throw him a bone. 'There actually is.'

He threw his hands up in praise. 'Okay, well, the Nancy Drew work about this particular shitemare can be shelved. It's not getting you anywhere, other than suffering from a drink problem and sending your relationship down the pipe.'

I'd known this was coming. I ran a hand through my hair and tipped my head back so I could avoid his stare, which was searing. 'What's she told you?'

'She isn't sleeping here anymore. She's hardly hearing from you. You're never present. Shall I go on?'

'Is this what Lena does,' I was face to face with him then, 'she just calls you to have a good fucking moan about me? Do you reciprocate? Is it a club with jackets and a membership fucking fee?' I threw my cold coffee out the window and dropped the empty mug to the floor with a sudden clunk.

'Volatile.' Duke snapped his fingers. 'I'm sure she said something about volatile moods as well.' He leaned forward to lessen the distance, and placed a hand on my knee as though trying to secure my attention. 'Doll, listen closely to this one, okay, because I'm saying this truthfully and with a lot of love. You. Are going. To lose her. Nod along if you understand me.'

I was closer to tears than I expected to be by then. Of course I understood. And of course, no one could blame Lena if she did leave. I was turning into a nightmare. *I'd* leave if it were an option.

'Okay, well that's that hurdle jumped. So, now we all understand that you might be about to lose her, I'm going to help you make sure that you don't...'

TWENTY-EIGHT

For a man who had never known the touch of a woman, Duke gave what I thought was relatively good relationship advice. He came up with a five-bullet-point plan of how I could win Lena back, which was something that I needed, given I wasn't entirely sure I'd even noticed how lost she was to me. When I tallied up the nights, I realised that in the last seven evenings, I had spent five of them alone – which I was still sober enough to know was a red flag. After Duke had gone, I showered, ate a solid breakfast of dry toast – one tiny mouthful at a time – and smoked another two cigarettes before dragging myself back into the office and trying to order it into something that didn't resemble panic as an art installation. The floor was pockmarked with paperwork, my laptop had a dangerous number of tabs open, and there were nonsensical Post-it notes *everywhere* around the room, as though a toddler had been given a stationery box to decorate with. The most telling note of them all being one that simply said: CALL SID. It was underlined three times. I couldn't even remember writing it down –

which subsequently meant that I didn't remember how my drunken self had planned to call a woman whose number I didn't have.

'But that's a problem for later,' I said aloud to Birdy, who was lingering in the doorway, watching from a safe distance. I screwed the note up into a tiny fluorescent-yellow ball and aimed for the same corner where I had thrown the other unhelpful shit. A hard sigh fell out that I hadn't realised I'd been holding, and I pushed my still-wet hair away from my face, with one hand getting caught in a tangle of knots en route. 'I'm a mess, Bird.' I looked around the space as I spoke and, while looking *slightly* better than it did half an hour ago, it was still nowhere near presentable. 'Not that it matters.'

I left, and locked the door behind me. If Lena did accept my invite of a home-cooked meal, the last thing I needed was for her to go snooping through the innards of the space. Though she still hadn't replied to the message I'd sent earlier – carefully crafted with Duke's guidance – so there may not have been a need for me to adopt the façade of normalcy at all. I could have continued to wallow in my what-the-fuck-has-my-life-become state quite peacefully for another evening yet. But that was something else Duke had continued to pep talk me about, too, as the morning had drawn on.

'Why the fuck aren't you panicking about someone outing my book as fiction?' I'd eventually snapped, somewhere around bullet-point three on the list of action points for loving Lena better.

He'd shrugged. 'If you don't know who it is or what they have, and there's no way of working either of those things out, what the fuck am I meant to be doing, doll? What the fuck are *you* meant to be doing?' He waited for an answer, but there wasn't one. Somehow, his blunt-force-trauma approach to the situation said everything and more about how to handle it. 'You can let it ruin your life *before* it happens, or you can ride it out *until* something happens. Do you want it to ruin your life now?'

That time, I had had an answer. 'No, of course I don't.'

'Well, there you go then. Bullet-point four...'

Of course, I wouldn't be listening to a word he said in respect to the book and the person who apparently knew the truth of it. But I could appreciate the approach all the same. Once the evidence of all my messy research was locked away, I trod back into the kitchen to make what must have been my sixth coffee of the day. I'd started drinking it to sober me up; at some point though, around the third coffee, I had reached a clarity of thought and calmness that would soon be ruined by one sip too many. Now, my approach was to drink my way back to that point, as though applying more caffeine to any situation would lead to peace of mind at the end of it. Still, what other option was there? It was that or gin, and I'd vowed to Duke that I wouldn't – at least not during daylight hours. So I made my coffee, grabbed my cigarettes, and my dog, and went back to the window. I hadn't checked my phone in at least an hour, so in danger was I of becoming the teenager who buggers their handset from locking and unlocking and locking and... all to check whether their crush has replied. So when I was perched in a comfortable position, I tapped the home screen and braced for disappointment – but instead there was surprise. 'You have one new message from...'

'Sid?'

I clicked into the social media messaging app and unlocked what turned out to be a conversation that I'd (drunkenly) started in the early hours of the morning. *How much memory have I swilled away?* I wondered as I skimmed my message to her – with, praise Jesus, minimal typographical errors – and saw that I'd contacted her under the pretence of researching a new book. I wondered then, whether telling that lie enough times might make it a truth; whether somehow, further down the line, I would be both talented and composed enough to spin a sequel out of this shitshow. For now, though, I had told the lie convincingly enough and asked whether she might be able to help with some old school photographs. There were people I needed to track down, and some people who were so long lost to me that I couldn't place their names, I'd lied again. Though that second point was perhaps a partial truth, given there were definitely people pictured in my spools of evidence that I wouldn't be able to put a name to even if they were to come and shake my hand at a book signing.

Sid wasn't one of them though. I could remember her clearly enough as the girl who threw the parties; the girl who took the pictures; the girl who would always lend a helping hand. Now she was a woman and nothing looked to have changed. She was happy to help, she said, could I do a Zoom?

'Because perish the thought anyone meets for coffee anymore,' I said as I started to draft my reply. Though deep down, I was relieved at the opportunity to stay in my hang-around-the-house clothes; not to be confused with my hangover clothes, that I had only just about managed to drag myself out of. I typed:

> Oh, you're a sweetheart.

> Zoom would be great. When suits?

I hit send, sipped my drink and queued up a cigarette. I had just about settled the butt between my lips when I saw the dots appear at the bottom of our chat window.

> Now?

Ten minutes later, there unfolded pixel by pixel a busy office behind Sid's fresh face. She did not have the complexion of someone who had been on the lash the night before; while I, on the other hand, was not the picture of health in my small Zoom square. Both of us waited for the audio to signal it had connected, smiling awkwardly through those moments of mouths moving while the internet connection looked not to have caught up with the greetings. Sid fixed her settings until the background blurred, but I had nothing behind me to hide; I'd strategically positioned myself in front of a bookshelf, such was the way with writers using video technology. Sid mouthed an obvious 'Hello' again but still nothing came through the speakers. In the silent seconds, I took a considered glance at her face and realised that – far from having changed drastically in the years between our talking – Sid looked every bit as handsome as she always had. In some ways, her dimple cheeks and colour blush were the same as the eighteen-year-old's I had said goodbye to at the leavers' assembly. But there were changes, too, glasses that she hadn't needed before, a more stylised haircut, platinum hair dye.

'Can you hear me?'

I shot back in my seat. From one extreme to the other, the audio had come through impossibly loud and sent Birdy scarpering across the opposite side of the living room.

'I'll take that as a yes.' Sid chuckled; a hearty, comforting sound somehow. I couldn't reason how someone I hadn't spoken to for so long suddenly felt so familiar. But the accompanying thought that came to a soft boil in the background – *It could be her, you know, you could be asking for help from the very person doing this to you* – created a clumsy tension in my stomach too. 'Jesus, Sally Pober, look at you!'

I managed a laugh. 'This is not me at my best.'

She waved the comment away. 'You're a bestselling author now, of course you were drinking on a school night.' She paused to sip from a glass of water that she'd picked up from off-screen. I was embarrassed that my boozing was so obvious to her. 'So, how's life in the fast lane?'

'Oh, it's more like a cycling lane, really,' I rebuffed the assessment. 'How about you? You're off taking pictures of the world, right?'

'Sometimes the world,' she shrugged, 'sometimes South London. That's where I am at the minute.' As though taking a cue she waved to someone in the blurred setting behind her then. 'I'm helping a friend with this fashion photography stint that she's doing. Well out of my comfort zone but the portfolio will probably benefit from something that isn't a stylised sunset and– I'm rambling already.'

'Ramble away,' I encouraged. I didn't have enough to say for myself to fill the *So how have you been?* small talk. We lived in a technology age; there was no way Sid hadn't at least given my name a quick run through an online search engine before speaking to me, which meant she already knew everything that I felt comfortable telling her. 'I didn't even know whether you'd be in the country when I messaged,' I pushed, hoping for subtle flattery. I'd watched her Instagram stories already; I knew exactly where she was, down to the postcode, before she'd even mentioned the place by name, thanks to one of her colleagues having tagged her in a reel showing followers where the studio was. Nothing is sacred anymore.

'Anyway, tell me about you. Tell me about writing!'

I tried for a playful groan. 'Honestly, it's turned me into a demon.'

'You must love it though.' I caught the hazy image of someone tapping her shoulder. Sid turned and spoke quietly to the person off-screen. 'Sorry,' she said as she scanned back to me, 'getting an ETA on when I'm needed.'

My stomach flipped at the thought of her leaving before I'd even had the chance to appraise the goods she might have. 'Do you need to...'

'No, no, I'm good for about half an hour. Which I hope is plenty of time to hear about your latest project? You're writing about school?'

'Well, I'm hoping to. But there are faces that I...' I huffed and shrugged, and Sid let out another burst of amusement.

'So you're treating me as a fact-finder?'

'More like a face-finder, if you don't mind being treated that way?'

'Treat me how you like, Pober, I won't say no.'

I felt a lick of warmth move through my face. *Is this flirting?* I wondered. To ground me back in reality I tapped again at my mobile and felt the sag of disappointment on seeing that Lena still hadn't replied. It became a tick, the tapping, the checking, that lasted through my half an hour video call with Sid – by which time, we'd agreed to meet for dinner anyway. I ended the call unsure of whether this was something else that I needed to feel guilt and sickness over, whether it was another way in which I was loving Lena wrong.

TWENTY-NINE

Lena rebuffed my offer of dinner, and for two days straight I suggested nothing but alternatives: *Dinner out somewhere? What about a cinema trip? Birdy and I could meet you from work and walk you home one evening?* I was suggesting anything by then to prove to her that a) I was committed to the cause and b) I was capable of leaving the house, which I soon realised my initial suggestion of a home-cooked meal did nothing to prove. After countless suggestions, she eventually took pity on me and replied with a yes to my offer of dinner with my parents. *Will Duke be coming too,* I wanted to ask, *is this going to be an intervention?* Though of course, after careful consideration – and a long walk with Birdy, that gave me my first burst of fresh air for the day – I realised it probably wasn't an intervention at all; what it was, was a test.

Lena had met my parents already, of course, but only a handful of times if that. I'd told Mum and Dad that they didn't need to come to the book launch – or any of the additional book launches disguised as different events entirely – so saturated would the evenings be with elbow-rubbing and fake smiles. That alone must mean it had been nearing a year since Lena had been in the same room as my folks.

'She wants commitment, Birdy,' I said quietly as we followed the cement tracks that weaved through our local park. 'She wants... to feel valued?' I wondered aloud while Birdy stopped for her millionth wee. While I waited for her I took the time to look around and spotted, directly opposite us, just a short walk and a road crossing away, a jewellers.

I'm a murderer who wrote a book about someone else doing the killing and now someone is threatening to out me, let's get married. Did they make a card for that? Was there an ideal setting for popping that particular question?

I was thankful when Birdy tugged to move along. When we stopped for another pee break shortly after, though, I pulled my phone out of my front pocket and keyed a reply to Lena.

> Dinner with my parents and my girlfriend would be lovely.

I lied.

> I'll ask when they're free.

Mum had done everything short of hanging bunting. The house had very obviously been cleaned from top to bottom, Dad was wearing a shirt I'd never seen before, and we were using the dining-room table, rather than the kitchen. All signs pointed towards Mum having made a ridiculous effort – supported further by Dad's unimpressed eye-roll as he welcomed us into the house, as though apologising in advance for–

'Girls!' Mum flocked towards us with a high pitch and welcomed us not one hug at a time, but rather in a joint hug that encapsulated us both at once. Lena and I shared a glance over Mum's shoulders while we could, and it warmed me to have that first show of closeness. The car journey hadn't been air-conditioning cold, but she hadn't warmed to me on the ride here either; opting instead to stroke Birdy, look out the window, and occasionally comment on the scenery we moved through. 'You both look so well,' she said when she unleashed us, holding us at arm's length then, with a palm cupped around a shoulder each. 'Though, Sal, you do look thin. Are you eating?'

'No but she's drinking,' Lena answered, and my eyes stretched. *Is this an intervention?* I thought again then, as I side-eyed her. But I noticed the smirk and realised, though the comment was cutting and too accurate, it was also said in good humour – or what passed for it at that stage in our relationship.

'You're such an only child,' I joked back, trying for a more jovial tone than she'd managed. 'I am eating, Mum.'

'Well, you'll definitely be eating today.' Dad squeezed past us all and Birdy dutifully followed him; she knew the weak mark for soliciting food. 'Your mother has made enough to feed you and all your readers, Sal.'

'So they can take Tupperware home!' Mum said over her shoulder.

Lena made a swooning expression. 'Who doesn't love leftovers?'

'My girl,' Mum said then, pinching her cheek softly, 'it's been too long.'

Lena reached for my hand, a small and quiet gesture; she squeezed and I watched her smile before agreeing. 'It really has been. But we're here now,' another squeeze, 'that's the main thing.'

Though she faced Mum, I felt somehow that we were having a very private conversation, too, and realised that the gruelling task of being normal, non-panicked and sociable for a few hours – while my mother force-fed me whatever was boiling, stewing and soaking in the kitchen – was worth it, for the sake of keeping a hold on one of the main reasons for my not wanting to get found out in the first place. *Her, of course*, I thought as I followed Lena into the living room, *so much of this is for her*.

And for her, I slapped on my best smile and answered *all* of Dad's questions about the book, which I took to be his way of apologising for and/or showing interest, despite still not having read it.

'You *haven't* read it?' Lena repeated, though I was sure I'd told her. 'It's a wonderful, brave thing, though, Vince, how have you...' She petered out when she saw Dad's shamed expression. 'I mean, of course, it's utterly horrific. But... I suppose, I saw so much of it being written, it's a different experience for me, isn't it,' she asked no one in particular, as she looked around us one by one but didn't wait for a reply before continuing, 'though I do wonder what this second book is doing to her.'

I squeezed Lena's knee under the dining table. 'Nothing,' I lied, and pushed broccoli to a different edge of my plate to where it had started. We were on our second course, but the threat of sickness was ever-present. Not for the first time in recent months, I wondered when

I'd last eaten a full meal. I managed a smile for Mum from across the table all the same, though, and purposefully shoved a forkful of pasta into my mouth, chewing while still smiling.

'What's this second book about then?' Dad asked.

My phone hummed on the table, a sharp vibration that signalled a new message. Duke had vaguely promised me news 'of something' that morning and asked me to keep the phone close by in case he needed me. It was potentially a welcome excuse to step into the garden for a minute and take a call.

'Can't you turn that thing off?' Mum asked, while next to me Lena craned across to see the message preview.

'Who's Sid?'

'Sid Stanton?' Mum leapt on the name. 'You and Sid are back in touch?'

I used my best, 'It's nothing,' tone. 'She's helping me with the second book, actually.' Of course, I hadn't mentioned Sid to Lena. The last thing any recovering relationship needed was the threat of an outsider, and even though there wasn't, and never had been, anything between me and Sid, there was always a quiet kinship between us for having both–

'You and her practically came out together when you were kids, didn't you?' Dad blurted, his face still angled at his food. Though he was occasionally slipping chunks of meat off his plate and onto the floor for Birdy to find. 'How is she, keeping well?'

'Did you have a little queers club?' Lena asked and I thought her tone was good-humoured. But then, 'Anything I should worry about?'

'Oh,' Dad's head snapped up, 'there was never

anything. Was there, Sally? You two just went through it together.'

'Lena, how old were you when–'

'Mum!' I cut her off, sensing where the question was moving. *How the hell did we get here?* I turned to Lena and apologised on my parents' behalf. 'You don't have to answer that.' She opened her mouth as though to respond but something in me – some deep-rooted panic response that was ready to throw sand on the growing fire around me – opted for a subject change. 'Lena and I are going away soon. Let's talk about that.'

Lena's eyes widened, only for a flicker of a moment – and I only noticed because I was watching for it. She reached up then and held my hand on the table; her wrist squashed against the screen of my phone, as though literally rubbing our happiness in another woman's face. 'Let's talk about that,' she agreed.

'To the coast?' Dad caught the conversational ball.

'To the coast?' I passed the question to Lena who made a noncommittal gesture. 'It's been a while since either of us have seen a beach, surely?'

Even though the gesture had been a forced one, the act of planning it out became a soothing process. Over dinner we talked about the benefits of holidaying inside the United Kingdom versus trying to leave it – 'With the dreaded fear that they mightn't let you back in,' Mum narrated – and how there was something to be said of the natural beauty in our own landscape. 'We had plenty of countryside treks in our day, didn't we, Luce?' Dad added, all the while using a bread roll to wipe up the remains of pasta sauce from around the edge of his plate. By the time Lena and I had settled on a clifftop setting with a beach view from every window as our ideal holiday spot, Mum was cleaning away dinner plates in a hurry with the promise that dessert wasn't far behind. Dad made an appreciative noise while next to me Lena made a small bloated one; it was a sound that you only recognise from familiarity and intimacy, no one else even seemed to have heard her. But I smiled over it as I handed the half-empty plate to Mum.

'You've left so much,' she critiqued.

'I was full from the starter alone.'

'Which you also left so much of.' She stacked the plates. 'Come and help me in the kitchen.' I opened my mouth to protest but didn't get far. Mum cocked her eyebrow and bunched her lips to one side; a disapproving expression if ever there was one. So I pushed my seat back from the table and quietly followed orders. 'We won't be long, you two chat away.'

Birdy followed us – ever the loyal pet, where food was concerned – though I felt bad that she and I had both left Dad and Lena without an easy buffer between them. *What will they even talk about?* I wondered as I reached up into the top cupboard to pull free four bowls for the dessert servings.

'Have you two been having problems?' Mum asked, unprompted, and I nearly dropped the crockery. I managed to set it down on the kitchen table with relatively steady hands before I answered.

'We're fine. What makes you ask?'

'Well,' she was pouring custard – fucking lashings of the stuff – into a glass jug to heat through in the microwave, 'something isn't okay. And if it isn't you and Lena, then it's you.'

'What?' I tried for soft outrage; nothing too over the

top, but enough to make her think I was irked by the suggestion. 'What's wrong with me?'

Mum leaned back against the work surface while the jug made its laps around the ancient microwave; its hum an ominous percussion. She folded her arms and eyed me up and down, as though searching for evidence of something. And like an intrusive thought my mind flitted back to my office; the photographs, the shaky notes pinned everywhere that had made me into a detective from a cheap rent-a-cop movie. *Don't think about the actual evidence*, I warned myself, knowing, of course, that would only make me think of it all the more.

'Months after Emma, it was like this.' I felt winded at the unexpected use of her name, so brazenly too. 'You're acting how you were when you were... I don't know, getting better, or trying to get better from it all. Shock, sadness, overcompensating with happiness.' She raised a finger then; the classic parental caution. 'You can't hide these things, Sally Pober.'

'Sid has texted again!' Lena shouted in from the next room. 'And Duke.'

It was the perfect excuse. I shrugged at Mum's accusations and rushed back to Lena, who was holding my phone in the centre of her palm like a blessed offering. I ignored Sid's message, of course, and clicked straight into Duke's instead, though it only read:

CALL ME. NOW.

FROM THE WOODS

I had never intended to write a book about Emma – about what happened to her. But during streams of counselling appointments, where memories bled into each other like a poorly constructed watercolour, the therapist I was seeing at the time suggested writing as a way to disentangle the truth from the trauma. It was understandable that not all of my memories were clear, she explained to me, but writing might be a way through the greyscale of truth and fabrication – or rather, truth and erasure, given that there was so much of what happened that I couldn't remember, or couldn't remember clearly enough for the information to be of any use. The police had stopped pushing me for the fine details after a while. Though they were always sensitive in their approach, I think they came to the conclusion they were chasing a ghost – and I was not a medium.

The man who took us may have taken other girls, other women; he may have taken people since, which is a thought that I still lose sleep over. I pace the rooms of my small home sometimes, wondering which part of the city he's in, whether he's in the city, even. On especially bad days, I wonder whether he's standing in front or behind me in the queue for my morning coffee, or whether he happens to follow the same route as me when I feel inclined to go for an evening run. It had crossed my mind, too, that he may even be at a book launch one day, when this story goes to print. When I first started to set it down, though, it didn't occur to me that the person responsible would care enough to make himself involved in the story for a second time – not least because I never thought that story, this story, would see the light of day.

I showed my counsellor the early writing, though, and it was her who suggested there might be something more here than catharsis.

'You could really help people, Sally,' she'd said.

And after years of carrying the survivor's guilt at not being able to help my best friend when she needed it most, the prospect of helping someone else was an appealing one. That's how *From the Woods* was born into more than a story told through counselling sessions, blossoming instead, into something that shows the human mind and body alike can recover from the most heinous of sufferings. It has taken time and will continue to take time, and I cannot claim by any stretch of the imagination that this was a solo endeavour – but I will save the specifics of that for the Acknowledgements page later in this paperback. I only return to these early moments of the book's conception as a way to explain the healing power behind having written it at all. I know there are some people who believe true crime is a throwaway type of storytelling, for non-fiction writers with a creative eye and a desire to spin a good yarn. For some of us, though, it's a vehicle through which we can tell our stories and air our pains, and maybe, maybe, heal.

I was ten chapters into the book before I realised I was writing chapters at all. I was barely out of my teenage years and still indoctrinated to the school of thought that all stories had to be told in the ABC order that they happened. When I was reliving everything through my counselling montages, though, it became clear that that wasn't how my mind thought of Emma's story. There were blind spots and I think there probably always will be – but perhaps that's the Kintsugi of the human psyche, the breaks are where hope can repair things.

THIRTY

Duke waited until I was a glass of champagne in – and Lena was taking a bathroom break – before he put two envelopes on the table and slid them across to me. I recognised the handwriting straight away – and though Duke hadn't seen the handwriting from the other notes, he'd evidently clocked the hand-delivered notelets, care of his office with no sign of a stamp. He cocked an eyebrow at me.

'I took the liberty of opening them.'

'It's illegal to open someone else's post.' I snatched at the contraband and half stood so I could awkwardly shove them into my back pocket. 'Since when do you go through my fan mail?'

'Colour me curious,' he sipped his drink, 'I told Kelly we were having some problems with abusive letters and that we needed a better screening process for what came through the office. She's very good at her job, you know? I think I'll keep this one for a while.'

Duke had a terrible habit of blitzing through assistants at an alarming rate. He consoled himself with the lie that it was a high-pressure job in a difficult industry. The reality was more that Duke was a nightmare to work with – and his clients weren't much better, myself included.

I set my elbows on the table and cradled my head. I was two days away from my dinner with Sid, though I knew already that she was having too much fun collating school materials, thanks to her frequent messaging. My replies were always polite, engaged and appreciative; secretly, I wished she'd hurry up and find me a suspect already – as though it would be that simple.

Duke snapped his fingers to get my attention. 'Nancy Drew,' I looked up, 'assuming you still don't know who this is?' He waited for me to shake my head before he continued. 'I think that when we do the radio interview later this week, we should go public with this.'

I jerked with such a force that I knocked over my glass. A waitress appeared before the spill of the drink hit the floor.

'I'm so sorry.'

'Honestly,' she rebuffed my remorse, 'it happens all the time. I'll get you a fresh glass and we'll get this cleaned right up.'

'You're fucking mental,' I said in an angry whisper when she was out of earshot and Lena was back in sight. 'You're fucking mental, and I won't do it.'

'Okay, well, we'll talk about it later,' he said, too calmly, and I could have clambered over the table to wrap my hands around his throat.

Lena landed hard on the cushioned bench alongside me and immediately tucked an arm around my shoulders for a squeeze. I had stopped sleeping and started to drink in secret – but at least she and I were getting on better.

Whenever she'd asked about the new book – which she had done, extensively, on the drive back from my parents' days earlier – I played the superstitious writer card and told her it was too soon to talk it over. Duke's news had been a helpful distraction against her questions, too, given that she seemed more excited than I could claim to be. And I hated the bones and mucous of my little letter writer for having taken white spirit to any sense of joy that I might carry in the face of all this – the excitement at having pulled the whole thing off. *Because you haven't, have you?* I heard in Emma's voice, and I tried to shake the spite of it away and tune back into Lena's question instead.

'I said,' she started a repeat, 'who do you think will play you in the film?'

'Come on, we don't even know that it'll get that far.'

'Sally, you're being a negative Mary Sue about this whole thing,' Duke cautioned me. 'Besides which, I don't buy champagne for any old shit. It'll come good, all of this will. Trust me,' he added, and I caught the sense that he wasn't only talking about the flickers of interest for the film rights to the book. Owing to its rolling status in the bestseller charts, no fewer than two film agents had expressed interest in the story – and had subsequently left me cursing my success as a result, because the last thing that book needed now was a wider audience.

I fidgeted and felt the crack of the two envelopes in my back pocket. 'I'm going to chase the waitress up with that glass,' I said then, and shuffled my way free from our booth. Lena said something by way of a reply but I didn't stop to listen. After rushing to the bar, I pulled both envelopes out of my pocket and one by one I tore them down their centres with the most aggressive rip I could manage. 'Excuse me.' I caught the attention of the server.

'Oh.' She turned with a fresh glass in hand. 'I was just bringing you this.'

'I'll trade you.' I held the torn letters up to her. 'Could you throw that in the bin for me, please?'

'Of course. If there's anything else I can be doing...'

'We'll give you a shout, thanks.'

Lena and Duke were falling over each other with laughter when I turned. And I couldn't stand the sight of either of them in those seconds. There was a violent bubble of something angry forming in my stomach that I knew was for Duke and not my girlfriend. But even the sight of her laughing and living and being blissfully ignorant to it all did something to me then, something that I didn't recognise or like. So instead of joining them I disappeared to the cover of the ladies toilets. I set my glass on a shelf and perched on a decorative armchair that served no real purpose at all, other than to signal we were in a high-end establishment that could afford surplus furniture by pretentious designers. It had been Duke's choice to come here. I pulled my phone free from my pocket and though there were no new messages from Sid, I clicked into our conversation anyway. Like making Tinder of my childhood, I swiped right, right, right on the images she'd sent me – a few of which featured Emma, but most of which didn't. There were so many faces I couldn't place. *How have I forgotten so many of you?* I wondered with further swipes. *How can someone so inconsequential to me be threatening to ruin my life?* Assuming of course, it was someone in these images, or other images that Sid might source. Assuming of course, it was someone, anyone, I still stood a chance of tracking down.

Aster listened carefully while I spilled my neurosis over her coffee table. I had asked her not to record the session, and she had adhered. I wasn't altogether sure what would come out, but I was sure that I didn't want an audio document of it all. We were back in her normal office for the appointment, and the brightness of the brilliant-white room stung my eyes throughout the hour – eyes that were already tired from having cried my way through the early hours of the morning, because alcohol is a depressant. *Who knew?* I exhaled hard in a long and slow breath, and tried not to let any other tears form.

'Lena doesn't know about the accusations,' I admitted then, 'she had no idea why I was crying this morning. It's the shittest part of her staying at mine again.'

Aster nodded. 'And you haven't thought of telling her?'

'No.'

'Or the police?'

'No,' I said again, but firmer. 'I can work it out. I know I can work it out.'

Aster flashed an expression that was at once both pitying and sympathetic – and I hated it. Though I found there were more and more things I hated lately: the people Birdy and I spoke to on our morning walks, the kind woman who always remembered my order at the coffee shop down the road, the property manager who had been helping me to find somewhere for mine and Lena's planned holiday. Their brilliant smiles and their perky attitudes were enough to cause a small demon in me to get on her haunches and growl. I often wondered whether it was the same demon who had killed my best friend – or whether there was more than one inside me. In the early drunken hours, when I was sad and scared rather than sad and angry, the thought of those demons alone was enough to induce tears too.

'When are you and Lena going away?'

'I don't know,' I answered with a wavering voice; I wasn't sure where the subject change had come from. 'Soon, I think? I have another two interviews this week and next, and then Duke has freed my schedule for a bit because...' *Because he thinks I'm cracking up.* I shook my head. 'Because he thinks I need the break.'

After his suggestion that I 'out' my letter writer on a national radio station, we had talked more, in private, about the whole stunt. The conversation had ended with me telling him to fuck himself and I felt certain that if I weren't such a veritable cash cow these days he would have dropped me on the spot. It had been a while since I'd checked over my contract with him but I was pretty sure abusive behaviours towards Duke or any member of his team likely weren't part of the package deal.

'I think he's right. The place you're going—'

'I haven't picked a place yet.'

'Are you choosing for the two of you?' she asked, in what sounded like a judgemental tone.

'I want to surprise Lena with somewhere. She wants clifftops,' I smiled, 'and a view of the beach from every window.'

Aster reciprocated my smile then. 'Don't we all? But can I make a suggestion?' I murmured a noise of encouragement and felt my stomach tense in readiness for it. 'Wherever you are, think about security for you both? Whether you work out who's writing these letters is inconsequential, Sally. You know in your heart of hearts what happened to you and Emma during those days, and there's no disproving that. But if they do turn out to be dangerous, in any way, the last thing you'll want is an isolated cabin in the woods.'

I tried to look for loopholes in what she'd said. But my heart of hearts couldn't find one. Instead I only managed a slow nod. 'I don't think Lena and I are about to stumble into a low-budget horror film, Aster.'

A small noise fell out of her, nearly a laugh but not quite. 'No, but then, neither do the people in the horror films.'

THIRTY-ONE

When it came to the radio interview, Duke was underhand about the way he seeded in my unwanted fan mail. He wasn't on-air with me. But he did make a point of telling Freya – the woman who would be interviewing me – that there were some hacks in the woodwork already, unwanted attention from fans who weren't really fans at all. The woman's eyes had widened at the mention of it, but like a true (un)professional she'd waited until we were recording the show before she asked for more information.

'Your agent, when he and I were talking earlier, mentioned something about aggressive fans, or superfans even? Do you feel comfortable talking to us about that, Sally?'

Now, while I liked Freya, and found her youthful enthusiasm endearing and encouraging, in that moment I could have happily leaned across the recording desk and slapped her pink-blossom cheek into a violent bloom. Because of course I wasn't happy talking about it, which was why it wasn't on our list of pre-approved questions. It was a mark against her insofar as professionalism – and I told her so afterwards. In that moment, though, with Duke lingering expectantly outside of the booth, all I did was smile and agree. Like the performance artist I had turned into: Sally the victim; Sally the writer; Sally the woman who escaped near death only to be plagued by superfans.

'I don't know that superfans is the right term,' I laughed, 'but there are certainly some letters, I get a few letters each week sent care of my agent, and there are some letters that have a... I don't know, an unpleasant tone, I suppose? But I think this kind of thing can happen in any industry, can't it? People who "make it" – I'm using air quotes, for the people at home who can't see me – people who make it will always have people who disapprove of their having made it, which I think is really sad, actually. But,' I tried to change my tone to something lighter, 'for every bad letter there are ten good ones, and I'm really, truly thankful to everyone who has read the book and felt moved, or encouraged or, I don't know, anything else that leads to some kind of personal development. It's amazing to know that a book, especially a book that was so hard to write, can do that for people.'

From outside the booth Duke gave me an 'Atta girl' wink and thumbs up. He was called away by the show's producer before I could mouth a 'Fuck you' by way of response.

The rest of the interview was smoother, though, and Freya managed to stick to questions we'd agreed to. Then came the portion of the show where listeners were encouraged to text in with their own questions, and I felt a vice grip around my stomach as Freya started to read them aloud into her microphone. Though the questions themselves were minimal, and instead there looked to be nothing more taxing than kind words and sentiment from strangers who were contacting the show to applaud my bravery on the one hand, and my writing skills on the other.

'The best true crime novel that Dominique from Weston has ever read, you heard it here first, folks. Sally, it's been a joy.'

'Likewise, Freya, thanks so much for having me.'

'We're jumping over to Donna for our latest weather report now, folks. Donna, what do you have for us?'

Freya flicked the microphones off and gave me the nod that recording had finished, and I disentangled myself from the headset at lightning speed. She thanked me again and again for the interview; I told her never to ask questions that someone hadn't agreed on. Her face dropped like I'd just told her that the moon wasn't, in fact, made of cheese, and that Santa Claus did once upon a time eat children.

'I'm so sorry, when Duke mentioned...'

'Don't sweat it. Duke says a lot of shit that he shouldn't. Honestly, it's been a pleasure.' I left her with a handshake and a smile, and went outside to tell my agent to go fuck himself for what I guessed would be the third time that day. I'd said it so many times now that it had lost its weight; I needed a new insult. Though I realised, too, that there was a great chance Duke might get sick of the insults and drop me – which was both a reason for and against hurling abuse at this point. 'What the fuck was that?' I angry whispered when I pulled him to one side of a crowded hallway. 'Superfans?'

'Sweets, before you go mad at me, you should know–'

'*You* should know,' I cut him off, without yet knowing

what the end of the sentence might even be. Part of me was almost relieved when he pressed his hand over my mouth to kill whatever was coming.

'What will you do when they find out it's fiction?' he asked with a cocked eyebrow. 'They texted the show while you were on-air. That's why the producer called me to one side. We officially owe them one for not reading it out.' He moved his hand away then, and I could tell he was braced for impact. But I had nothing. I could only shrug, shake my head and push a hand through my mess of hair. It worried me that I might look as shit as I felt then. 'Are you okay?' he asked softly, as though not wanting to trigger the crouched anger.

I sighed. 'Does it matter?'

'Sal...'

I held a hand up to stop him. 'I have dinner to smile my way through now and I need to grab a shower beforehand. We'll... I don't know, we'll talk, another time. I'm done on this for the day.'

'Tell Lena I said hello,' he shouted after me as I paced away from him.

And I would, whenever I saw her next.

Sid was wearing a high-necked black top, denim-blue chinos, black and white Converse and a wide smile. She looked gorgeous. And the sheer thought was enough to send me clutching at my stomach with guilt. There was a stab of literal pain in my abdomen so severe that I paused midway on my walk through the restaurant and clutched at my gut. She stood, and her concern was obvious. But I only waved it away and continued on my walk to our secluded table for two at the back of the room – just as I'd requested. I wasn't looking for intimacy, only privacy, though I realised in those final few seconds how easily the two things might be confused in this setting. She didn't sit back down, but instead waited for me to join her at which point she pulled me into a hug that felt overfamiliar for someone I hadn't seen in years, though, perhaps, just the right amount of familiar for someone who I'd been texting most days since having tracked them down on social media.

'Sally Pober, get a look at you.' She unleashed me from the hug and stepped back, as though distancing herself well enough to assess me properly. After she'd looked me up and down she said, 'Are you okay? It looked like something hurt you halfway here.'

To which I said, 'I have a girlfriend.'

I presented the information in a small, neat nugget. The sentence so blunt that she was observably surprised by the announcement.

'Oh-kay.' She hesitated before adding, 'That's great.'

I laughed then, and revelled in the sensation of ice-breaking. Our awkward introduction was out of the way, and Lena was on the table. 'It was guilt, when I saw you,' I added. 'It suddenly occurred to me that through all of this, I hadn't mentioned her once and...' I petered out, but Sid autocompleted the sentence for me.

'And you didn't want me to get the wrong idea,' she said, taking her seat at the table again. I sat opposite, and did my level best to avoid eye contact. 'Okay, I see how I *could* get the wrong idea. But, Sally,' she reached over and placed a hand palm up on the table, 'you absolute loser, I didn't think this was a date.'

Even though Sid had aged, for a flicker of a second I

saw her exactly as she used to be – right down to the same term of endearment she used to use too. I placed my hand in hers and, as she gave me a gentle squeeze, I finally managed eye contact – and then a smile.

'You must think I'm mental.'

She tilted her head from one side to the other as though weighing the thought up. 'Actually, I think you're very sweet. But you have a girlfriend, and this isn't a date, so I don't think you need to be *too* worried about old friends catching up, and one of those friends dumping a boat-load of photographs on the other in exchange for their next book being dedicated to them.' I burped out a laugh; an abrupt sound that perfectly captured just how much she'd caught me off guard. 'Okay, the dedication might be reaching.'

'I can manage an acknowledgement.'

'I should fucking think so, for this lot.' She reached for something out of sight then, and her hand reappeared holding a thick, padded envelope that she dropped on the table with a soft clunk. 'These are copies of *all* of the hard-copy photographs I've got from when we were at school.' I was already reaching for the goods when her hand disappeared again. 'And these are the digital versions of things I didn't keep the hard copies of.' Finally, she dropped a USB stick onto the table too. 'I took a lot of fucking pictures when we were kids, do you know that?'

I laughed, but already I was thumbing through the images. It was a montage of memories and misspent youthful moments, and I saw Emma's face littered throughout like a small beacon – or a lingering threat.

'There are quite a few of her in there,' Sid said, as though noticing the same thing I'd noticed. 'Anything with Emma in I actually tried to group together at the front, because, well, I didn't know how easy it would be to see them.'

I froze on a cluster then, Emma pictured in one pose after another. Sid leaned over to look at what had caught my attention, but she didn't add any narrative to it. Instead, she gave me a second to quietly inspect the youthful glow of my beautiful best friend – who I'd killed.

'I don't remember this party,' I said, skipping to the next image. 'When...'

'Maggie's sweet sixteen. You were away with your folks, I think?'

I half remembered. There may have been a full memory there – no doubt consisting of sulks and complaints on my part, at having to miss a school social event that I would have likely been desperate to attend – but I was too distracted, too busy trying to remember faces and slot everyone into place and–

'Who's this?'

Sid leaned further across the table but I spun the image round for ease. It was Emma – at Maggie's party still – with watercolour-drunk eyes, a wide smile, and her arms draped around a girl I couldn't put a name, or even a greyscale memory to. *Do I know you?* I wondered, while Sid took her turn inspecting the image. *Did I ever know you?* There was something loosely familiar about her but still...

'Weird thing, *I* don't remember her either, but the more time I spent with photos from that party,' she reached over to take the prints from me and dealt a selection of them onto the table as though she were a card dealer, 'the more I started to see her.'

This mystery girl and Emma were pictured in various states of drunkenness, delighted with themselves in every shot. But no matter how hard I stared at the images in front of me, I still couldn't put anything to the girl pictured. I could only shake my head, stare harder, narrow my eyes to a squint as though there would be a clue hidden somewhere in the backdrop – some lit neon sign saying, *Yes, this is the girl you're looking for.*

'I guess you don't know her either then?'

I shook my head. 'I don't know who she is, no.'

But I'm sure as shit going to find out...

THIRTY-TWO

Lena was lying with her head on my stomach. Meanwhile, Birdy was at the bottom of the bed making soft dreaming noises. I didn't wake her; I lived in fear of pulling her from some wild dog dream where she was queen of a landscape and I was ripping her from her throne. Lena sighed then, too, though I knew she was awake; it was only a quiet, content noise, something I hadn't heard from her in what felt like months. *Has it been that long since this mess started?* I ran my fingers through her hair and down her back until another noise emerged, and she huddled closer against me. It was the first time we'd had sex in weeks, that much I was certain of. The night I saw Sid, Lena had texted me to ask where I was:

> Home. Getting an early one. Radio interview wiped me out.

And I'd been so plagued with guilt about the lie that in the days since I'd been the carbon copy of what a perfect girlfriend should look like. Birdy and I had met her from work; I'd cooked dinner; I'd even put lunch in a Tupperware box for the following day. And last night, after sitting cross-legged on the living-room floor looking at hillside holiday lets and eating pizza for two hours, I'd taken her to bed and loved her for a while. I was terrified that she'd be able to tell my mind was elsewhere for much of the time we were together – but she hadn't said anything yet. And I wondered whether my lying skills were escalating to a degree that even she couldn't tell what was truth and fiction with me anymore – which would, admittedly, make life that bit easier.

'It was so nice seeing your folks the other day, wasn't it?' she asked then, out of fucking nowhere it seemed, and it made me wonder where *her* head had been. 'We should try to do that more often.'

I lingered over how to answer. I wanted something noncommittal insofar as making plans with my parents, but relevant enough to show I'd paid attention. 'You must miss yours a lot. I can't even imagine...'

Lena had lost both parents in a car accident seven years ago, before I'd even known that she existed. She hadn't gone into the details, and it was hardly something I was ever likely to push her on. But every now and then she'd make a comment, or she'd pause too long in the hallway to stare at a photograph of me with my parents, and those moments made me wonder how much grief she must still be carrying. At the very beginning of us, when I'd told her about Emma, she said that was something else we had in common – that loss, that grief. I'd nodded along and remained quiet and sensitive. Astute Lena had let the topic slide from then on in the same way that I let it slide with her parents. She seldom asked about Emma at all, and I'd never been more grateful; now, the very sound of her name caused a spasm in my stomach so violent that more often than not the anxiety was audible.

'Only as much as you must miss Emma,' she answered.

And there it was: the spasm; the churn.

'Ha,' she struggled up onto her elbow and faced me, 'hungry much?'

'Starving,' I lied. *But thank fuck for the topic change.* 'Breakfast?'

'No can do.' Lena was up and out of bed then. 'I'm on an early shift and I'm already against the clock and...' She petered out when she checked the screen of her phone. 'Weird.'

'Context?' I pushed myself upright and dropped my head against the wall.

'I've got a text about a delivery?'

'I assume it's weird because you're not expecting one?'

'Yes, dummy. Hm.' She pocketed her phone, buttoned her jeans, and leaned over to kiss Birdy. 'If the offer of food is still going later, though, I wouldn't say no.'

'Deal. We'll eat out. You can choose where.'

'You're spoiling me.' She leaned over to kiss my forehead.

I managed a tight smile. 'I'm trying to.'

'I'll have a think about dinner and text you? I love you both,' she said from the doorway. 'Don't work too hard, okay? This second book is already worse than the first one was.' She winked and kept her tone light, but I knew there was an undercurrent of sincerity to what she'd said too. I heard the door slam seconds later – then the first lock, then the second.

I clambered to the bottom of the bed then, and buried

my face in the fur of Birdy's warm stomach. 'Fucking hell, Bird,' I said into her, 'she has no idea.'

I had already scoured through the images Sid had given me. Any picture where that girl was featured, I set it to one side. Despite our putting our heads together, neither Sid nor I had been able to place her before the night was out. I'd graciously accepted Sid's offer of her asking around her school friends then – *our* school friends, if only I'd kept in touch with people from that time. But after Emma I'd wanted a clean slate.

'And look where that's got me,' I said aloud to no one while I shifted position on my office floor. I uncrossed and recrossed my legs and looked again at the timeline of images I'd made featuring the girl in question.

Emma was in most of the images, but not all of them. I took that as a positive; if she was pictured with other people, reasonably, other people might just remember who the fuck she was. But whenever she was pictured with Emma, they appeared to be especially friendly: laughing, hugging, pretending to share from the same beer bottle. And the images of her and Emma had another distinctive feature too: I wasn't in any of them.

It feels cliché to say that Emma and I had been stitched together at the hip. But we had been. Right down to planning out our horrific scheme to get famous overnight. The thought that rang around my head, though, was the horrible and ugly possibility that I hadn't been the only person she'd approached with the idea. *But would it have been you?* I picked up a snapshot of them sitting side by side on a fallen tree in front of a roaring fire and I tried to remember why, why, why I hadn't been at that party, or camp-out, or whatever the fuck it was I was looking at evidence of. Sid had assured me she could find out; she said something about group chats; something about closed Facebook groups. *Why wasn't I nice enough to keep in touch with any of these people?* I tried to match up faces around Emma and her unknown friend and pair them with pictures of people I actually recognised, snapshots where I was present, with people who passed for friends at the time. I was desperate to reach out to any of them, but even when I started to cross-match faces and names, I couldn't fathom how the hell I would introduce the plea: 'Trying to track down this girl I can't remember whose name I don't know. Can you place her?' There was no easy or natural way of doing that! I ran a hand through my hair and closed my eyes for one breath, two breaths, three–

My phone hummed around the floor. It was only a message, and only from Duke, so I happily ignored it. We were on speaking terms, friendly terms, even, but at that exact moment I only had energy enough to be kind to Lena or Sid – anyone else and it was wasted. Whatever he needed he could wait; if he couldn't wait, he'd call.

I'd already sent copies of the images to Mum and Dad to see whether they recognised the face that I couldn't. Mum said there was 'something' about the girl but she couldn't place her exactly. Meanwhile, Dad had clicked his fingers down the phone line and said, 'I know that girl.' And hadn't been able to expand further. 'Okay, well I need that girl so if you think of anything I can actually use, give me a call,' I'd snapped back, and I hadn't been able to bring myself to apologise yet.

The phone hummed for a second time and I huffed,

thinking it would be Duke again, pestering again, but when I looked it was–

'Lena...' I snatched at the handset to open the message and like small rubber bullets the words hit me one after the other:

> Flowers are beautiful. Thank you.

I panic-clicked into Duke's message then too, wondering whether there was a round-robin delivery of floral arrangements making its way around the city but:

> Nice touch, Pober. She loves the flowers. Knew you could do it. Let's interview prep soon. D.

I immediately hit call – on his number, not hers. He answered after the third ring but I interrupted his hello.

'What fucking flowers?'

There was a long pause before he said, 'Should she not have told me?'

Why was she telling him anything, anyway? How did they suddenly become so fucking close? I didn't know whether the questions were formed of jealousy or suspicion – but neither of them felt like the most pressing issue then. 'Duke, *I* didn't send Lena flowers.'

'But she just texted, like, ten minutes ago to say–'

'I know, she texted me, that's the only reason I *know* about the flowers. Fucking hell, Duke,' I struggled to my feet, 'she only popped home to get her shit from work. What if there's a card? What if there's a card that she hasn't read yet?'

'Okay, so Lena has a secret admirer, potentially, but a) you two are solid and b) Sal, you can take some healthy competition from someone unoriginal enough to send...' I didn't know how osmosis worked exactly, whether it was the sort of thing that could move through technology – or whether Duke and I were somehow so cosmically intwined now that we'd become a pair of those sad fuckers who can feel what the other is feeling. But when he petered out and the line went deathly quiet, I knew that he knew. 'You have to go to her flat.'

'And what, break in?'

'You don't have a key?' He sounded outraged.

'Why the fuck would I have a key? We're always here because of Birdy.' She whimpered at the sound of her name and I crossed to the doorway where she was watching the drama unfold. I wondered whether this was the equivalent of a soap opera for dogs; watching their owners in private to see the many and varied ways they collapsed into themselves whenever other people weren't around. Or whether Birdy, too, was in fact bored of my shit now.

'New plan,' Duke brightened, 'give me half an hour and I'll meet you outside Lena's building.'

'And what, *you'll* break in?'

There was another long pause then before he admitted, 'Yes, that's what I'm thinking of doing. Do you have any issues with that, because if you do then we can always let this shit play out naturally and hope for the best instead?'

I could have wept. In that moment, I could have let my tired legs fold beneath like a paper crane structure; I could have crushed my body against the cold surface of the floor. And I could have cried until my dehydration was diagnosable, my chest was thrumming with palpitations and my body throbbed and ached from the exhaustion of weeping my small and fucked-up heart out.

'Do I take that as a yes?'

I leaned against the doorframe and took a shaky breath. 'I'll see you there.'

'Brilliant. Bye for– Oh, Sal, don't bring Birdy, okay?'

I smiled down at the small and adoring eyes looking up at me, and I felt a wave of sickness that she had absolutely no idea what an utter shit I'd been my entire life up to – and including – now. I crouched to give her another stroke and then I reluctantly agreed to Duke's terms. Whether Birdy was bored of it all or simply entertained, I still didn't want her to see what her mum was about to do.

THIRTY-THREE

Lena's building turned out to be a cheap place to bribe your way into. Somehow, by the time I'd locked the office, had a rushed panic attack in my bathroom, double-locked the flat and made my way to Lena's flat, Duke was already standing in the open doorway. He looked despicably smug with himself. I leaned over and set my hands on my knees while I panted air back into my aching chest – 'You really should think about working out more, doll, just for your health, you know?' – and I tried desperately to hold back what I thought felt like a third wave of tears ebbing and flowing behind my eyes. I managed to stand up straight then, and steadied myself against the wall. Now I was upright, Duke flashed me a fresh packet of bobby pins and despite the discomfort coursing through me I found that I managed a laugh.

'I was a teenage reprobate, don't you know,' he said with a small bow. 'But it turns out I didn't even need these.' He pocketed them again and stepped back, opening the door wider and welcoming me in. 'I told the caretaker you think Lena is cheating. Turns out he doesn't like her very much. If he ever sees the two of you together, try not to look too happy, okay?'

My mouth bobbed open and closed as though running on automatic. But I had nothing. I could only manage another huff of a laugh.

'Come on, I've done my part.' He nodded into the flat. 'You're going to have to cross the threshold at some point.'

'This doesn't feel right at all,' I managed then.

'No, it's been a while since I invaded someone's privacy like this, it has to be said. But hey ho, needs must. Get inside.'

I took hesitant steps – a teenager following their parent's instructions – and shuffled past him, into Lena's hallway. We hardly spent any time here, she and I. I'd always used Birdy as an excuse though I'd never really known whether that was the reason – the only reason – or whether she just made it easy to stay at home. Lena had nested at my place; she had a drawer, and space in the wardrobe, and hair bobbles in the bathroom. In short, I had afforded her just enough to feel like I was complying with everything that so-called women's magazines told us that we women should demand in our partner's homes. I'd never asked for anything in return at her place, because Birdy – Birdy again – meant that I seldom spent a night here, even in the earliest days of us seeing each other. Once I'd stepped into the space, though, I instantly realised that this – a home – was another thing I'd deprived my partner of.

Where my flat was light, airy, and open, with minimal decorative embellishments, Lena's was darker, cosier, lived in – despite the fact that she did so much of her living at mine. The sofa was old, beaten up but comfortable-looking, and it sagged only at one side; another marker of my quiet denial of her needs. There was an open magazine on the coffee table and a mug that hadn't been moved back to the kitchen; another mark of Lena's nesting habits that sat awkwardly against my own. The smell of the place was distinctly Lena, too, her perfume and her body and the way she must have brewed a coffee to take to work with her, the smell somehow trapped in the open-plan living space. That was about the only thing that our homes shared: a floor-plan, the one thing neither of us had any say on at all. Her flat was smaller than mine, admittedly, but the living room fed into the dining room that fed into the kitchen, and I found myself stopping to survey each space as I went.

'Why are you looking around the place like you haven't seen it before?' Duke asked from somewhere behind me. I heard a drawer open and I snapped round to see what he was doing. 'What,' he shrugged, his hand still clutching the handle, 'you seem to be taking your time and I've got to do something to keep busy.'

I snapped then, as though something in me had timed out. The sand had run through straight back into the earth and at the bottom of my hourglass there was rage and irritation. 'Aren't you in the least bit fucking concerned about all of this?'

Duke's eyes widened but only for a second before narrowing. 'Sally, unless you bumped off Emma in secret, staged her having been snatched and,' he waved a hand around then, 'Christ, whatever else that fucked-up man did to you both, unless you staged every last second of it, the worst, the absolute *worst* thing that can happen here is some bad press. And I've already played the Capote card.'

I reached out a hand to steady myself against Lena's

dining table. Duke's answer had winded me; a hard punch right in the soft core of my belly. And no sooner had the impact spread across my abdomen, I felt myself doubling over and there were colours and breathing was harder than it should have been and there were no colours then, only black and hard breathing and–

'Sally? Sally, sweets, listen to me, listen to my breathing.' Duke crouched in front of me – *When did I sink to the floor?* – and breathed slow, in through the nose, out through the mouth, as though he were my Lamaze partner. 'Breathe with me, doll, okay?' He pushed hair away from my face and I realised then that I was sweating, too, my forehead dampened like a mother preparing for childbirth. I worried what horned creature would come out of me. *But have I already given birth to that?* I tried to shake the thought away and follow Duke's breathing until my chest was steady enough to speak again.

'I'm sorry,' I forced out, each word a small labour, 'this is all getting to me. It's getting too much.'

'I can see that, sweets.' He touched my cheek gently with a tenderness I didn't recognise in him. 'Let's check over the flowers and get the fuck out of here. I'm buying you a drink.'

Duke stood and held out a hand for me to grab onto. Once he'd tugged me into an upright position he moved in for a hug – 'Don't, Duke, I'll cry.' – I wasn't ready for the contact. Instead, I slowly trod away from him and into the kitchen, where there was a brilliant white bunch of unopened lilies standing boldly in a vase on the countertop – *Do people send lilies when someone has died?* – and they were turning towards the sun of an open window, as though they deserved to be there, as though they'd made themselves at home. Between two of the flowers I could see a small card poking free and I plucked it as though stealing a petal. Under the lip of the red envelope there was a card with an image that matched the flowers, only they were pictured open, with pollen spilling free, as though giving the recipient a view into the future. Confirming my own wicked premonition, I opened the card and found it, the dreaded message, the *What will you do when they find out it's fiction?* A lazy refrain to my entire life now. I considered throwing the flowers straight into the bin, but of course there was no way for that to go unnoticed. Even pocketing the card, I knew would be a considerable risk; it hadn't been opened before I got to it, but Lena might have at least noticed it was there. Whether she'd say anything – whether she'd worry that someone had snuck through her home – I didn't know. But I reasoned it was a bigger risk to leave the card than it was to take it. For good measure, I took the plastic stalk the card had been fixed to as well, in a bid to minimise any evidence.

'Well, whoever the fucker is, they know– Duke! What did I say?'

I rounded the corner to find Duke rummaging through the same drawer he'd opened when we first arrived. He'd clearly tossed it, moving one thing out of the way of another to get a look at what was hidden there.

'What if she notices someone has been through that?'

'Please,' he was holding what looked like a photograph, 'it's a junk drawer, no one ever knows the order they put things in here. Besides, look at how cute this is.'

He handed me a picture of an older couple. They were standing in front of a waterfall background, a scene dressed in heavy greenery, fresh leaves and sunlight. It was the archetypal photograph from a holiday, with the man and woman pictured smiling so wide I thought their faces might crack open. The woman looked around the age of my own mother, though she was dressed in a more daring fashion; probably befitting of the weather conditions, I thought. She donned a bikini top and a sarong so see-through that she may as well have not worn it at all. Her hair – a mess or mangle of curls – was half up, half down and there was something about that that I recognised. She was wearing sunglasses but on her head rather than her face, and I wondered whether she'd removed them for the picture. Meanwhile, the man looked a little older; there were more wrinkles, visible even from the distance the photographer stood at, small crow's feet around the eyes that marked years of laughter, I wistfully thought. He was wearing knee-length shorts with a leaf print on them and nothing on top, showing off a tattoo sitting squarely over his heart, though I couldn't make out exactly what it said, only that it was writing and even he looked, somehow, like someone I might have seen before or–

'It must be her folks,' Duke said, interrupting my scrutiny. 'There's a whole bunch of snapshots.' He'd been flicking through them, I realised, while I inspected this one. 'But there's this, too, which is uncomfortably cute.'

He handed me a postcard that read *Welcome to Australia*. It showed an image not altogether dissimilar to the one in the picture I was holding, though the postcard didn't have the happy couple pictured, only a scenic view instead. I flipped it over to find the handwritten note Duke must have been referring to:

We decided to make the postcard better with our own version. Miss you pumpkin. Wish you were here. Mum and Dad xxx.

In the top-right corner, where the address was fixed, there was a handwritten date: July 2022.

'One year ago…' I said aloud. But Duke didn't understand why it mattered.

THIRTY-FOUR

'Who lies about their parents dying? Who does a fucked-up thing like that?'

Aster had only been able to offer me a telephone appointment. But I wasn't in a position to turn down small mercies, so instead I'd thanked heaven and told her that I could talk whenever. It sounded like she was on the move, in her car perhaps, or at the very least being driven somewhere. I thought I could hear heavy traffic in the background. Though that may have just been blood rushing through, too, around my ears, a baseline static that had been there for two hours now while I'd paced my living room and tried to find rhyme, reason or logic with what we'd found at Lena's.

'How can I trust her? How can I trust *anything* she tells me now?'

I thought I heard Aster sigh. 'Have you ever lied to Lena?'

The question floored me – even though I knew it was fair, even though I knew it was reasonable, and even though I *knew* Aster was doing me a kindness in speaking to me at all, I still found myself barking into the phone – 'What the fuck does that have to do with anything?' – like emotional Tourette's erupting out. When she didn't answer I breathed in deeply and apologised. 'I'm freaking out,' I added, as though that were an excuse.

'I can tell.'

After an uncomfortable pause I admitted, 'Yes, I've lied to her.'

'About important things?'

'Yes.'

'There's no way of knowing what Lena's relationship with her parents is like–'

'It's good enough for them to wish she were in Australia,' I interrupted.

'At the time. A year isn't seven years, admittedly. But it's still a mighty long time in which something can happen, relationships can break down, people can look for a fresh start.'

But we'd been together when that postcard arrived for her. I perched on the edge of the sofa and rested my elbows on my knees. 'It's still a big lie.'

'It is. But as we've already covered...'

'People lie about important things,' I auto-filled the sentence.

'They do, and if it's something Lena doesn't want to talk about, well, I'm afraid there isn't much that you can do other than respect that. It may be a rabbit hole she created, at the time, for whatever reason, that she now can't back out of. But again, it is her right to keep things to herself.'

I forced out a slow and shaky sigh, and tried to murmur a noise of agreement, though I knew it wasn't convincing.

'Besides which,' Aster added, 'I'm curious to know exactly how you'd even approach this subject with Lena, given the circumstances under which you found out her parents were alive.'

I managed another shaky breath. 'I thought she was keeping something from me,' I lied, 'and I was right,' I added, as though that justified the actions.

'Let's unpack that, shall we? Knowing what you know now, do you think your breaking into your partner's home was acceptable?'

'When you put it like that...' I started, my tone petulant but jovial around the edges. But there was no joking my way out of this, no sarcastic self-defence mechanism. I had breached Lena's privacy doing what I did – and my penance was losing faith in her entirely.

There were very few people in the world who I could turn to with relationship problems. Though there hadn't exactly been many before that point in time. Prior to Lena, there hadn't been anyone who I felt drawn to enough to even venture into a full-blown relationship with – at least, not as far as I was concerned. There were likely some ex-entanglements who would have called what we had a relationship, hence their displeasure at my having called things off with such abruptness. But from the first time we'd met things had been different with Lena; there'd been an irresistible pull, as though I were coming home to something, someone I'd already known my entire life, and I'd only somehow misplaced it before meeting her. Which is why the thought of her lying about something so significant had cut through to my core – even though I knew that that made me a dirty, raging, flaming hypocrite. Still, I needed help on what to do next and how to handle it all – how to *feel* about it all, even though Aster had always been quick to tell me that we could only feel what we felt about anything, and that it wasn't something we could control. *But God loves a trier*, I thought as I pulled my chair under the table and quietly thanked the waitress for the menu she'd just handed me. I hadn't been able to stomach food for the last day and a half. As far as Lena was concerned I was at home nursing a stomach bug and I was in no state for company; that had been my cover. But there was no way I could keep that lie going in a restaurant of all places, and certainly not meeting–

'There's my girl!'

'Hi, Dad.' I stood up to greet him and fell into his open-armed gesture. I could have cried against the soft of his chest but instead I only turned a little closer into him and pulled in the smell of home. 'Thanks for coming.'

'As though I'd turn down a lunch in the big city.' We both took to our seats then, and I handed him the menu. 'Mind you, getting out from underneath your mother's feet without giving the game away was no easy feat. I think she thinks I'm having an affair.' He chuckled at the thought, and somehow it warmed me, that the thought of cheating on Mum was not only improbable – it was laughable.

'Well, whatever you want, it's on me.' The waitress appeared then, as if by magic, and asked for our drinks order. 'I'll take a double gin and tonic, thanks. Dad?'

His eyebrows were raised, and I wondered whether this luncheon would shortly turn into a diatribe about my drinking. 'I'll take a pint of Diet Coke, thanks.' Dad waited for her to disappear before he commented at least. 'Things must be bad.'

I made a huffing noise. 'That's just my lunchtime drink, Dad.' I tried to joke it off, as I would do with anyone else. But I could see that he wasn't buying it. 'Okay, things aren't exactly great.'

'I thought as much.' He put the menu down then, as though signalling that I had his full attention. 'Shall we get this out on the table now, before we fill it with food, or do you want to draw it out?'

The options weren't exactly great, either way, but doing it before lunch would, I thought, at least salvage some time where Dad and I could just be having a father and daughter date before he disappeared off home – and that wasn't an opportunity that presented itself all that often. So I pulled in a greedy breath and asked the question that had been rattling around my mind for the morning.

'What's the worst lie you've ever told Mum?'

'Ha! I already don't like this game.' But from my deadpan expression he could see there was no joking in me. 'Can I tell you the worst lie she's ever told me instead?'

Dad's tone was more serious then, but still an unexpected laugh erupted out of me at his idea of the trade-off. 'It's not exactly a lie if you know about it.'

'What if she doesn't know that I know about it?'

'Oh my...' *Do I want to know this? Really?* I worried that I was about to create another black hole of mistrust by hearing Dad out. Though I countered that worry, too, with the reality that whatever the lie was it clearly hadn't been detrimental enough for Dad to leave – or even confront Mum, by the sounds of it. 'Okay, I... Whatever it is, I promise I'll never tell her.'

'Okay.' He looked out of the window as he spoke, and a sad expression washed over him, and the wave of nerves that hit the wall of my stomach was of winter storm intensity. 'Your mother was married before me. It was a short-lived thing, as best as I can tell, but still. We'd been married for just under a year and I was planning, well, this elaborate silly thing, and I needed a copy of our wedding certificate.' He turned to me then, and flashed an unconvincing smile. 'Paper, that's the tradition for your first... Anyway, I requested a copy of the certificate but there was a mix-up at the office, and I wound up with a certificate that had your mother's name, and some other bloke's beside it.' He paused the story when the waitress came over with our drinks, and we both took our turns in thanking her. By the time she was leaving, his face was its usual happy-go-lucky again and his tone had loosened into something light-hearted. 'Bonkers, isn't it?' He sipped his drink. *Bonkers was a fucking understatement.* 'But you must never tell her you know, Sally, okay? Our secret now.'

I ignored his question and pressed on with my own. 'Who was he?'

He shrugged. 'I've no idea. Hardly matters now, does it?'

It felt like a theatrical slap; one side then the other. I was painfully aware that I was sitting there with my mouth dropped open, but I couldn't close it for fear of the burn the shock might cause once I'd swallowed it. *Is everyone a liar?* I wondered then. *Have I been making too much of everything all along?* Though a laugh huffed out of me at the thought – as though I could reasonably align any of this, any of *their* secrets, with the ones I'd been carrying with me for years.

'Now, are you going to tell me what this is about?'

I hesitated a second before answering. It suddenly struck me that, while feeling my feelings was fine and all, I might still somehow have completely overreacted to the lie. *Is it the lie itself, or the lying that bothers me?* But either way, I self-critiqued, I had no right to hold it against Lena. *She's been sleeping with a murderer for two years, after all.* I washed the thought down with three large mouthfuls of gin and tonic. Then flashed Dad a tight smile.

'No, actually,' I managed a laugh, 'I don't think I am.'

Dad joined the laugh, but in a blissful and confused sort of way, then he brought his glass up to chug his own few mouthfuls. I was scanning the rest of the restaurant by then, looking for faces I might know, trying to spot my fellow liars – which I firmly believed, by then, was absolutely fucking everyone. Though my thoughts occasionally clouded over with distractions – Emma, *What will you do when they find out it's fiction?* Emma, murder, fiction – the saving grace of discovering Lena's lie was that I'd become blissfully distracted from the messed web of my own. I'd often thought that we – as a race – could justify near as damn it anything with our *'But at least I didn't do that...'* attitude. And there I was, using everyone else's misdemeanours now as a benchmark for my own, as though anything compared, as though anything *could* compare to murder. Yet–

'I actually have something to tell you about your mother, while it's just us.'

'Have you had a chance to browse the menu?'

'Could we have another minute, please?' I snapped at

the waitress who had managed to manifest at the least convenient moment. Dad's sentence had my stomach in a vice grip already. I was prone to assuming the worst in any given situation and he well knew it. 'Is she sick?'

'You were rude to that woman,' he said in a lowered voice.

I waved the comment away. 'So I'll leave a tip. What's happening with Mum?'

He sighed and stared into his drink for two, three, four seconds. I was about to snap him out of his trance state with another question when he said, 'She really didn't want you to know, and I said there was no chance of you not finding out, yada-yada. It's all in hand, anyway, because we've spoken to the police–'

'The police?'

It wasn't a theatrical slap that time. Instead, it was waiting for smear test results. It was confessing something embarrassing but necessary to your parents. It was being reprimanded for not knowing the answer to something in class. A medley of experiences that make the floor precarious beneath your feet, knowing any moment it might give way entirely and–

'See, she got this flower delivery a day or two ago.'

FROM THE WOODS

Even though there were other people – better-placed people, professionally speaking – to hold my hand through it all, Harry, as I know him now, seldom left my side throughout the investigation. Whenever there was an update – even if the update was that there still wasn't an update – it came from him. In those months, he became an additional member of my family somehow, and I'm not sure he's ever lost that role either, though I can't imagine how he'll feel about reading that. It may be an inappropriate thing to say about the man who investigated your kidnapping, but there it is in black and white. Harry was supportive and gentle and everything that a good uncle should be; I won't say father, at the risk of doing a disservice to my own who was, of course, golden throughout it all too. But Harry had no obligation to care for me how he did, and I suppose that's what makes me especially grateful to him.

'Are you just going to slip out of my life now?'

The investigation into the kidnapping – into Emma's death – hadn't ceased entirely. But we were being informed, one non-update at a time, that sooner or later resources would have to be pulled. There were other cases, more active cases, and there was only so much the police could do without further evidence appearing. I prayed for it; not because of Harry but Emma, who'd only had memorial services and columns in newspapers and had, to my deep pain and irritation, seen no justice at all, despite the efforts that had been made.

'I don't think we'll ever *really* be out of each other's lives,' Harry had said, throwing a smile to my parents who were also there at the time of this talk. I remember my teenage self feeling like it was a break-up, as though Harry was explaining why he had to leave me now – or at the very least, step away. *It's not you, it's us.* 'There are other cases that I need to be working on too.'

'I understand,' I think I said – or I like to think I said. Though maybe I only mean that I understand now; at the time, I mightn't have done. 'But there's no new evidence at all?' I remember asking. I had made this into a refrain; the criminal case equivalent of 'Are we there yet?'

Harry had flashed my parents a thin smile and then turned back to me. 'There isn't yet, but that doesn't mean there won't be. Leads turn up all the time, people make mistakes, other people remember things. There's still a chance that we're going to crack this, and I don't want you to think otherwise.' He reached across to grab my hand then, and squeezed. 'There's always a chance of things changing.'

A similar version of this conversation happened again when Harry asked me out for coffee to, it turned out, tell me that he was leaving the police. He didn't say whether he was retiring or moving professions and it didn't feel like my place to ask. I only nodded along with an expression that I hoped showed understanding, while he explained that he was tired of the dead-ends and the cold cases and the–

'Dead girls?'

He'd given me a sad sort of smile and said, 'Yes, the dead girls.'

I don't remember much else of the exchange after that. Though I do remember a strange sense of déjà vu after we'd settled the bill for our drinks and migrated outside. I'd hugged him and wished him well, and said something else, too, to the effect of *don't be a stranger*, or *make sure you keep in touch*. 'I want to know how life works out.' I smiled, and Harry shrugged.

'Who knows, kid. There's always a chance of things changing.'

THIRTY-FIVE

Despite leaving the city a good hour ahead of time, I hit so much traffic and so many diversions along the way that I was the last person to arrive. Alongside Mum and Dad's car there was Harry's old Mustang – because after leaving the force he slipped into cliché – and there was another car that I didn't recognise. It was an iconic Mom-Mobile though, practical to a fault with more seating than any one person could ever need. I wagered that DS Worsley must spend her free time shuffling about parties of children, when she wasn't contending with parties of criminals. I sucked in a greedy breath before I got out of the car and held my hand flat and level, to practise being steady. I'd told Lena that I was meeting Dad to plan a surprise birthday thing for Mum and that I'd be out of the city for the afternoon; she'd offered to stay with Birdy, which I'd gratefully accepted. *Though Christ, if I don't need you now, Bird.* I clenched my hand, opened it again, and took another deep breath. The individual fires in life were each distracting me from the other. Lena's lie had pulled my attention away from the flower threat; the flower threat had now pulled me away from Lena. But I found that this morning, when she'd arrived with treats for Birdy and a hug for me, the contact, the seeing her, it was too welcome and familiar for me to resist the gentleness of it. I'd decided then that I needed something in life that was untouched by deceit – which is perhaps why her own had hurt quite so much – but at least mine was still trapped in a locked box.

'For now,' I said as I swung the car door open and climbed out.

Dad waited in the front doorway as I trod up the gravel to the house. 'We're in the garden.' He leaned forward to kiss me then, and grabbed a shoulder on his move away. 'Everything okay, Sal?'

'Of course.' I forced a smile. 'I'm worried about you two.'

'Well,' he stepped aside to welcome me in, 'we're pretty worried about you.'

Mum and I had had two Grown-Up Conversations – both immediately before bed, as though she were finding a way to tuck me in – since Dad had confessed his sins to her and told her that I knew about the flowers. During each phone call she asked the same questions that she had asked every night when she put me to bed as a teenager – after Emma. *Are you okay? Is there anything you need? You're sure there's nothing we can be doing?* Anyone would think the flowers had landed on my doorstep, the way she was acting. Though I realised there was a quiet consensus that the threat was one that applied to me as much as it did to Mum – which was true, I supposed, but no one else could know that. I hadn't confessed to my own delivery, to my own unwelcome love letters. When Harry had called me the day before – asking if I wanted to come along to this 'informal chat' – I had mentioned nothing of my own hushed torment. I'd only agreed, asked a time, and promised not to be late.

'There she is,' Mum said as I stepped out into the garden. She was up and out of her seat, and then she rushed into me with such a firm hold that I wobbled on my feet. 'I'm so glad Harry called you.'

'Me too.' I managed another smile as she pulled away. 'Who doesn't love a garden party?'

Mum walked with an arm around my waist, guiding me as though I were a sick patient in need of physical assistance. *Mental, maybe, but physically I'm just about fine*, I thought as I took the empty seat; one positioned in the shade. Harry reached over for a squeeze of my forearm. I was next to him, and I wondered whether Mum's seating arrangements had been deliberate.

'Good to see you, kid.'

'Harry.' I managed another wide smile. I was beginning to think I should have wired my jaw in place for the meeting, such was the growing need to maintain an '*Of course I'm okay*' façade. 'DS Worsley, nice to see you,' I said and then spluttered a laugh. 'God, what a strange and awkward thing to say, under the circumstances.'

'Hot or cold drink, Sally?' Dad asked, before Worsley could answer.

'Cold, please.' *And if you could douse me in ice, too, that would be brilliant*. I felt my temperature rising. The day was an unusually warm one for the time of year. But I was all too aware what the fever of panic felt like. I recognised it in the heat of my spine, in the sweat where my upper arms rested against my ribs. Dad leaned over to pass me a glass of what looked like home-made lemonade and I was disappointed to see my hand shaking when I reached for it. I hoped that no one else had noticed, but then I saw Harry's raised eyebrow, and felt Mum squeeze my knee beneath the table. I was a mess and people were seeing it. But at least now I had an excuse.

'Emma, we thought it was right for you to be here given that this involves you as much as it does your parents.'

It felt as though Worsley had thrown her hot coffee in my face. I sat there willing an answer to come but found that whenever my mouth bobbed open, nothing emerged. I managed a glance at Dad, then Mum. But they were both suffering the same shock as I was; someone had just recast their murdering daughter as a dead girl.

'Sally,' Harry finally managed. Though he aimed it at Worsley rather than me.

I'd never seen her embarrassed before. But there was a pink blossom forming in her cheeks and a dumbstruck expression spreading over her face, and something about seeing her so entirely thrown by what had happened was so pleasing, so reassuring somehow, that my own sweat and panic ebbed.

'Sally, I– Jesus, I'm so–'

I held my hand up to stop her. 'It's fine, really,' I lied. Because of course it wasn't fine. *None of this is fucking fine.* I sipped my drink and waited for the grown-ups to talk, and when none of them did I kicked the ball myself. 'So what are we doing about this nutcase that has sent Mum flowers?'

Dad snorted a laugh. 'Well, that's broken the ice.'

Worsley managed an awkward, nervous smile. It didn't suit her at all, to be floundering quite so much. But it was good to know that something could shirk the cocksureness of her character on occasion. 'We've been in touch with the florist who took the order for the flowers,' she started, and soon slipped back into her usual business tone. Meanwhile, I felt every word like a hot needle in a patch of skin: the florist seared through my sternum; the flowers through my stomach. I tried to steady my breathing with a long exhale but it was hard for that sort of thing to go unnoticed with one or both parents glancing at you every few seconds.

'It was cash, you said?' I double-checked, matching it against my own flower deliveries. Lena's had come from a different florist's to my own delivery but the modus operandi had been the same: ordered under Emma's name, paid for in cash.

'And what about camera footage?' Mum asked, sounding every bit like she knew the proper procedure for these things. I wondered whether it was the side effect of too many ITV dramas, or whether it was muscle memory from the last time she'd been drawn into a police investigation – which had been my fault then, too, I reminded myself with a spasm of guilt.

'Near useless.'

'But we have some,' Worsley added quickly, as though to undercut the pessimism of Harry's answer. I thought I saw a look swapped between them. The detective reached out of sight then, one hand digging around in a bag under the table, I guessed. Dad took the opportunity to (s)mother me.

'Do you need anything, Sally? Another drink? We haven't even offered you anything to eat, Christ, Luce, do we have snacks?'

Mum set her hand on his forearm for a squeeze while I answered. 'I'm fine, Dad, really.' I tucked my hand around my glass of lemonade that was bleeding condensation over the table, creating a pool I thought Mum was probably desperate to mop clean.

'This is what we've pulled from the camera in the shop.' Worsley set an image on the table between us all, and suddenly Harry's pessimism became entirely justified. It was a person wearing a hoodie – that was it. From the still shot in front of us it wasn't even possible to determine the sex of the culprit; their build didn't give anything away, assuming that you could tell anything by build these days. When no one commented on the image, Worsley layered another one, two, three images over the top of each other like a cheap attempt at a montage. 'We got live footage of them in the shop, and we also managed to get some street footage that shows the direction they came from too. Unfortunately, we've spoken to the florist and owing to the footfall through the place, she isn't sure she can really give us anything like an accurate description, but still...'

A long and laboured pause elbowed between us all then, until Dad eventually picked at the corner of it.

'And?'

Harry, with his understated smirk, looked vindicated. 'That's all, folks,' he said in a jovial tone. Worsley opened her mouth to defend her corner but Harry raised a hand to stop her. 'I'm being unfair, I know, so it's worth saying this isn't at all a reflection on Michelle and the work her team is doing. There really is just nothing to find, until something else happens.'

'Assuming something else *does* happen,' Worsley snapped.

I was present enough to be aware of the tension then,

but I was still lingering over Harry's use of Worsley's first name…

'And do you think that's likely?' Dad asked.

'Never mind whether it's likely,' Mum intervened, 'what protection are you putting in place for Sally in the event that something *does* happen? We have to assume it will, don't we?' She looked from one grown-up to another but excluded me from the questioning, and just like I was the survivor of a recent kidnapping again, I was relegated to the role of the girl who had made it home – rather than an adult with a voice.

There was another look passed between Harry and Worsley, and I imagined, somehow, whole mouths full of words contained in that look. There was clearly something more to say, a risky suggestion to be made, and they were bartering for You're It. When Harry shifted, inched forward slightly to lean his elbows on the table and flash that thin smile, I knew he'd lost.

'How would you feel about taking a break?' He made the suggestion to Mum and Dad but then turned to me. 'All of you, taking a break.'

'I'm in the middle of a book promotion, Harry.'

'A break from what?' Dad asked.

'A break from living in our homes,' I answered. 'That's what you mean, isn't it?' When Lena's flowers had arrived, and it became clear that her address was no longer a kept secret, it occurred to me then that our holiday to celebrate the end of the book promotion would need to be bumped up to a holiday in the middle of the book promotion – but I'd wavered over the idea. I'd been too busy looking through images, reading Leavers' Books, toying with the idea of calling– 'Have you spoken to Peter?'

'Christ, Peter,' Dad groaned, as though he'd only just remembered that Emma had a family too.

'We have,' Worsley answered, 'and he's had no suspicious deliveries, no contact, no anything. We have told him the situation, though, and he's as troubled as we are, as you are, obviously, which is why we think the safest thing–'

'Is to kick us out of our home?' Mum said. She made the suggestion sound preposterous. 'And Sally?'

'She's due a holiday,' Dad answered and my head snapped round to him. 'Don't look at me in that tone of voice, Sally Pober. You've been working like a wild thing on this godforsaken book and look where it's got you.'

It felt like the parental, literary equivalent of, *You were asking for this.*

'Now, Vince, before we lose ourselves on this, why don't we take a minute, take a walk around the garden, and come back to this? Could everyone do with a minute?' Harry said then, looking from one person to the next. Everyone reluctantly agreed, and Dad was the first to slam his chair outward from the table and disappear into the house. Mum dutifully followed, after flashing a tentative smile at her guests. I didn't go anywhere though. I only sat and practised breathing, and wondered which holiday cottage I should hastily book for myself and Lena. I recognised Harry's tone well enough to know there was no fighting it. This decision had already been made.

THIRTY-SIX

When it was a matter of health and safety – *life and death?* – Duke took a disarmingly sympathetic approach to my work schedule – or rather, the task of rearranging my schedule. I explained what had happened with Mum, Dad and the police, and once the pound signs had cleared from his eyes – I thought I could see him working out the narrative arc of a sequel already – he assured me that nothing was more important than my safety. 'None of it is anything that can't be moved,' he'd promised. Bar one last little event...

It turned out to be an interview between myself and a reputable bookseller in one of the city's biggest bookshops – in front of a live audience.

'You take the piss, do you know that?'

'What?' Duke was rubbing my shoulders – like a trainer in the ring – and staring back at me from the mirror opposite us both. He'd insisted that I have my make-up done before the event, on account of 'looking like shit' without a face on. I'd told him that lack of sleep will do that to a girl, but his sympathy must have timed out by the time of that conversation because here we were, having a girls' afternoon out. 'I just want you to look your best, okay? We're expecting a lot of people there this evening.'

'What's a lot?'

He shrugged. 'A hundred, maybe.' When my eyes widened he rushed to reassure me. 'There's security on the door, and there will be security dotted around the place while you're speaking too. Honestly, sweets, it's the most secure book event that I'll have done in my entire goddamn career.'

'Here we are!' said the bright-eyed and bushy-tailed assistant who'd been left in charge of my face. She'd been looking for a precise shade of lip-liner, and she'd fluttered away like a stunned butterfly when she'd realised she didn't have a sample of it to use. Now she looked renewed, as though finding the liner had relieved her of every ill in her life. *Lucky bitch.* I tried to match her smile in the mirror. 'Relax your mouth for me please, my lovely, that's it.' She concentrated with her eyes narrowed and her tongue piercing out from her lips, only the tip, and there was something endearing about the expression. When she was finished she stood back like an artist might, to take a look at her canvas whole. 'Just beautiful, babes, honestly, ten/ten, would take to a book-launch event.' She smiled and scrunched her shoulders up as though they were part of a single gesture. I couldn't return it, though, with my lips so thinly traced on. I left the chair worried to change my expression at all.

By the time the event started – three hours later – I had laughed so much at people's reactions to my make-up that there was a good chance none of it was left on at all. Lena's face had dropped when I walked into the flat to get changed into my dress earlier and I'd immediately erupted in laughter so violent that I was dabbing tears away from my eyes after two minutes. Now, around the room various other friends and colleagues were trying to hide their reactions, too, under thinly veiled comments like 'You look so different!' and 'Well, this is a change'. It felt like a quiet game of bingo that I was playing with myself – given that Duke had rebuffed my suggestion that he join in the bingo antics too. It had been enough of a distraction to help me coast through to the start of the event with minimal panic, though, and anything that allowed for that was a welcome thing.

Lena was sitting at the back of the room alongside Harry, who had come, he said, because he wanted to support me. I thought the more likely reason was that he wanted to make sure a nutcase didn't jump up midway through the interview wielding a bouquet of unwanted flowers – or something worse. And it wasn't until that thought struck that a too familiar hum of bees sounded in my ears, as though someone had lifted the lid on a hive. The room oscillated between too loud and too quiet and I found my only way of following instructions was to wait now until someone physically led me onto the raised platform and showed me to my seat.

'Do you need anything?' the helping hand asked, and I managed a head shake.

'Sally, it's an absolute joy to meet you.' The woman in front held out her hand and I was still socially savvy enough to recognise the cue, despite the necklace of stingers that felt poised around my throat. 'I'm Olivia, I'll be hosting the interview this evening. I assume Duke showed you the questions already?'

But she didn't wait for an answer before hollering for the same helping hand and asking for glasses of water for us both. I'd already turned down water. But Duke hadn't shown me the questions. *Has he shown me the questions?*

'Sally, you look peaky, are you okay? Can someone hurry up with that water?' This wasn't Olivia's first rodeo; I could see already. She herded people around with the confidence of someone who lives and breathes this industry, and I could only hope that some of her energy might rub off on me before the first question was asked. I braved a look into the audience then, as though scouring for faces that I didn't recognise – and of course, there were tens of them. But then there was Lena's; Lena's beautiful, reassuring, familiar face at the back of the room, beaming as she held up two hands positioned in such a way to form a floating heart. And everyone else fell away.

Apart from Olivia, that is, who was waving a glass of water in my face.

'Good evening, everyone!'

I was hardly through a mouthful when she called everyone's attention to the front of the room where we were sitting. I was painfully aware of the audience looking at me while I wiped my mouth clean, and it was only when I looked down at the bloodied smudge on my hand that I remembered the clown face I was wearing. *I'll bet it's a clown face now*, it occurred to me as I tried to rub the mark clean without drawing too much attention to my fidgeting hands. But of course, everyone could see everything from this vantage point; *anyone* could see *anything*. And I suddenly felt painfully vulnerable –

vulnerable, and sick. I swallowed back the burn of bile in time for Olivia to finish her practised introduction, and I tried for a wide smile when she turned on me with her first question – 'What's life like in the fast lane of writing?' – though I was aware, too, that thanks to my clumsy mouth wipe, my smile might already have been Why-So-Serious wide.

I feigned a laugh. Lena would be the only person in the audience who could tell – and there was something comforting about that. 'I don't know that I'd call it the fast lane. I spend most of my days play-acting that I'm a detective in a B-movie with my notes and my stickers and pictures.' Another laugh. 'I'm sure if you ask my partner she'd say it was like living with a crazy woman.' I moved to turn then, to isolate Lena out from the audience and show her off and to bask in the novelty of having her there – it was the first event she'd been able to make it along to – but then my stomach turned, a churning, building wave. *Do they know what Lena looks like? Am I giving her away if I mention her?* I swallowed the thought – the sting of paranoia – and styled out the sideways glance as an innocent look into the crowd. And I decided I mustn't make eye contact with Lena then, I mustn't blow her cover.

'Am I right in thinking you're working on a second book already?'

I couldn't blame her for asking. After all, it was the lie that I'd told them all. So I agreed, with the hesitant nod of an interest-shy writer who doesn't want to talk about their project.

'Anything you can tell us about?' She leaned in to ask the question, as though I were taking her – and an entire room full of people – into my confidence. But I only mimed drawing a zip tight across my lips and then threw an imaginary key into the front row. Olivia laughed. 'Understood! Let's talk about *From the Woods* instead...'

From there the questions were rapid-fire:

'Was it difficult to write the book?'

'Did you find that you were writing it with Emma over your shoulder?'

'How do your parents feel about the work?'

'Emma's parents?'

'Are you in touch with anyone else from that time?'

On and on it went. It was, I imagined, how an interrogation might go. *So perhaps this is practice for the future.* I winced and sipped another mouthful of water. Soon, it felt like answering on automatic and I hoped the answers were passable, but given the intermittent laughs and sounds of sympathy that rippled across the crowd, I gathered I must be doing okay. Though the relief – the clear smear, the A on a test, the 'We haven't found any evidence' relief – when Olivia said, 'My last question then...' I murmured along in agreement – encouragement, even. *Yes please, Olivia, let this fucking end.*

'Weren't you worried, at all, writing this whole book about a man who was never...' she hesitated then, and I realised that either Duke hadn't shown me the questions, or Olivia was going off-script – but whichever it was, it was the first time Olivia looked nervous. 'Writing this book about a man who was never caught. He could be out there, still, surely, reading away at everything you've said and...'

The question died, but I got the gist. The room was pin-drop quiet and I couldn't decide whether I was hearing a clock tick or my own heartbeat keeping time in my ears. I sucked in a greedy breath and looked out into the crowd. *It could be any single one of you. You could be right here, in front of me.* Despite myself then, I groaned. An audible noise of absolute dismay that everyone must have heard – including Olivia, who leapt to the rescue, leaned across to squeeze my knee, and then cut her own question off at its cord. I imagined it live and kicking still in everyone's mind though; this bloodied and crying creature that they were all too desperate for an answer to. I wanted the confidence, the arrogance, to say that I hadn't been worried – but of course, whether or not any of that were true, I should have been.

'Worried or not, I think you're bloody brave and utterly exceptional. A round of applause, please and thank you, for Sally Pober!'

And the room went wild.

I looked out to try to spot the single person not clapping. *Are you withholding praise from me, stranger? Or would you mime it all the same?*

'It was an unfair question,' Olivia said in a low voice as we both stood, and I bit back on agreeing with her. 'You were fantastic, and it's been a pleasure to meet you, Sally, honestly. Can I get you a drink?'

'Wine, please,' I managed.

I looked out into the crowd who were freeing themselves from their seats and making their way to the various watering stations pinned around the room. Lena was making her way to me from one side; Duke from the other. And then I felt my phone thrum twice in my front pocket. I had time, I wagered, so I struggled the handset free to see that at some point during the interview Sid had messaged me –

> Does the name Fleur Ellroy mean anything to you?

But the two most recent messages were from a number I didn't have saved:

> Lovely interview.

The first message read.

> What will you do when they find out it's fiction?

THIRTY-SEVEN

Fleur Ellroy meant nothing to me. Sid recognised the name, she said, but she still couldn't place the girl. She'd kindly offered to do more digging, and I wondered how much more digging I could let her do before I had to put her on some kind of payroll for it. But I had dug as far as I could go. I contacted my school – our old school – and said I was doing research for a new book, was there anything they could tell me? A young and seemingly star-struck receptionist spouted something about GDPR before he lowered his voice to a near whisper – 'I can't find that name on our system, not from your year certainly.' – and all that left me with was the option of trying the same lucky line with every other school within a travellable distance. It was feasible, of course, that Emma had friends in other places. *But why only when I wasn't around, and why had Emma never told me about her?* I wondered as I fidgeted with the corner of Emma and Fleur, their arms wrapped around each other, a beer bottle in Emma's hand signifying some party or another. There was a mixture of people in the background, those I recognised and those I didn't. But it was Fleur's face I kept coming back to. There was something familiar about her now, something I couldn't quite place, but after so long spent locked in an office with the same handful of images, I began to wonder whether the familiarity was a fabricated thing; whether I recognised her now, simply because I'd spent so long staring at her. There were at least two occasions that I could name, since the interview – since the long and winding talks with Sid – where I had imagined Fleur in the wild: once in a coffee shop; once in Aster's waiting room while I was hanging fire for yet another emergency therapy session, where I achieved nothing more, it seemed, than testing Aster's patience. Though of course these wild sightings were nothing more than imaginings either. From looking over snapshots of my own teenage face, I was all too aware of how physical appearances might change from teens to twenties to thirties, which made the mysterious Fleur even more of a needle to try to find.

'Sal, are you nearly ready?'

I snapped my head around to Lena lingering in the open doorway of the office and even then I had to blink away images of Fleur's teenage face, drunk on teenage years, happy hormones and cheap booze as she was in all of these pictures.

'I'm just packing up.'

Lena's foot fidgeted at the threshold but she didn't tread in. She knew the rules. 'Remember you're not meant to be taking *loads* of work with you. We had a deal.' As though in support of Lena's reminder, Birdy let out a small grumble then, from her spot just inside the doorway: the one woman allowed in here with me.

'I know, I know,' I gestured to the photos, 'only a few bits.'

'Work free, Duke free.' Lena laughed. 'Okay, probably not *totally* Duke free. But beach walks and hot chocolate and windswept photos, those were my terms.'

I managed a smile. 'I remember, and I stand by the agreement.'

She was hardly asking for much, I knew. But the enforced break away didn't have the same ring to it for me as it did for her. Though of course, Lena didn't know it was enforced. She didn't know Worsley had recommended a break from the city; Harry had encouraged the suggestion; my parents had insisted, using tones they hadn't taken with me since I was a teenager. To Lena, this was the holiday I had promised her – and it assuaged my growing tumour of guilt for me to tell myself that that was all that mattered, that her faith in the make-believe was enough.

The journey had taken a solid four and a half hours – including pee stops for Birdy and two smoke stops for me, and Lena said nothing both times – with Spotify skipping through our favourite songs as we went, allowing for sing-a-longs and too many memories to flood in. For days I had been reliving school years on repeat, trying to place Fleur in some or any of the memories. But Lena had insisted on recapping all of the times we'd heard this track or had sex to this track or happened to catch this band live – and the enthusiasm had exhausted me, along with the drive. Besides which, I was scared that an influx of new memories would be enough to force the old ones further into the recesses – as though that were how long- and short-term stores worked – so I was hesitant to play her games. By the time our satnav was cutting out from crap signal coverage, we were wedged on a country road that meant meeting an oncoming vehicle would have sent us reversing all the way back to the beginning, and at least that gave me an excuse for quiet, for concentration.

Had Fleur been at Emma's last birthday party?

'Are you thinking about her?' Lena asked, when we peaked at the end of the road and landed back in what passed for civilisation.

The question startled me. 'Who?'

'Emma.' She said her name softly. 'You always get that faraway look when...'

I shrugged. 'I guess I am, a little.'

Lena reached across and squeezed my thigh. The gesture somehow made me jump. 'Hey,' she soothed, 'it's okay to be thinking about her. I think about her too, sometimes. I just never say.'

I juddered the car before regaining control of the clutch. 'Why do you think about her?' The satnav still hadn't stirred back to life; I was driving blind, but Lena's admission demanded more of my attention then.

'Because she's important, isn't she?'

I narrowed my eyes to peer at a road sign before making a sharp turn right. 'She is,' I admitted, 'she always will be, won't she?' *For so many reasons.* 'Can we not talk about her while I'm driving?' I huffed a laugh. 'I'm trying to work out where–'

'Oh, here!' Lena pointed to a sign that I'd missed. 'Wiles Cottage, that way.'

There were two more country roads and no more questions. But there was an audible gasp from Lena when we finally rounded into the track that led to the holiday lease we had for the next two weeks. The cottage was the picturesque spot that we'd been promised. On the drive along the path towards it, I skimmed the area for nearby neighbours and saw none. We were only a short drive from the coastline, but it looked as though we were cruising into isolation. Lena made more appreciative noises the closer we got. Meanwhile, my stomach only churned at the sight of the clifftop close by; it essentially formed the front garden of the property. But heights had made me weary – since Emma, strangely – for that sensation of wanting to jump. Aster told me it was a normal human reaction, that most people thought of jumping but never did; *most people*, I parroted to myself the first time she explained, *meaning some of them must–*

'Jesus, this is amazing,' she announced as I brought the car to a stop. 'Birdy, let's go.' She opened the passenger door and one after the other both of the women in my life escaped the stuffy vehicle and ventured onto the landscape. Birdy squatted every two metres or so, play-acting at being a dog set on marking territory. But Lena was making straight for the cliff edge. I knew she'd be brave enough to look down.

I made laboured efforts to undo my seat belt and disconnect my phone from the car's stereo system – and I took the chance to check for messages while I was at it.

> Still nothing. Ha. Seriously. Who the hell is this woman?

Sid had written. My thumb hovered to tap back a message but I'd barely managed a syllable when there came a knock at my window.

'Tell Duke to leave you alone for five minutes,' Lena

said through the glass, 'we literally just got here. We at least need to unpack the hot chocolate first.'

It pained me, her assumption that it wasn't another woman at the end of the phone screen. Even though it wasn't like that, I reminded myself, as I hit the lock button. But somehow, that didn't make it feel any less of a betrayal.

'Okay, okay,' I wedged my phone into my pocket and reached for the door handle, but Lena was already opening it from the outside, 'but I'm not going near that cliff edge.'

Lena looped arms with me and started to march me in the direction of the cottage. 'Bloody right you're not,' her tone was light, jovial, 'knowing you, you'd go and jump off the sodding thing.'

'Birdy!' I used her as an excuse to ignore Lena's comment, and paused on the pathway until she caught up with us. 'They said something about a key box.'

'On the wall.' Lena pointed. 'Actually, shall I get opened up and you can get started on the car?'

Then I did laugh, a curt 'Ha!' that caused Lena to spin around and face me. 'What?'

I put a hand either side of her waist and pulled her towards me. 'I notice how I'm getting the short straw in this situation.' Lena didn't answer, she only leaned in and placed a single kiss on my lips and somehow the gesture was enough to snatch a breath out of me. She gave me a second for my lungs to catch up after she pulled away. 'You're with me for my muscles, aren't you?' I asked.

In a deadly serious tone she answered, 'No, I'm with you for the millions I'll inherit in royalties if I can stick around long enough.' But after a beat of silence had passed she belched out her own laugh. 'Yes, yes, I'm with you for your muscles. Go, make sure the kitchen bag is one of the first. I want that hot chocolate.'

'You're obsessed,' I shouted after her, before turning to tread my way back to the car. It gave me time to tap out a quick reply to Sid –

> I'm going to check death and marriage records.

– and stash my phone back as though it were contraband. Lena was so determined for this to be a proper break from... well, everything, it crossed my mind that if I used up my daily technology time too quickly, she might confiscate the rights altogether. But by the time I'd reached the boot of the car there was already a hum in my front pocket, as though Sid had only been sitting there, waiting on a reply like a patient Birdy waiting for me to come home from an event.

> I've got a theory. Lemme try something. Get back to you.

When I opened the boot the first bag to fall free happened to be the one rammed with food: a tub of Cadbury's hot chocolate tumbled and bowled somewhere beneath the car, and it felt symbolic, somehow, all of my hot chocolates rolling away in one sweep. I turned my phone off then, and started to collect the perishables that Lena had packed for us – because of course, she'd taken care of the sensible things. One after the other I picked up items that I loved and she hated, and with each there came a pang of love so pronounced that they were one by one nearly enough to wind me. I added to the promise I'd made to Lena then – 'No, I won't be on my phone too much.' – and made a quiet promise to myself to be present, to enjoy what we were sharing, to *not* think about other women constantly, even if the other women were dead, missing, or helping me to conduct a secret investigation into both of those already listed.

Lena appeared at my side while I was struggling to hold the handles of the first food bag in the bend of my arm, so I could load my hands with what looked like even more food bags besides.

'Why did I find this at the front of the car?' She threw the hot chocolate tin in the air playfully and caught it again.

'I love you.'

She looked taken aback. 'Where did that come from?'

I kissed her on the cheek as I passed. 'It's always there.'

And that, I told myself, was what I needed to hold on to. *That* was why I needed to be here.

THIRTY-EIGHT

In the first two days we walked thirty-six kilometres – according to our respective Apple Healths. *Because perish the thought that everything isn't monitored these days*, I thought as I slammed closed a cupboard in the kitchen. I couldn't find the coffee, and I wondered whether Lena had hidden it in a quiet exchange for the cigarettes I'd been smoking. As though it was ludicrous that any one person might have as many as two vices. By day three of the holiday Birdy was exhausted, and I was steadfastly refusing the possibility that we leave her at home for the day which meant, much to Lena's dismay, we were staying home for the day too. I'd told her to go out alone, explore the coastline. 'That wasn't the point of the break,' she'd snapped, sounding every bit like the clingy teenager. And now the coffee was nowhere to be seen. On second thought, she may have snatched it away after the non-argument simply to spite me.

I opted for tea instead and left the bag in for two minutes longer than recommended because I needed something that would clamber out of the cup and gently tap me around the face. I'd hardly been sleeping. Instead, I had spent most of the midnight hours in a velvet-crush armchair in the living room; one of two that had been positioned with a view out of the wide bay window, offering a sight of the clifftop and shoreline just beyond it. That's where Lena was now, nursing a cup of hot water with a lemon slice. It felt as though she were slowly turning the holiday into some sort of detox camp. Next thing, she'd confiscate my phone entirely and flush all of the chocolate bars through the rubbish disposal – which felt like an uncharacteristically American thing for any countryside British home to have. But we'd both been enamoured with it when we first realised what it was.

Birdy and I watched her from the doorway, neither of us quite brave enough to approach. I checked my phone again in those seconds and sighed heavily at the sight of no signal bars, still. I had managed to swap all of three messages with Sid since being here – neither of us having made any headway on Fleur in that time either. Not through lack of trying on Sid's part; though on mine, I could only do so much in the handful of hours a day that Lena didn't roast me for being at my laptop. I told her that writing was important and back to back on both days now she'd huffed at me as though I were telling a childish fib.

'You can use my phone if you need to make a call,' she'd said then, without even turning. And I wondered how readable my frustration must be, through the expression of a sigh alone, that she could tell the cause of it without even checking. 'I'm sure your parents are fine, wherever they are, but whatever.'

I hesitated, lingered over the lie I might tell in response to the offer. But instead I only managed a 'Thank you'.

'It should be on the kitchen counter. The password is your birthday.'

The sentiment felt like an insect sting sitting in my sternum. *See how much she loves you*, I thought on the tread from one room to another. Birdy followed behind, dutifully and determinedly on my side, no matter how much of a shit I was being. I reasoned that I had made it through the first two days on best behaviour at least; surely that deserved a call to the outside world.

I unlocked Lena's phone and, on autopilot, keyed *Mum* into her Contacts – and there it was, the reminder that Lena could be a shit too. I lingered over her parents' number for a second too long before clicking into her call records. *How often do you call your parents if you're actively telling people that they're dead?* The only numbers listed were mine and Duke's, punctuated very occasionally with names that I recognised from work. After navigating back into Contacts, I started to think the unthinkable: *I could just call the number*. It would give me a definitive answer, rather than encouraging this watercolour uncertainty; the faint wisp of doubt that tumbled in only occasionally, like smoke fumes through a part-open window. I hit dial before I could entertain anymore back and forth thinking on it, and with a shaking hand I pressed her mobile to my ear. It rang once, twice, and with each shrill hum I thought maybe, just maybe I'd got it all wrong and then–

'Hello, flower, how are you doing?'

I disconnected the call and threw the handset on the table like it was a hot pebble, the burn of it leaving a mark in the folds of my palm. My breathing became laboured then, and I tried one shaky breath after another but found the chest pains were coming already and there was an all too familiar feeling of something like worry, something like panic, something like no one can be trusted and—

'Sal? Sally, what happened?'

Lena crouched down to be level with me. I hadn't felt my knees buckle but at some point I had gone from upright to origami-folded without knowing it was happening. I pushed wet hair away from my forehead and felt the damp of my skin across my temples too.

'Breathe with me,' Lena instructed, as she slowed her own breaths as though presenting a tutorial to someone new to this atmosphere. I wondered how many times a day she must do this for people at work. 'Sal, babe, breathe in a little for me, okay?' I nodded and tried to focus on her voice, on the things about her voice I recognised. I tried to forget the memory of her telling me about her parents, the soft whimper that had come whenever she talked about the accident – the accident that hadn't happened. 'Did something happen, are your parents okay?'

'I...' I had to pause to force out a long breath. I still couldn't look at her. 'I didn't get that far. I'm sorry, I... I'm not even sure... I think I just need some air.' She helped me up without instruction then, as though recognising the beginnings of a bigger struggle as I tried to push myself back to an upright pose. 'I'll be... It'll all be fine. I just need some air. Christ,' I pushed away hair that had tumbled forwards in the move, 'I don't know where that came from.'

Lena cupped my cheek with a warm palm and gave me the tenderest of looks and my stomach rumbled like a forgotten pot. 'Shall I come with you, to get some air?'

I managed to shake my head. 'Honestly, I'll be okay once I've done a lap of the garden. Can I...' I gestured behind her to where the phone lay on the table. 'I didn't even get to call.' Lena turned and passed me the handset.

'Don't be long, okay?' She leaned forward and set a kiss in the centre of my forehead. 'Whatever just spooked you, I don't want it happening on a clifftop,' she tried to make it sound like a joke, 'you're my wild horse, Sally Pober.'

I had the heartbeat of one in those moments, and the sweat sheen of a filly outrunning a larger breed.

'It's not even about Lena, I know it's not about Lena. Testing her, checking her parents' number, it's just about control, right? In that moment, that was the only thing I could exercise control over and now I'm panicking and after this I'll be distant and then I'll go back and forth on whether I can accept the lie, or confront her,' I paused to suck in a greedy breath, 'when really the person I want to confront is Fleur fucking Ellroy, to ask what she knew about Emma, and what Emma told her, and whether she's the one sending the fucking flowers and,' another breath, this one more laboured, 'I don't even have a signal for you to call me back, I'm using Lena's phone because the signal on my one is like a bloody disappearing act, so I'm cut off from the world and trapped with a woman who's lying to me and...' The realisation hit me like a well-placed coin in a two-pence pusher; everything falling at once. 'She's also trapped with a woman who's lying to her. Lying about much worse things. Creeping around behind her– Christ, I got there, Aster, I– You don't have to return this message, just, thanks.'

I disconnected the call and clicked into Lena's

contacts. I didn't mind her knowing I'd left a long and rambling message for my therapist. But I could do without her knowing that I'd dead dialled her very alive parents while she wasn't looking. I told myself that would be the last of the deceptions now. I'd use Lena's phone for actual emergencies only, and while I was telling myself that lie, a message arrived from Duke. I lingered over whether to click into it or not, whether to peer through the Venetian blinds of what they said when I wasn't looking. In the end, the temptation of that window was too much, and I opened her inbox.

> How's she being? Still trouble?

But there was no message before that. Any conversation threads they shared had been deleted. I checked WhatsApp but there was nothing there either, and I couldn't imagine Lena and Duke having swapped idle chit-chat via emails. But– *Still trouble?* I parroted back. *When have I been trouble?*

I made a montage of my behaviour from the last two days – long walks, hot chocolate, fish and chips, and too much sex – and tried to trace the thread of trouble that Lena might have reported back on. *But it had been my best behaviour*, I reassured myself. Though before I could fall further into the rabbit hole of frantic wondering, Birdy appeared, bounding towards me where I lingered at the bottom of the garden. Lena must have let her out, and I wondered then whether it would only be seconds before Lena herself appeared, too, following Birdy's trail.

'Have we been trouble?' I crouched to talk to her and ran my fingertips underneath her small beard and chin. Birdy tipped her head upwards to encourage more of the same, but there was one more thing I needed to do before Lena caught up with me.

I pulled my own phone from my back pocket where it was stashed, lifeless. In the last two days I had managed to snatch wisps of signal in two spots – standing next to the car, and here, at the bottom of this fairy-tale garden space – though it was all smoke, mirrors and minimal cellular coverage that often didn't stretch as far as a phone call. I might get a text to Sid, though, I might–

But Sid had gotten to me first. There was one new answerphone message waiting in my inbox, a hovering ambiguous symbol, and I wondered whether Sid had left the key to Fleur Ellroy right there in a pocket of my iPhone handset – just out of reach. *'You do not have enough signal coverage to complete this action'* multiplied by three. My service provider chanted the reminder in a bored tone every time I hit the dial button and then Lena was in view, and the opportunity was slipping, and Sid was caught in the cobwebs of my inaccessible inbox and–

'Did you get through?' she asked, all smiles as she looked down at me where I was still crouched level with Birdy. 'Your parents?'

I passed her phone up to her. 'I called Aster instead.'

Rather than taking the phone from her standpoint, she kneeled to be level with us both. 'I know I was testy earlier, but I'm really proud of you, you know? Like, for everything. For trying to take a break, for limiting the work you're doing,' she huffed a laugh, 'for nearly going cold turkey with your phone. I know it's hard to be present, babe, but I'm grateful, honestly.' She set a hand on Birdy's head, the white crown between her ears. 'Both of us, aren't we, beautiful girl?'

Birdy grumbled – under the soft pressure of the head

rub, I thought, rather than anything Lena had said. But still, what could I add now that she'd brought Birdy into it? I couldn't accuse her of lying, nor could I admit to my own. I couldn't listen to Sid's message, nor could I call her back. I couldn't enjoy the holiday, nor could I admit to such a thing either. So I stayed there, ducked low and kneading at the soft fur of my dog, oscillating between everything I could and couldn't do; a pinball lost in the workings of a rusted machine.

THIRTY-NINE

I must have doubled my average step count for the day while I paced from one side of the restaurant front to the other. I told Lena I was coming for a cigarette – which had also been true – though the main motivator was to try to get signal enough to listen to Sid's message, which had remained locked in my inbox for three days now. During my allotted internet hours I'd resorted to emailing her, to no avail, and I'd started to do my own research into Fleur Ellroy while I was at it. I hadn't got any writing done – and I scolded myself for that, as though I, too, believed I was working on a second book – but I had ruled out marriage and death certificates that were attached to that name, from people of around the right age as well, so at least I wasn't chasing a complete ghost; though in many ways it felt like it. I found that I was dreaming about her too, a thin wisp of something that I would reach out to grab the throat of, only to have her disintegrate underneath me. And I was dreaming of Emma more, which I thought was an understandable side effect of it all.

I had enough signal bars to text Sid for the third time:

> I'm trapped in a land of no telephone poles. What did you find out?

But I didn't have time enough to wait for a reply before I saw Lena waving at me through the front window of the eatery to signal that our food had just arrived.

We had both opted for locally caught fish baked in a lemon-and-herb sauce with twice-cooked chips. We were sharing a bottle of white wine; there was a candle on the table and pale music in the background and everything about the evening should have been fucking delightful and yet! I forced a slow breath out through my nose and pasted on a smile before I looked up to meet Lena's stare.

'It looks bloody brilliant, doesn't it?'

I nodded. 'Fantastic. Let's...'

But she cut off my encouragement by reaching a hand across the table. It was palm up, calling to me, and I matched the gesture. Even though for two days now my tired body had been in such an exaggerated version of fight or flight mode that I found now even the slightest touch of anything against me caused an uncomfortable prickle over the affected patch of skin. Still, I squeezed her hand back and kept the smile fixed in place.

Lena didn't say anything. She only gave me this look; this lingering, love-stuffed look. And I felt a stab of discomfort in my stomach for how disconnected I felt to her. If we'd been at home, she would have been sleeping at her own apartment – or I would have been sleeping in my office, under the pretence of working. Here, there was nowhere to hide, and I was beginning to worry over how many cracks she would inevitably see in this close proximity, with nothing else to do all day but watch me unravel.

'Anyway,' she said, as though she'd spoken beforehand, 'let's dig in.'

There soon followed a string of appreciative noises and small talk, and when Lena asked whether I'd managed to get through to my parents yet – I hadn't – there was a knot of something in me that pulled tighter. Whatever it was, it was the sort of bind where you gave up even trying to undo the folds of it; you would either accept that the knotted thing must stay such a way, or you'd cut the cord entirely for freedom. *Ask about her parents*, I thought then, an involuntary flutter of antagonism, an extra voice in me that couldn't forgive Lena her sins, even though I was allowing her to live in ignorance of mine. But I couldn't ask, of course; it would be the equivalent of cutting the cord – which was a thing I wasn't ready to do, though a part of me wondered whether it was coming. I still loved her, right down to the core of my belly where I kept my happiest feelings. But the convoluted weave of life was becoming too hard to shield from her, and I wondered how much longer I could freefall through this without confessing to her that–

'What do you think of the food?'

'It's gorgeous, isn't it?' It tasted like ash. 'We should ask for the recipe, try to make it while we're here.'

She froze with a sauce-soaked chip halfway to her mouth. 'Seriously?'

I laughed. 'Is it such a wild idea?' It was of course, wild and completely out of character, and absolutely not something that I would have suggested had we been at home living our normal lives of hidden panic. *But I have to fill the hours somehow*, I thought, *I can't be doing nothing anymore.*

'Okay,' she put the chip in her mouth and spoke around it, 'okay, I'll go and ask.' And with that she was up, heading in the direction of the kitchen door with the energy of a woman on a small mission. I imagined the waiting staff were ready for a complaint, but I saw their show of delight when Lena expressed our enjoyment of the meal, a request for the recipe, a thumbs up from her to me as a waiter disappeared into the kitchen. I'd been so focused on Lena that I didn't register her phone, sitting on the right-hand corner of her side of the table, until it hummed alive with a new message. I checked my own then, in case the signal bars were catching, and behold, there was a message from Sid –

> Can you talk?

– and I felt a gut twist of frustration that she couldn't tell me whatever the news was via a text message, email, or even a carrier pigeon. I replied –

> Will try to call later. What's happening?

– and then I checked Lena's progress. She was talking to a waiter still, waving her hands in what I perceived to be excitement. And just like that, something got the better of me.

I leaned over to Lena's side of the table and tapped at the screen until it came alive with colour. There was one new message from Duke – only this time, I didn't have the chance to read its contents.

The problem with paranoia is that it's tautological; a mental sensation where even the mere entertainment of the feeling somehow feeds the concern that the feeling exists. Am I being paranoid, or am I paranoid for thinking that I'm paranoid? It was a serpent, jaw unhinged and teeth clamped tight around its own tail, but there was no breaking the infinite loop of such a religious figure. I spent the next day with my worries swallowing and regurgitating themselves, like a wild animal stocking food for its young. Every time Lena's phone sounded, I wondered whether it was Duke and, if it was, what they could possibly be talking about. I didn't know when they'd become quite so close, or why, but somehow it felt like the walls of a home collapsing, whole chunks of plaster coming away in my hands through to brickwork and plasterboard beneath, and it crossed my mind that if the walls were allowed to disintegrate entirely, all manner of untamed creatures would spill out into the wilds of our rented cottage, claw at the paintwork and chew through the soft furnishings. I was imagining all of this on the second day of solid rain, looking out to the view of the clifftop. The sealine was a charcoal boundary that had been smudged with a wet finger, and claustrophobia became a bedfellow to my distrust.

Lena came up behind me, a soft-footed thing but still my ears twitched at the sound. When she set her hands on either of my shoulders I flinched and she cooed me with comfort that ran through me like an unoiled and ancient hinge.

'Hey,' she lowered herself to speak closer to my ear, 'where are you?'

'Here.'

'I don't think you are, Sal.' She rounded the armchair and dropped to a crouch in front of me. It was a strange battle of feelings that warred in my stomach when I looked at her then, the belief that she would never hurt me taking a knuckle-duster to the lie I knew she'd packed our life with, sparring with the constant chronic knowledge that I was a liar too. But a worse one.

'You're going for a run?' I asked, noting her sports gear. 'You'll get washed away.'

She smiled. 'It's a cleansing. You should come with me.' I saw her side-eye the table where I had a neat gin and a packet of cigarettes perched. I wasn't smoking in the holiday let, but I liked to have them close. 'A run will be better for you than either of those things.'

I made a point of reaching out to grab my glass. 'Don't be so sure.'

'Okay,' she stood, 'if you're not going to talk to me, I'll get out and maybe we can try again when I get back.'

'Why are you and Duke talking so much?' I asked the question to her retreating figure. My eyes were still fixed ahead, and I wagered that Lena must have been five steps behind my chair by then, but she hurried back before she answered.

'Jesus, is that what this weirdness is all about? I stole your friend?'

'He's my agent.'

'But he isn't allowed friends?' Her tone was escalating to irritated, so I made a point of keeping my own as deadpan as I could, despite the early indicators of an earthquake that were stirring in my abdomen and up through my ribcage.

'He is. I just didn't realise you two were–'

'Equally as worried about you? Well we are. So if you must know, we're texting because he's checking firstly that you're okay, and secondly that I am. But if you're that uncertain of us both, a gay man and a lesbian woman, you're welcome to read through my messages.'

It was a false floor. If she gave me her phone, she would back-pocket the opportunity to look at mine – and there was no way I could hand over that bow-wrapped bundle of evidence for her to scour through, especially not with the twenty-seven failed calls to Sid's number in the last day. But still, I remembered how her messages from Duke had been cleared the last time I'd looked, and I wondered whether it was cockiness on her part that made her sure I wouldn't want to check. Unless she'd offered knowing I wouldn't surrender my own handset in exchange, in which case the entire offer was gesture only and– *Hello, serpent*, I thought, greeting my intrusive paranoia with an equally intrusive thought. I rubbed at my forehead and reached for the gin glass.

'I'll take that as a no.'

But by then there was something on its haunches in me, saliva dripping from exposed teeth and a rumble in the throat. Instead of a howl or a roar, though, it emerged in an accusation, bloodied and exposed on the cream rug in front of me.

'I know your parents aren't dead.'

For the second time I heard her footsteps pause. I knew it was only one, two, three seconds but time became elasticated and the quiet stretched on for what I thought must have been days trapped in the façade of only a couple of heartbeats – or a few, given the pounding in my chest.

'I'm going for a run.'

The next sound was the front door closing. The rain thrashed hard against the window in front of me as the wind changed direction again, and again I thought of Lena being washed away. Then I stood and started to scour the cottage. She never took her phone on a run.

FORTY

I threw Birdy in the car and left. It crossed my mind to pack my things, to let Lena get home, soaked and sopping from a ridiculous run in ridiculous weather. But despite the low-bubble rage in my belly, I couldn't bring myself to put her through that worry yet. Instead, we battled the elements – Birdy in her car seat next to me – and drove until civilisation struck and my signal bars were strong. The rain had made coverage even worse, so it took a longer stretch before the 3G became consistent. Now, even though we were surrounded by coffee shops and eateries, I had no inclination to actually leave the car. I pulled into a car park with a sea view, dropped my head back and rolled down the windows enough so I could breathe in the grit of the landscape – but not so far that the landscape came swilling into the car with us. Birdy clambered out of her seat then, but instead of migrating over to my lap – which would have been her usual manoeuvre – she put two small paws on the passenger door of the car, angled her snout at the open window and inhaled hard. A small and hurried series of sniffs followed.

'We're not going for a walk in this weather, Bird.'

But that wasn't what had caught her attention. When I practised my own deep inhale, I realised it must be the nearby fish and chip stand that had grabbed her. It hit my stomach and my olfactory senses at the same time, and while my brain told me I wasn't hungry, that I couldn't possibly stand the thought of eating, my stomach told me otherwise, and it communicated with such a low rumble that it caused Birdy's head to snap around.

I dialled my parents' number and Mum answered on the second ring.

'Sally, are you okay? Christ, we've been calling.'

The many missed call alerts and messages were still pouring into my handset, a slow and steady arrival of worry and interest that my network carrier would only give me one message by one, as though that organisation was also trying to withhold essential information from me.

'Lena said she'd texted you? I'm sorry, Mum, I've got no fucking signal–'

'Language,' Dad cautioned, and I realised then, she must have me on speakerphone.

'I haven't heard from Lena,' Mum picked up, 'I texted her two days ago asking how you were both getting along. I didn't mention the... well, the situation. I only asked how the holiday was and it delivered and then she didn't... I texted again, yesterday, I think, was it yesterday, Vince?'

'Sally, are you okay?' Dad pushed, ignoring Mum's question entirely.

I didn't know how to answer other than to lie. 'Of course, absolutely. Lena's signal must be playing up as well. We're fine, all three of us are fine.' I imagined Lena running through coastal wilderness somewhere by now, her cheeks red from the increasing slaps of cold and her short fringe plastered to her forehead. 'Lena's gone for a run so Birdy and I have escaped to the land of telephone poles,' I forced a laugh, 'are *you* okay?'

There was a long pause before Dad answered. 'We're home.'

The knee-jerk feeling was jealousy. I suddenly ached for my window seat, my secret cigarettes and my office that harboured more information than I'd managed to bring with me. Smoking on the outside porch and limiting my research time to a mere two hours a day had become tiresome already – and the ebb and flow of distrust and suspicion wasn't helping matters. It crossed my mind, some time on the drive out to this point, that the problem wasn't Lena and her cotton-thread lies at all. *Hadn't you already realised that?* I thought, but somehow the thought arrived in Emma's voice and I had to physically shake my head to clear it.

'Why are you home?'

'Because your father would rather be hounded by a stranger delivering flowers than spending time with your Aunt Liz.' Relief washed through me; the normalcy of her answer made something in my sternum slowly start to heat through. 'So we've come home and we're just... I don't know what we're doing. We're waiting, like you. When are you back, love?'

As soon as possible. 'I don't know, honestly, Mum. We've got the cottage for another week but...' I flirted with the truth. I reached over for a comfort stroke of Birdy but she was still perched to pull in every ounce of chip shop she could through the small space available, and I resolved to get her a sausage once I'd escaped the call with

Mum and Dad. 'But it's hard, being away from everything.'

'I bet no signal is killing you,' Dad said.

'But the book is still doing well,' Mum chimed in, as though that would be of some comfort. Of course, I knew the book was doing well. *From the Woods* was still sitting in the top ten of various bestseller lists, and I was still getting emails from Duke's assistant – not Duke himself, I'd noticed – with various offers of work, all signed off with a reassurance that I didn't need to decide anything right away and that I could get back to her whenever.

'Thanks, Mum. Look, I just wanted to check in while I could. I'd better get a move on back to the cottage before Lena thinks we've abandoned her. But look, stay safe, okay? Call Harry if you need him, call Lena if you need me. I love you both.'

They chorused, 'We love you too,' before we disconnected the call – but somehow, something about it felt inexplicably final.

I pulled Birdy in for a kiss before I climbed out of the car and into the falling flood. The chip shop was empty now, everyone having taken refuge in their cars, homes, hotels to hide away from the onslaught of ill weather – which at least meant that getting served didn't take long. I went back to the car with a large sausage that I broke into bite-sized chunks for Birdy, who inhaled every piece as though she hadn't eaten for weeks on end. Then she turned her attention to my own small parcel. I hadn't been able to help myself once I was in the shop, my stomach having emitted another low growl that made the server narrow her eyes at me as though I might have a hell hound hidden at my feet. I unwrapped my cone of chips – that was more a small bundle in vinegar-soaked paper –

and pulled in the smell; though it was less a smell, and more a package of memories featuring childhood visits to the seaside; the first time Emma and I went away with school and got drunk underneath a pier; the time I waded out into the sea at high tide after Emma had died and–

My phone hummed and pulled me out of the ocean by my hair. I had thirteen unread WhatsApp messages and two new voicemails. But somehow, the chips – and the salt sting memory of that time in Brighton – seemed altogether more important now than gaining any contact with the outside world, even though that had been the main reason for the journey.

I pinched a thick chip, blew on it and touched it to my lips how a mother might with a mouthful of purée, before offering it to Birdy. She sniffed, scowled and pulled away, so I threw the chip into my own open trap instead. The hunger hit me once I started eating and I found I pulled in one mouthful after another, wedging chips together in a wad and eating them in two bites at most; another mouthful already queued up before I'd finished the present one. I wiped the grease of one hand against the side of my jeans and reached for my phone to try to multitask through the binge. There were seven WhatsApp messages from Sid, and what looked like only one voicemail still; the same one, I assumed, from the other day.

'Sally, it's me. I have something, something I think might be big. Can you– Will you just call me when you get this, please? I– I need to talk to you and–'

I hit three to delete the message and called her back straight away. The panic in her had at least paused my eating, giving me the chance to catch my breath while the phone rang out three, four, five times.

'Thank fucking God,' she answered, 'who the hell doesn't have coverage in this day and age?'

'I emailed you!'

'Okay, well,' she lingered and I thought I heard the click of a mouse in the background, 'I haven't been at my emails, clearly. I've been on a shoot in Leeds and– Do you know what, not the point, it doesn't matter. Are you okay?'

Why is that the first question people ask? I wondered whether there was a standardisation scale for okay-ness that I wasn't privy to – or maybe one that us damaged types, as a breed, weren't privy to, which was part of what made the question such a hard one to piece together an answer for. The more I considered it, the more I thought I hadn't been okay since Emma; which is to say, I hadn't been okay since I murdered my best friend. It was a thought that rolled around more frequently now, not the okay-ness necessarily but the thought of Emma, the thought of what I'd done to Emma and what I deserved now, whether I deserved this slow taunt that had taken my body into a needled vice and–

'Jesus, Sally, did you lose signal already?'

'Sorry, no, I'm here. I'm okay, of course.'

Because of course, it was easier to wade into the shallow waters of okay, rather than to push the questioner into the deep end, leave them to doggy paddle in your panic and smut and shit, which was your own standardised measure of being okay – because that's how damaged people lived. I tried to look beyond Birdy's window but the steam of our respective foods had clouded every outlook; the only smudge in it all being the soft impact of Birdy's breath on the passenger side pane.

'Are you okay?' I asked then, because I realised I'd skipped a beat of etiquette.

'I am, but look, I found out some stuff about Fleur and I don't think it's all stuff you're going to be happy about.'

To date I hadn't found out anything about Fleur, and that hadn't made me happy; it stood to reason that I may as well try not being happy about some things I did know instead. Sid was obviously superior in the research department I decided then. It had only been, in hours totalled, a day of googling variations of Fleur's name, scouring social media sites and crawling over and under death and marriage certificates – only to find nothing. Though of course, through my hurried searches in the quiet of a backroom in the holiday let – while Lena had been stood outside the closed door with a stopwatch, I was sure – an even more disturbing thought about Fleur had occurred to me: *What if she has nothing to do with this?* I had pinned my hopes on a girl I knew nothing about and yet, I had made her the most likely suspect in the whole investigation. I had already decided she, yes, *she* who I couldn't place from years of living in close proximity – albeit one person removed, through Emma – was the person sending me notes, having flowers delivered to my loved ones, and surely, quietly, preparing to out me for what I was. But what if it's not her? What if it's all sullied time, swilled down an open drain?

'Are you listening? You're really quiet and I've no idea when I'm losing you and when I'm not.'

I huffed a laugh. 'You're not losing me.'

'Okay, school years and yada-yada, all that aside. So she wasn't in our year at school, but she was a year below us, at Hard Castle.' Hard Castle had been the roughest school in the area, I remembered. Mum had once cautioned me and Emma for simply having walked past the place on our way home from netball practice. 'One or two people have told me her and Emma were close, one or two have said that they weren't really close at all and Fleur was a clinger-on who Emma moaned about a lot in private.' *But not to me?* I still couldn't make sense of that; a missing link that I needed to fall into place but the constant background rush of information from Sid made it impossible to step back from the puzzle and survey the bigger picture and she kept talking and talking until I begged her to take a breath and she said, 'Sally, look, I found out why Fleur is so impossible to find, okay? That's what I'm getting to here. Fleur isn't Fleur anymore; she doesn't exist.'

And just like that, the rain stopped. In the abruptness of sudden onset deafness, I opened and closed my mouth to pop my ears in case the rush of blood had momentarily switched off the sound but no, someone had only finished wringing out the clouds.

'I don't think I...'

'She changed her name, Sally, is what I'm saying.'

Fuck. 'Did someone tell you that, or–'

'No, no, I found her, Sal, I found people who know her, now, and...' There was a horrible hesitation then, the type that comes before a life-altering blow, and somehow I knew, in the core of my sternum, everything was about to change. 'Sally, you actually know her.'

FORTY-ONE

I was sitting at the dining table when she came home. Positioned at the head of it, as though I were about to hold an official meeting – or an interrogation. In the time that I'd been out, Lena must have come and gone from her run because she wasn't wearing her gym gear anymore; her hair was bone-dry but scraped back into a high ponytail and it gave an over-exposed view of her face. When she leaned in the doorway with her arms folded and her stare fixed on me, I searched each square centimetre for anything that I might recognise, or re-recognise, something I had seen before that I might now see again, conjoined with whatever it was that had attracted me to her in the first place. The first time I'd seen her, something in me ticked over – or maybe, stopped ticking altogether. The internal bustle of automatic machinery paused for a second and I knew, instantly somehow, that she was the person to take a chance on. *And now look at us.* Her eyebrows were even, her nose perfectly formed and centred, and her lips were neat, though I knew that when she eventually spoke – one of us would have to – the left side of her mouth would tuck up slightly more than the right; the product of a lazy dimple.

'I guess we need to talk,' she said, when my stare had lasted too long or when she'd become bored with the waiting, maybe. Her tone was flat, neutral, and it made it impossible to judge whether she was angry or nervous; I only knew that I was both.

Under the table I clenched and unclenched both hands to steady them, before I moved one up towards the two pictures that lay waiting. I pushed them forwards, in her general direction, and waited for her to step into the room to gain a better vantage point for seeing them. An internal metronome kept time for me and I tried to set my breathing to it, but still I could feel the confused flutter of a lost sparrow, hopping up one rib at a time as though scaling a wall out of me. Only when it reached the top, it invariably found itself knocking against the bone and cartilage that kept it trapped in a guilt cage. It tumbled down to the base of my stomach and started the process again each time. And I wondered whether, if I tipped my head back and unhinged my jaws to make myself a crocodile, would it see the light and come fluttering out, leaving only a mouthful of feathers.

Lena didn't say anything to begin with, only made a small 'Hm' noise. But after surveying the photos for a second or two longer, a quiet 'Oh' dropped out of her and landed on the table space between us like a pebble.

'I suppose your parents being alive should be the least of my concerns now,' I managed, though my voice shook with it.

Still, she didn't say anything. Instead, she pulled out a seat at the opposite side of the table, dropped into it, and pulled the photographs closer to her. She studied one then the other, squinting as though inspecting them for one detail in particular. I wondered whether she would ferret a jeweller's loop from her pocket.

'You look different.'

'Mm,' she put the second photograph down, 'people change as they grow up. And I'd be lying if I said there wasn't a nose job in my very late teens. I had this accident and got a huge...' She petered out and a sad expression took over her face then, as though something uncomfortable were just dawning on her; I thought it must be the memory of the accident but– 'I suppose I can't talk to you like that anymore.'

It was a knee-jerk reaction to smile then. 'Please do,' the shake now gone in my voice, 'given that I don't know a single fucking thing about you, it would be nice to hear some stories from your past.'

'Don't be like that.'

'Don't be so calm!' I slammed my palm against the hard wood of the table to punctuate the point. I couldn't find reason in how quickly the feelings had turned over in me, as though someone had taken a paddling drill to the thick mixture I had been carrying for weeks, months now, and there was no predicting what feeling might come to the surface next.

'Emma used to say you had a temper.'

And there it was, her name, writhing on the table between us.

'Don't say her name either.'

'She always said you were forever telling her what to do.'

'I wasn't, she wouldn't–'

'She did.'

It felt like the beginning of a sparring match, as

though unknowingly I had stepped into a ring of barbed fencing and this woman – this total fucking stranger – was circling me in it.

'Was it you, sending the notes, sending the flowers? Was that all you?'

I needed to know how many networks of lies there were, how many hidden things to be unearthed. Lena wasn't Lena, but that didn't make her the letter writer either. Quietly, I waited for her answer while she fidgeted with the corner of one of the photographs in front of her: an image of Fleur – *Lena* – and Emma at a party together, as it seemed they always had been.

'I thought I'd be fine with it,' she eventually said, 'I thought I could see the book and the fame and– I even thought I could read the book and not react too much, but I just couldn't, you know?' She looked at me then, narrow-eyed. 'To see you lying how you were, and getting so much fucking credit for it too, and– Jesus, if it didn't just stick in me after a while.' She dropped the photo and picked up the other in its place; they both looked sober in this second one. 'Duke mentioned, an off-handed comment was all, that you were already getting fan mail and I thought, okay, I can work with that. It was going to be a one-time thing but then I saw your reaction and so help me God, Sally, somehow it was like I revelled in it and–'

'That doesn't make sense,' I cut through her, hell-bent on taking a scalpel to the disfigured explanation. 'You're making it sound like you haven't been planning this all along, like you haven't *lied* throughout our entire relationship, Len– Fleur.'

She winced when I used her real name. 'You're paranoid if you think that I got into this two years ago planning some sort of take-down, Sally. How important do you think you are?'

A gaslight went on over my head. There was nothing quite as damaging than to hear someone who doesn't appear paranoid telling you that you are; nothing quite so validating to paranoia, to have someone weaponise it for you.

'When we met, you knew who I was?'

She nodded, slowly, as though hesitant in the admission. 'You don't look so different.'

'Why didn't Emma ever introduce us?'

'You're asking the wrong questions.'

'And I'm expecting some fucking answers.'

Lena sighed then, *actually* sighed, as though bored with this already, and I felt the sparrow thrash and knock and tremble.

'She said you two shared everything, it was nice to have something that was "just hers".' I took note of the air quotes, as though she'd ripped the phrase from Emma's own tongue. 'We bumped into each other at some netball match or another, you hadn't been able to make it. I blocked her and we both took a tumble, and ended up falling over ourselves with laughter, much to the dismay of our teammates.' She smiled as she spoke and I could see this was a fond memory for her. I hated that. 'We kept in touch after, she invited me to some parties, I invited her to some. She tried to plan a kidnapping with me.' She looked up from the photographs then, and fixed me with a hard and uncomfortable stare. 'But then, she was always choosing to take you to certain things over me. I guess there were just times when you were more appropriate.'

'I don't know what you're talking about,' I answered, following the instructions of an internal voice that parroted *deny it, deny everything*. 'Emma and I were kidnapped. A man took us and–'

'Sal,' she waved away my storytelling, 'if we're going to be honest, we may as well *be* honest. Don't you think?'

'After Emma died...' I petered out when I saw Lena hold up a finger to pause me.

'After you killed her?'

I let the accusation hang there. Until now, no one had known. No one in the world had known the truth of my so-called survivor's guilt, or the burden of having carried such a dreadful thing on my back for so long. The lie of Emma's death had heavily weighed me down and now, somehow, having been unburdened from it, I found breathing hard, felt my chest heave and shudder like an engine with a clapped-out part and I couldn't get anything steady. There were too many colours and everything got loud and–

'I need water.'

Lena pushed back from the table. 'I'll get–'

'You stay where you are. I'd choke on anything you brought me.'

The sink was on the other side of the kitchen; I wasn't sure that I could make it. Instead, I pulled open the fridge and took orange juice from the door, and drank it straight from the carton. I chugged and chugged as though I could wash away the bad feeling, starting from the inside, all the while thinking, *Lena hates this, Lena hates it when I drink something shared straight from the bottle.* When I finally came up for air another thought washed in: *But does she?* There was no way to unpick the stitching, to disentangle truth from make-believe. I didn't know whether Lena's favourite colour was green, or whether she loved Chinese more than Indian, or whether she'd always turned *Moulin*

Rouge off at chapter twenty-two of the DVD throughout her teenage years to ensure the story had a happy ending.

'I really didn't plan for this, Sally.' She'd left the table too by then, and lingered on the boundary of the room as I drank again to busy my mouth. 'I didn't start this thinking, *Ooh, one day I'll out her for what she is.*'

I spluttered and wiped my mouth clean. 'No? It was just an idea that came to you when you saw... what? The reception to the book, the work I'd put in to fabricating it? What was the tipping point?' I reached out to hold the work surface, to have something firm and footed in foundation to steady myself. 'Everything, our whole life together, it was a lie, wasn't it?'

Lena bunched her mouth to the side as though really considering the question. 'When I saw you in the city it was a complete coincidence. Of course I recognised you, and I knew where from, but I didn't approach you with ill-feeling, Sally, I didn't approach you with... this, all of this in mind.' She used a consolatory tone, as though we were only talking about an amicable break-up, as though one of us had cheated and we were trying to find a way through. 'Not all of it was a lie, Sal.'

'Only your name, and your entire life history, your reasons for being with me?'

She huffed. 'I've been with you because I liked you. I was willing to put things with Emma to one side–'

'I *murdered* her!' I shouted the admission at a volume I thought might shake the supporting pillars of the house. 'I murdered her, *Fleur*, and you were willing to put that to one side?'

The kitchen clock counted out six seconds before she answered. 'I don't suppose there's any coming back from this now, is there?'

'No, there fucking isn't.'

The more we talked, the more it crossed my greyscale mind that I wasn't the only unhinged woman in the room; that maybe, teenage behaviours aside, I was the more level out of the two of us now. Lena looked disappointed at the prospect of there being no way out from it all. But we were in that same barbed ring still, circling each other, waiting for the first strike, or pin manoeuvre. And whether through self-defence or spite or something altogether different, I found that I wasn't focused on her at all then; I was staring at the knife block instead.

'I think we need a walk,' Lena said, and I thought she must have noticed. 'I don't think you're likely to get away with murder twice, are you?'

'I don't think a walk is going to help matters.'

'No,' she came closer then, eased the orange juice from my hand and set it on the side, 'but it gives us a neutral landscape, don't you think?'

I didn't want neutral. I wanted to take the thickest blade and drive it deep into the stomach I'd kissed so many times, either in passion or compassion or even just jest. Something in me wanted to force it right into something of hers; something that would hurt, something that would bleed. But dousing the fire of those thoughts was the ember flicker of another: *Is that how it had felt with Emma? Do you want it to be different, this time?*

'Fine,' I agreed, because I didn't want there to be a 'this time' at all. 'But I need for you to tell me what she told you.'

Lena smiled and stepped aside so I could get to the doorway before her. 'Everything.'

From a distance, anyone admiring our silhouettes could have been forgiven for thinking we were an ordinary couple. The rain had eased, and we had migrated towards a stone bench that was fixed near the edge of the clifftop, leading away from the holiday let. The wary heights that had seemed so scary when we'd first arrived here didn't hold the same threat anymore. The worst had already happened, I thought, how could a tumble from a ragged rock face make anything worse?

Emma had told Fleur everything; that much seemed true. Lena explained how Emma had told her she was frustrated with school, with life, even with me. They had been swapping ideas for getting famous quick, both as invested as the other, and something about that reality – Emma sharing those frustrations, those ideas – forced a pain to settle in the well of my stomach. Emma had asked Fleur whether she would be willing to try the plan – the same plan she and I had eventually gone through – but days after first mentioning it, Emma rescinded. 'She took back the offer,' Lena said with a sad tone, 'made it sound like it was an utterly stupid idea, one that we could never go through with. It was about a week after that that I heard the news, two young girls gone missing, one of them wound up dead.' She turned to me then, and spoke in a tone that was too friendly. 'Things must have got real bad, real quickly in that bunker, huh?'

I couldn't answer the question. But there were more of my own still waiting. 'When you met me, why did you...' Speak to me, like me, let me love you for a while; there were too many ways to end the sentence. 'Why did you let things happen between us, why didn't you tell me who you were, about Emma?'

Lena sucked in a mouthful of air, as though fuelling

herself for a long answer. 'You're not a bad person, Sally, not *now* anyway, you just did a bad thing. I didn't know whether you knew me, whether Emma had even said anything about me, but you clearly didn't recognise me and I guess a part of me had always...'

'Always what?'

'Wondered.'

She was crazy, of course. Though I wasn't sure I was in a position to judge.

'And now, now you know me, now you know for certain, what happens? Do you tell everyone the truth of what I did, the truth of the book?' I spat the questions at machine-gun pace, but Lena only shrugged.

'It was just gentle taunting, Sally. I honestly never thought that far ahead and... I still haven't thought that far ahead.'

Gentle taunting, I parroted, *gentle taunting* where I had lost sleep and alienated friends and family and believed, for a moment, that my family was in danger; *gentle taunting* that saw me trapped in a seascape with a woman who knew, who had known for years, that I was a murderer but who had, what – stuck it out with me anyway? *Gentle taunting*, and I was up and off the bench, pacing and pushing my hands through my hair, only then realising the sweat sheen on my forehead and the rising heat that was moving from my pelvis through my gut and into my shoulders. *Gentle taunting* that had brought us here, to a literal stand-off and–

'What if we walk away?' The suggestion echoed out of me like a belch and my eyes widened; Lena's did too. But I believed, deep in the steam and panic of my body, I believed there had to be a way out.

'An amicable break-up, you mean?' Lena shook her

head. 'I know you, Sally. There's no way you can go in for that, not after this.'

'What do you think I'm going to do?' I spat back with my arms outstretched and my palms open to her. The problem was, she *did* know me – but I didn't have a clue what would clinch this for her. This beautiful, mad stranger I'd been left with. But still, I haggled for freedom; at least for the option of it. 'It's not like I can run back to the city and bad-mouth you, Lena. Look at the fucking situation I'm in.'

She smiled; that lopsided lazy smile I had looked up to during so many blissful and quiet mornings in bed. Our entire relationship was now two simultaneous images: one, where it was backlit in romanticised lighting, a gentle glow around every memory of her; the other, where the edges were thumb-smudged and impossible to see clearly, authentically. *Because nothing about it was authentic*, I thought then, and an animal sound tripped out of me that turned Lena's apparent smugness to an expression of sympathy. But I didn't want it; I didn't want this unknown creature to feel anything other than disinterest. I wanted her to be so unfathomably bored and detached from my life now that she simply slipped free of it.

She stood from the bench then, too, and closed the distance between us, and I recognised the look she wore. It was the prelude to a kiss; it was morning coffee and surprise flowers, the latter of which would never have quite the same feel to them now, no matter the sender. She looked at me with warmth and duvet days and hand holding, and I wondered then, whether Lena, *my* Lena, who literally cared for people for a living, was trapped in there as a duality with Fleur. Fleur who felt burned and bitter and crisp still, from Emma having chosen me. *But look how that worked out for Emma,* I wanted to say, *didn't she get her comeuppance already?* Though of course, this wasn't about Emma's comeuppance; it was about mine. Lena tucked her hand to fit beneath my right ear, and I felt the heat of her palm lean awkwardly against my neck. She kept looking at me as though she were only Lena, as though she were only loving me, and I thought too fast again that maybe if I pushed her in the right direction, we could both escape this – amicably, leaving as strangers who had nothing, wanted nothing to do with the other. If I said the right thing; if only I found a way to push–

'I've got it, babe,' Lena said then, and she managed a soft smile with it. 'I think I've worked it out...'

FROM THE WOODS: EPILOGUE

I never expected this to be a book that had an Epilogue. In my mind, once the story was told, that would be the end of it; I suppose I saw it as a purge. It was for readers – I don't know enough about the industry, to be honest, I never listened closely enough – but maybe reviewers, too, to form their opinions and share their thoughts, without an addendum, without a *And then this happened...*

Of course, I never imagined *this* would happen. That holiday was meant to be a break to recoup energy lost through writing, and researching, and book promotion. It was never something intended to frame an Epilogue, nor news reports or articles or online think pieces. The holiday was never intended to be the preface to a funeral either. When the break started, it was everything both of us – all three of us, because Birdy has never turned down a visit to the beach – needed. Or I thought that was the case. I was in regular contact with Duke throughout because he was worried, too, and although I was worried still – and told him so throughout our exchanges – I never imagined how worried I needed to be. As someone in my profession, too, I'd hoped, or I'd always hoped before this, that this sort of plan would be easy to spot from a clear coastline mile away. Though people have told me that perhaps it wasn't a plan, maybe it wasn't planned at all – which somehow makes it worse.

Throughout the events and the readings and the signings for *From the Woods*, Sally and I spoke of Emma often. I knew that the book, far from being cathartic, had in fact stirred things afresh for her. But she had me and Duke and her therapist, she had parents who loved, and love, her deeply. I'd thought she was coping, despite the bad days; despite the worried texts to Duke. I was mistaken. Sally's suicide is an absolute tragedy and I wish, wish, only wish, I had got to the edge quicker, got to *her* quicker. There's no changing this now though. So all I can say is thank you, to everyone who has read and continues to read Sally's work. You keep her and Emma alive – and there are loved ones who are especially thankful for that.

Lena and Birdy
2023

THE END

ALSO BY CHARLOTTE BARNES

SUSPENSE THRILLERS:

Intention

All I See Is You

Sincerely, Yours

The Things I Didn't Do

Safe Word

Penance

The Good Child

CRIME:

The DI Melanie Watton Series

The Copycat (book one)

The Watcher (book two)

The Cutter (book three)

ACKNOWLEDGEMENTS

When I was writing *A True Crime*, I put a call-out for people on my Facebook page for people who didn't mind their names appearing in the book. Now, those kind people are seeded throughout this story; sometimes as minor characters and sometimes as absolutely essential ones. So to everyone who gifted me their name for this, thank you, and I hope you spot yourself in these pages.

As always, thanks and gratitude has to go to the wider crime writing community for their support, and to everyone at Team Bloodhound for their work on the book. It has, over and again, been a joy to work with you all.

A NOTE FROM THE PUBLISHER

Thank you for reading this book. If you enjoyed it please do consider leaving a review on Amazon to help others find it too.

We hate typos. All of our books have been rigorously edited and proofread, but sometimes mistakes do slip through. If you have spotted a typo, please do let us know and we can get it amended within hours.

info@bloodhoundbooks.com

Printed in Great Britain
by Amazon